I0731027

PRAISE FOR RAISING A DEMON

Selection of Five Star Reviews from Goodreads

I loved it! The characters were funny and likable. I found that it was an easy reading story and I hope to see more of these characters.

This is my first book by Amy Cissell and I really enjoyed it...in fact it was hard for me to put down. I loved the references to the shows Supernatural and Lucifer...both favourites of mine.

I loved this book, it is entertaining and the characters are pretty awesome. Evie is a single mom, who is sent into a crazy "revelation week" from hell (pun intended) and we discover that there is a lot more that meets the eye in sleepy Eden Valley. I'm curious about the other characters and what will happen next in the series. I just found a new series to look forward to and I think if you like fantasy, urban fantasy and hotness everywhere, this book is just for you.

I thoroughly enjoyed Evie's story. A fresh new take on a midlife crisis! All of the characters are so well developed and a joy to read. I loved Evie's friends and family and Lily especially is a precocious little girl. Even Luc's brother and sister were fun to read. I am definitely looking forward to the next book in the series!

DEVIL AND THE DEEP BLUE LAKE

AMY CISSELL

BROKEN
WORLD
PUBLISHING

DEVIL AND THE DEEP BLUE LAKE
Amy Cissell

A Broken World Publication
PO Box 11643
Portland, OR 97211
Devil and the Deep Blue Lake
Copyright © 2021 by Amy Cissell
ISBN 978-1-949410-32-7 (ebook) ;
ISBN 978-1-949410-33-4 (paperback)

Cover Design: Cissell Ink
Edited by Suzanne Lahna, The Quick Fox
Edited & Proofread by Christopher Barnes, Cissell Ink

All rights reserved. No part of this publication may be reproduced, distributed, or transmitted in any form or by any means, including photocopying, recording, or other electronic or mechanical methods, without the prior written permission of the publisher, except in the case of brief quotations embodied in critical reviews and certain other noncommercial uses permitted by copyright law. For permission requests, write to the author at editors@brokenworldpublishing.com.

This is a work of fiction. Names, characters, businesses, places, events, and incidents are either the products of the author's imagination or used in a fictitious manner. Any resemblance to actual persons, living or dead, or actual events is purely coincidental.

Eden Valley

Raising a Demon
Devil and the Deep, Blue Lake
Valley of Angels
Guardian of Eden

Eden Valley World Novellas

Match Made in Hell
Fall From Grace
Hell's Bells
Heaven Sent

for me
and
for all the therapists
I've tortured over the years

ACKNOWLEDGMENTS

So many thanks to my advance readers! Y'all are beyond fantastic.

I'm grateful to my editors Suzanne Lahna of The Quick Fox and Christopher Barnes of Cissell Ink for their feedback, plot hole discoveries, comma rehabilitation, and insistence that I add some descriptions and character emotions (ew).

CONTENT WARNING

This book contains depictions of alcohol abuse, drowning, near child drowning, and bi & homophobia on the part of one character. It also has mentions of suicide and mental illness.

CHAPTER ONE

"**G**enevieve Kane, if you don't open this door right now, I will..." Evie's voice trailed off. She was probably trying to think of a suitable threat that might get Viv off the couch.

"She'll sic her demon fiancé on you," Bev said. "Or, if you're being particularly stubborn, her demon spawn. Both of them."

Viv sighed and pressed her index fingers against the bridge of her nose. Evie and Bev had been pounding on her condo door for the last fifteen minutes. If it went on much longer, someone would call the cops.

She knew what they wanted. Had known they were showing up. But her stupid flashes of knowledge seldom gave her enough warning to avoid uncomfortable situations, just enough to brace herself.

The knocking stopped.

"Viv?" Evie said, tentatively. "You know we love you, and ordinarily, neither of us would push you to see us if you really didn't want to, but we're worried."

"Please let us in," Bev said through the door. "Thirty minutes of conversation is all we're asking. If you want us to leave after, we'll go. No questions asked."

"And no repercussions," Evie said. "We'll be here for you when you need us, but right now we need to make sure you're okay."

Viv walked to the door but didn't open it. She dropped her chin to her chest and wrapped her arms around herself.

"I wish—" Evie's voice was interrupted by the hollow sound of a hand clapping over her mouth.

"Don't say that," Bev said.

"Shit. I didn't mean…"

Viv rolled her eyes and sighed loud enough for it to carry through the door. She unlocked and opened it. "Thirty minutes, and then you leave." She turned and walked back into her apartment, poured herself a glass of wine, and sat down in the overstuffed recliner.

Evie and Bev exchanged glances and settled onto the couch across from Viv.

Viv looked at her friends, fingers tapping on her knee. She looked at her smartwatch, then up at the women across from her. "Twenty-seven minutes."

Evie crossed her legs and leaned forward. "Viv, I know this year has been hard, and I know that Eden Valley is the last place you want to be. But you're shutting us out, too. Bev and I don't need you to come to us for our monthly brunch. We just need you."

Bev fixed Viv with a hard stare that Viv couldn't escape from. "You know I would move heaven and hell for you. Either of us would. But we can't help you if you won't let us in."

"I didn't even think that would be a literal situation ever, but here we are." Evie spread her arms to encompass the condo.

Evie and Bev leaned back, watching Viv expectantly. She took a large drink of the chardonnay she always had on hand thanks to an old lover who'd become a good friend. Her gaze dropped to the table separating her from her friends. It might be a narrow coffee table, but it felt like the gulf she'd put between them was widening the longer this went on. The visions that had been mere blips when they started in April of last year had picked up in frequency and intensity, if not usefulness, in the intervening fifteen months. They'd started in Eden Valley, and every time she went back, they'd ratcheted up another notch. Staying away was the only way she could protect herself, something her friends wouldn't understand. She took another sip. "Twenty-three minutes."

Evie sat up straight, folded her hands on her lap, and said, "We've been friends since we were in fourth grade. That's thirty-six years of history. In that time, we have seldom fought and, until a year ago, we've never gone more than a day without speaking. Bev and I have dropped so many balls with you, taken you and your trips back to Eden Valley for granted. I don't know how to make it up to you. Tell me what you need, and I'll do it. *We'll* do it. But I will not let this friendship die until you look me in the eye and tell me it's already buried. Can you do that?"

Cold spread through Viv's body, and a lump grew in her throat. She needed to tell Evie and Bev to go in a definitive enough way so they never came back, otherwise they'd keep bothering her until she eventually broke down and gave in, making everything even worse. She didn't know how many more visits she could make and still come back to Seattle as a semi-functional human being.

She'd broken up with so many people, hated it when the people she was dating got too pushy and asked for too much. She could use the same strategy here. Viv hardened herself, set her jaw, and looked Evie directly in the eye. "It's over. Our friendship ran its course at least a decade ago, but we were all too stubborn or too stupid to let it go. But now, I'm taking control of my life and telling you to leave. Delete my number. And don't come here again."

She almost winced at the look in Evie's eyes—she'd never seen her friend look that hurt and lost except when her daughter had been kidnapped by a King of Hell.

Evie dropped her eyes and cleared her throat. "Okay. If that's what you want. You can close the door, but I never will. Say the word and I will drop everything for you." She stood up.

Bev grabbed Evie's arm and yanked her back down. "By my calculation, we have almost fifteen minutes left. Evie's said her piece, and you've said yours, but now it's my turn."

Viv squirmed under Bev's steely gaze.

"Genevieve Kane, you are being an absolute idiot. Don't sit there and pretend this friendship was over a decade ago. We walked into hell together last year to save Evie's daughter, and I would, by all we hold sacred, walk right back into hell again to save your sorry ass. If you're going to end this, throw away everything the three of us have been through, then at least have the decency to be honest about it."

Viv's jaw dropped. She'd never heard Bev lose her temper like this. Not when her adopted daughter Shelby had destroyed her garden in a fit of PTSD-induced rage. Not when her parents had forgotten to show up for graduation leaving Bev the only person to walk off the stage with no family to meet, and not when Joanne Olson—now Sheriff Mills of Chelan County—had thrown Bev's backpack that contained her favorite jeans, two first edition books she'd saved up for months to buy from the local used bookshop, and her second-place science fair project into the lake the last day of freshman year.

Bev was tapping her foot and waiting for a response. "You have approximately three minutes to tell us what the hell is going on before I let Evie wish it out of you."

"Her wishes on people only work if the subjects were already inclined to make those decisions," Viv muttered. Dammit. She hadn't meant to say anything.

"Oh, you want to tell us the truth," Bev said. "You just won't admit it." Her voice softened into the warmth more typical of Bev. "Viv, c'mon. If you can't trust us, who can you trust?"

"This isn't a path you have to walk alone," Evie said, laying down her best compassionate mom voice—the one Viv heard her use when Lily was in trouble and Evie was trying to coax her out of her defensive shell and back into the sunshiny girl she usually was.

She was resolute, though. Being alone was better than asking her friends to carry her baggage. Again. She opened her mouth to tell them that, then surprised everyone by bursting into tears.

VIV SIPPED a glass of wine on the rooftop bar Bev and Evie had dragged her to. She caught her reflection in the mirror behind the bar and winced. She looked like hell. No—she'd had a fling with a demon who'd been hotter than the hell she came from, and Sam looked infinitely better than Viv did right now.

After she'd started crying, Bev and Evie had fallen into "Mom-mode." Evie'd pushed Viv into the shower and talked her into getting dressed while Bev cleaned up the place and dumped the takeout containers and empty wine bottles that were littering the kitchen. Then, they'd dragged her to this bar, grabbed a table in the back with a clear line of sight to the bar and the entrance, and looked at her expectantly.

The weight of what they wanted her to say pushed her head between her shoulders until she was hunched over her wine.

Bev and Evie waited silently. Viv knew they were giving her time and not making her feel pushed aside by chattering to each other, but the silence was heavy and felt like judgment. She took a deep breath, flicked a long strand of jet-black hair behind her ear, and looked at her friends—her best friends.

"I'm sorry." As a start, it wasn't bad, but Viv knew it wasn't enough. She picked up the bar napkin and twisted it in her hands before shredding it into narrow strips. A flash hit her, the blinding headache close behind. She pushed back from the table just in time to avoid the tray of half-empty glasses that dropped onto the edge of the table and crashed to the ground where she'd been sitting an instant ago.

"I am so sorry!" the server said. "I can't believe that happened. I'll be right back to clean this mess up. Why don't you ladies move to that table." She gestured to the nearest table that had recently been vacated. "Don't take your drinks—they might have glass in them. I'll get you fresh glasses and a bottle. Obviously on the house."

Viv tried to breathe her heart rate into submission. She grabbed her purse, shook off the shards of glass and wiped it off with the rag offered to her by the small horde of bar employees who'd descended to clean up the mess of broken glass and spilled alcohol.

The women settled at the new table and had been there less than a minute before their server was dropping off fresh waters and a bottle of wine with three glasses. "It's a good thing you moved when you did!" she said. "I'm so glad that tray didn't hit you."

"I'm just lucky, I guess," Viv said, forcing a smile. The stabbing pain behind her eyes was dulling a bit, and her peripheral vision was slowly returning. She couldn't see well through the lights flashing in her eyes yet, but color was returning to her world, and she could see well enough to find the now-full glass of wine and down it like a college student in a tequila shot contest.

"Are you okay?" Evie asked. She poured a little more wine into Viv's glass, but it was not a full pour. Viv knew Evie was thinking about the empty bottles Bev had cleaned up earlier.

"Fine," Viv managed. She rubbed her temples and tried to bring the world back into focus. As long as she didn't get another vision, she'd be fine in about ten minutes. Wine numbed the pain that came with the flashes of insight, and wine kept them from happening. Wine and staying away from situations where she interacted with people and events that might need predicting.

"I'm going to the ladies' room," Viv said. "Be right back." She jumped up and ran away from the table before either friend could offer to come with her. Instead of using the restroom on the roof, she darted downstairs, bumping into the walls like a pinball ricocheting off the walls of a machine and activating too-bright lights.

She walked up to the bar. "Two shots of Jameson." She tossed a twenty down on the bar. The bartender brought her the whiskey. She took both shots, one after another, and slammed the glasses down on the bar.

"You're not driving anywhere, are you, ma'am?" the bartender asked.

"Nope. I've got my designated busybodies upstairs," Viv said. She turned around to return to her wine and saw Bev behind her.

"I was coming to check on you," Bev said, disappointment and worry radiating from her. "To make sure you were okay."

Viv bit back every excuse she wanted to make and every angry thought that wanted to burst forth.

"Let's go back upstairs," Viv said. "I'll try to explain."

VIV SAT DOWN, conscious that she'd spent most of the afternoon squirming under the gazes of her friends but not telling them anything. Instead, she'd cried, showed off the unpredictable and useless "gift" she'd gotten courtesy of the portal to hell that had opened in Eden Valley the year before, depositing Evie's long-lost love —and the father of her child—back in town, and done secret shots in the middle of the afternoon like a kid hiding from their parents. In other words, she was winning the friendship game.

When she'd gotten back to the table, the wine was gone, replaced with glasses of iced tea. A cheese and charcuterie tray showed up moments later.

"I don't want to push you," Evie said. "But this isn't like you. You're acting out of character, and you're trying to run away from us."

Viv felt resolve solidify in her chest. Evie was right. She had to tell someone. Carrying this alone was killing her. She took one more minute to push away the envy she felt—Evie's gift was useful and didn't cause killer headaches, and Bev hadn't gotten anything but the brand that marked her as hell's—and to make sure there weren't tears lurking in the corners of her eyes waiting for the dam to burst and flood what little dignity she had left.

"It's the damn flashes of intuition or knowledge or whatever you want to call them. I thought they'd go away if I left Eden Valley. Every time I came back to visit, it got worse. Things were clearer, no more vague urges. I know what's going to happen and how to change it. But I don't always know in time to do anything. And the headaches…" She trailed off, nausea twisting her stomach. She tried to remember the last time she'd put anything in her stomach that wasn't coffee or alcohol and came up fuzzy.

Viv made a cheese and cracker plate for herself and scarfed down a few bites, washing it all down with iced tea.

"I'm sure you've tried everything to get the headaches under control," Bev said. "So I won't offer suggestions unless you want me to."

Viv ticked off on her fingers. "OTC pain killers, meditation, acupuncture, yoga, Imitrex, Oxy. I've visited specialists, neurologists, naturopaths, chiropractors, reiki healers, and some shady guy in a back alley building who was probably doing illegal things in the other room but promised he was the second coming of Christ and had the ability to heal anything demon related. The only thing that dulls the pain and keeps the flashes from showing up is alcohol."

Evie reached across the table and grabbed Viv's hand. "We one hundred percent believe you. But you have to know this isn't sustainable. It isn't healthy. How are you keeping up with work?"

"If I stay home and don't encounter anyone, it's not as bad," Viv said. "I get up early, get through everything I need to do for my clients, and then..." She trailed off. They'd already seen her home and her behavior today; she didn't want to admit that the wine or—if it was a particularly bad day—whiskey was now an almost daily habit.

"That explains why you don't want to come ho—back to Eden Valley," Bev said. "But it doesn't explain why you stopped taking our calls. You know we'd come to Seattle for brunch if that's what you needed."

"You think I wanted you to see me like this?" The anger was building again, and with it the headache that the whiskey had dulled. She yanked her hand back. "I know I'm a mess. I know this isn't sustainable. Not all of us were lucky enough to end up with a supernatural shoplifting ability, a hot guy, and a new baby. Not all of us got to avoid it altogether. That's why I didn't call. You can't understand what I'm going through, and I can't hide my resentment. I don't want your judgment *or* your help. I don't need an intervention. I don't need either of you."

Viv watched Evie's posture straighten and her face harden. Evie's eyes narrowed; her expression shuttered. Viv had been on the receiving end of the Addams stare before, but that'd been from Evie's mom Hope, and it'd been almost thirty years since she'd been subject to it.

"I didn't want to have to do this, but I see now there's no other way." Evie leaned forward and captured Viv's gaze. "We are taking you back to your condo. You are packing your bags. And you are coming home."

Viv wanted to argue, but with the weight of Evie's gaze on her, she couldn't fight back. Either something had happened to her will, or Evie's had gotten a lot, lot stronger.

Evie smiled, but it didn't quite reach her eyes. "It's amazing what two half-demon babies will do to a woman," she said. "I don't even have to wish out loud anymore." She threw several bills on the table and stood up.

Viv had no choice but to do the same, and the horrifying part was, she no longer wanted to resist.

CHAPTER TWO

V iv sat at Bev's dining room table, holding her face in her hands. Her head was pounding. It wasn't the "vision" headache. This was a hangover—something she'd gotten increasingly used to over the last year.

"Here, drink this," Bev said, shoving a glass of orange liquid in front of Viv's face.

"Sports drink?" Viv's nose wrinkled as she regarded the neon beverage.

"It'll help," Bev said. "And if it gets bad, let me know, and I'll take you to the hospital."

"If what gets bad?" Viv asked, downing the drink. It was replaced with another and a steaming mug.

"Drink the broth, too." Bev sat down across from Viv and watched her alternate between the two. "Withdrawal. I don't know how much you were drinking and for how long, but I will not risk you. If you start shaking or sweating, we are out the door and at the emergency clinic. If you think we should go now, let me know. Don't lie. Don't prevaricate."

"Where's Shelby?" Viv asked, ignoring the question for now and finishing her liquids. Her stomach growled, hunger and nausea warring for supremacy.

"She and Lily had a sleepover at Kevin's—those three kids are even more inseparable now than ever—and were headed to swimming lessons, then Evie's from there," Bev answered. "Do you think you could tolerate a smoothie? Or how about scrambled eggs?"

"Smoothie. And it's just a hangover. A really, really bad one, but only a hangover." The humiliation she felt at not only having put herself into this situation, but having others see, was as present as the headache drilling into her skull. Then Bev's words—and the casualness with which she said them—hit her. "Kevin's? Since when?"

Bev moved to the kitchen and Viv followed. As Bev moved around the kitchen grabbing fruit and yogurt and juice, she said, "Since Hell. Kevin's mom, Aurielle Jones—Elle—started going to school functions. She gave us her phone number and invited me and Evie to tea. I don't know what to make of it, but it's good. We've had brunch."

"She's your new brunch third?" Viv asked, failing to keep the bitter note of jealousy out of her voice.

"She's the fourth of five ladies who brunch," Bev said placidly. She turned on the blender.

"Five? There's five of you now?" Viv asked as soon as the blender stopped and the echoes of the noise no longer reverberated in her head.

"Yep. Evie, me, Elle, and Sam."

"That's four," Viv pointed out. "And why did you invite Sam? She's a demon."

"So are Lily and Alex," Bev said, pouring the thin smoothie into a tall glass and handing it to Viv. "So is Luc. Sam is Evie's almost sister-in-law. She rented my cabin to stay in Eden Valley close to her nieces. We brunch. And the fifth is obviously you, dummy."

Viv closed her eyes and took a deep breath, trying to drown the irritation. She'd skipped the last—she counted on her fingers—five brunches. She hadn't been back to visit since just after Alex was born —her tiny birthday twin—and only a couple times before that. Shit. She hadn't seen her honorary nieces more than two or three times in the last year and had missed Lily's eleventh birthday and Shelby's twelfth.

"I am awful," Viv said, taking a sip of the smoothie and willing her stomach to accept it without protest. "No wonder you replaced me."

Bev sat down across from Viv, handed her a cup of coffee heavily dosed with fresh cream, and took a drink of her own black coffee. "You're not replaced, but even if that were the case, it means it took two other people to take the place of one Genevieve Kane." She reached out and put her hand on Viv's forearm and squeezed until Viv looked up at her. "You're not replaceable, Viv. I'm sorry we didn't come check on you earlier. I knew something wasn't right, but I thought you were putting your broken heart back together and wanted to give you time and space. And I was too wrapped up in my own stuff. I failed you, and I'm sorry."

Viv blinked back tears. She'd never been much of a crier, but Bev always knew what buttons to push to pull her emotions to the fore-front. "You didn't fail me, Bev. You and Evie are the best parts of my life. I failed myself and you guys by fucking up this badly." She took another sip of the smoothie and let the cool liquid soothe her nausea.

Bev smiled at Viv. "We could play the self-recrimination Olympics, but I'm not sure that's the best use of our time. I have to go to work in a little bit. Will you be okay on your own?"

Humiliation threatened to burn away the cooling effects of the smoothie. "I'm not going to raid your liquor cabinet, if that's what you're asking," Viv said.

"It wasn't, but you wouldn't be able to, anyway. This is currently a booze-free house. Not because of you, before you get defensive. It's been an interesting year for everyone." Bev grabbed her bag from the hook near the door, pulled out a key chain, and handed it to Viv. "This key will open the medicine safe in the linen closet in case you need more aspirin, and if you need a knife or scissors or anything sharp, the smaller key will open the drawer next to the stove."

Viv took the keys and tried to make sense of the info Bev had just dumped on her. She opened her mouth to ask, but Bev shook her head. "Later, babe. Right now, it's all about you. How are you feeling?"

"Hungry. Nauseated. Headachy. But surprisingly not terrible," Viv replied.

"Finish your smoothie. Evie will be here in about fifteen minutes to hang out. If you think you're up for it in an hour or so, you can try some solid food." Bev grabbed a blazer she'd slung over the back of the chair. "I'm so sorry I have to leave. I've taken so much time off this year that I need to at least make an appearance in the office today. I'll be home before Shelby gets home, and you won't be alone."

Viv plastered a smile on her face and flapped her hands at Bev. "Go. I promise I'll be fine until my second babysitter gets here. I have your number, and I promise to call if I start to feel worse."

Bev hesitated, then flung her arms around Viv and kissed her forehead. "I missed you, and I'm glad you're here, even if the reason sucks."

"I'm glad I'm here, too," Viv said. She stilled in Bev's arms and tested the unexpected feeling for the compulsion Evie had created the day before and was surprised to realize every word was genuine.

As soon as Bev walked out the door and Viv heard her car drive away, Viv found a portable coffee mug, dumped her coffee in it, and, after slipping her shoes on and grabbing her shades, walked out the door. The door clicked behind her, and she paused until she heard the automatic lock engage. She walked down the street and headed through an overgrown alley that hadn't seen car traffic in years. The drying grass rustled against her jeans, wafting the sweet smell of summer towards her.

The sky was bright blue, uncharitably unmarred by clouds and the sun, already warm even this early, chased away the cold she'd been unable to shake for months even as it intensified the throbbing hangover pain behind her eyeballs. Viv strode through Eden Valley, hoping her determined stride would discourage anyone from approaching her. When she got to Main Street, she looked around from the shadow of the gas station awning; then sure the coast was clear and neither Bev nor Evie were close, she darted across the street, took a sharp turn into the city park, and skirted the trees at the edge of the park until she got to the trail that started in the park and wound its way around Eden Lake. Once she was a few yards down the trail and not visible from either the park or Main Street, she rolled her shoulders and winced as everything and more popped with the release of tension that'd been piling on for far too long.

Viv walked slowly down the trail. It'd been a long time since she'd been to this part of the lake—she usually hung out at Evie's—but she was sure there was a… There it was. A bench, nearly hidden by the low shrubs and high grass that edged the trail. Viv pushed her way through and settled onto the bench. It was clean and afforded an unobstructed view of the Lake with the Cascade Mountains rising dramatically on either side. The air was clear and crisp, and tendrils of mist rose from the water.

The sun was warm on her back, but the cool breeze coming off the lake balanced it perfectly. No matter how much she ran, how many times she professed to hate the town where she'd lived since she was nine, the town her mother had grown up in, coming here was coming home.

Viv leaned back and tipped her head up, letting the sounds of the breeze rustling the leaves and the trill of birds lull her into an almost meditative state. It'd been a long time since she'd allowed herself to be alone with her thoughts. She'd spent most of the last year either working or drinking, and, if she was honest with herself, the years before that either working or distracting herself with whomever she was dating at the time. When she found herself between relationships, she threw herself into work and exercise classes—cardio classes, Zumba, spinning. She'd stopped running about a year before her trip to hell when the meditative calm she'd always loved became another place for her negative thoughts to clamor for attention.

The one time she'd tried therapy to work through her mother issues, she lasted three sessions before ghosting her therapist who'd insisted she needed to spend time with herself before she could figure out where to go and what to do. He'd had the unmitigated gall to tell her she'd let herself be defined first by the mother she'd spent the last forty-plus years disappointing, then by her friends who she constantly compared herself to, and then by the series of relationships that never seemed to go anywhere, leaving nothing of herself to be defined by what she wanted. He'd offered up what felt like so much critique of her character, her reactions, and her coping mechanisms—which used to be exercise instead of alcohol—and no guidance or even leading questions about how to begin to heal.

Viv finished her coffee and pushed her shades on top of her head. She winced as the sunlight hit her, bringing fresh waves of nausea and stabbing pain. She put both feet on the ground, closed her eyes, and did the breathing exercises she'd picked up from a short-lived meditation kick when she thought she could learn to let go of her thoughts and rise above the anxiety, self-loathing, and depression that had dogged her for too long. When the hangover-like symptoms dissipated to a manageable level, she slowly opened her eyes.

She'd been gone too long—she knew Bev and Evie would be worried about her, and she didn't want to be a bigger jerk than she'd already been. She grabbed her phone, didn't check the messages or voicemail, and dictated a message to Siri, letting them both know she was okay.

She hit send and heard the *ping* of an incoming message. Viv shot to her feet and looked around. Adrenaline surged through her body, freezing her like a deer in headlights. Evie was on the trail behind her, baby on her chest, and a disgruntled expression on her face.

Viv watched as her best friend looked around, then plunged through the underbrush towards Viv.

"You are a world-class jerk," Evie huffed. "Not only did you disappear without a note, knowing we were worried about you—alcohol detox is no joke, asshole—you made me go for a freaking hike, carrying a wiggly baby, when I still haven't recovered from pushing this ungrateful demon with her giant demon head out of my body."

Evie collapsed on the bench, and Viv sat down gingerly beside her.

"Sorry," Viv said in a small voice she barely recognized. "It's just a hangover, but I didn't think it through."

Evie blew out a long breath. "It's fine. Really. I get why you'd need some time, and I know why you're here."

"You do?" Viv asked. She'd thought her propensity to hide in plain sight over the years had gone unnoticed.

"Of course. This is the bench where you, me, and Bev swore to be best friends forever, where we became blood sisters." Evie held up her hand. A small, silvery scar on her wrist flashed in the sunlight. Viv held her wrist up to display a matching scar. "But you should've left a note. I didn't tell Bev you were missing—she doesn't need the stress— but I had a momentary freak-out." Evie looked down at Viv, and Viv couldn't read the expression in her eyes. Evie said, wry grin spreading across her face, "I need to apologize."

"For what?" Viv wracked her brain, but all she came up with were her own shortcomings.

"I pushed you. I used the power I've gotten from Luc and my children to force you into something you didn't want to do. I know I'd do it again, but I took away your choice, and that was wrong."

Viv shifted her gaze to a point over Evie's shoulder and twisted her hands together. "It's okay. I really believe you couldn't have made me do anything I didn't want to, even if that want was buried pretty deep down. Thank you for caring, for not giving up on me."

"Always," Evie said. She pulled Alex out of the baby carrier on her chest and fanned herself. "These baby wearing contraptions are hot."

"May I?" Viv asked, holding her arms out towards the baby. She was grateful for the change of subject and unworthy of having a friend who could read her so adeptly.

Evie handed her over. "Be my guest. If she goes for a boob, let me know and I'll feed her. Hopefully, she won't need a change immediately. I didn't bring the diaper bag."

Viv sat down and cradled the baby in her arms. She raised Alex close enough to breathe in the fresh, sweet baby scent of the baby's perfect, if relatively large, head. "She's so big," Viv said, inhaling deeply through her nose.

"She's six months old," Evie said.

There wasn't a hint of censure in her friend's voice, but it didn't prevent a swell of guilt from rising. At this rate, between the waves of guilt and fear and self-loathing, Viv was going to get washed out to sea—or lake, she amended as she looked over Alex's head at the impossibly blue-green body of water in front of her—by a cliché tidal wave of emotion.

Evie, seemingly oblivious to the storm of emotions vying for prominence in Viv's chest, rolled her neck and arched her back. "And she is heavy. I think I know why people in their forties—at least this woman—shouldn't have kids. I thought carrying Lily around was bad enough eleven years ago... I am so much older and stiffer now." She opened her eyes and, with a final grimace, sat down next to Viv and followed her gaze out to the lake.

"I still have trouble being close to the lake for too long," Evie confessed. "Knowing that *something* is in there. After almost losing Lily and my dad last year... The only good thing is that for the first summer in as long as anyone can remember, no one drowned last year."

Eden Lake was still this morning, like an unmarred mirror, perfectly reflecting the mountains rising in a semi-circle around it. "I love it," Viv said. "But I get why you wouldn't. Not saying I want to ever go out on it again—there isn't anything that could ever get me to touch that water—but I spent a lot of hours on this bench growing up. Every time I needed to escape my mom and didn't want to be around people, I came here. I don't like the stillness, though. It's easier to let it pull out all the negative feelings when I can count the waves."

Concentric circles, narrow at first, then widening, appeared in the middle of the lake. Less than a minute later, gentle waves lapped the beach in front of them.

Viv and Evie froze, staring at the waves that hadn't been there before and had no obvious source.

"Um... Wanna go get breakfast at the diner?" Evie asked, putting the baby carrier back on and holding out her arms.

"Abso-fucking-lutely." Viv turned and glanced behind her. The waves were dissipating—almost gone—and a pair of emerald eyes appeared above the water's surface in the center of the lake. She blinked, and they were gone. A ghostly image of Bev took its place, hovering above the water and holding something that Viv knew was a body. One more blink, and the lake was once again placid, not a wave marring its surface.

She braced for the spike of pain that accompanied her flashes of knowing, but nothing came. She didn't release the tension in her shoulders, though, until she and Evie were on the trail and headed back towards the park.

CHAPTER THREE

V iv stood in front of the mirror in her borrowed bedroom trying not to count the days she'd been in Eden Valley. She never stayed longer than five days—it made it harder to leave. There was a compulsion that took hold; it felt like the town didn't want her to go.

Knowing what she knew now—what she'd learned last year about the hungriness of the lake being not just anthropomorphic and Eden Valley being a hotspot for demon activity—it made a little more sense that the town would have a supernatural hold on those it considered residents, but it still rankled as she found her free will and drive slowly leached from her body.

Viv sighed. Right now, there was no help for it. She could work here as well as anywhere, and she wasn't sure that returning to her condo in Seattle would be healthy. At least here, she had her friends. It was hard to admit how much she'd missed them, missed the kids, in her self-imposed exile, but watching Shelby, Lily, and Kevin flit back and forth between playful children and miniature adults gave her hope that there was a light at the end of the tunnel.

Being continually head butted by Sprinkles, Lily's three-headed hellhound currently masquerading as a Bernese Mountain Dog, was the icing on the cake. Viv loved animals, but hadn't been allowed a pet growing up, and when she bought her own place, it seemed impractical to get one. She worked constantly and when she wasn't working, she was socializing. Her condo wasn't big enough for a dog to stretch their legs, and her furniture wasn't cheap enough to risk leaving it alone with a kitten.

"Viv! Are you about ready?" Bev called up the stairs. "No rush if you aren't, but I need more coffee and if we aren't leaving soon, I'll make another cup here."

Viv sighed. Her hair was a mess—the undercut she'd meticulously maintained for years had grown out and was shaggy, and her natural jet-black hair and the fading pink and blue streaks were sporting grey roots. She hadn't grabbed her makeup. Or cute clothes. Or the supply of contacts she hadn't told anyone she needed. Viv glared at her reflection, at the borrowed, too-big grey t-shirt sporting a trans pride flag and a "Support Trans Kids" logo, shoved her glasses up her nose, and headed downstairs.

"I need to go home," she proclaimed as she walked into the kitchen. "I need a haircut, clean clothes, and makeup. And other things."

Bev looked at her, then did a double take. "You are wearing glasses," she said. "I'm sorry. You probably knew that, but I had no idea…"

Viv huffed out a breath. "I didn't grab anything of use out of the bathroom. Including my contact replacements. I guess it's a good thing that I always have a pair of glasses in my bag, but I hate that I have to wear them."

"They're cute," Bev said, getting closer and narrowing her eyes at her friend. "I can take you back to grab whatever you need tomorrow —or, better yet, you can give your keys to Luc along with a list of what you need, and he can grab everything Monday. I know he's headed to Seattle for some kind of work conference and will be back on Wednesday. We can wash your clothes—it's no big deal, really—and you'll be okay for a few more days, right?"

Viv looked down at her feet. She knew Bev was right, that she shouldn't go back right now, but she was itching to get out of town before it was too late. She shook her head, but her words betrayed her. "That's fine. I'll make a list. Although asking Lucifer, Prince of Hell, to pack some underwear for me is...weird."

Bev grinned. "He's seen underwear before, you know. And if you want something small before Wednesday, I bet Evie can get it for you. Unless she's angry, her control is a little shaky—Luc says it's the after-effects of having a baby—but it's better than it's ever been before."

Viv thought about having access to her contacts so she could ditch her ridiculous glasses that made her feel her age and the creeping mortality she'd been hiding from for years, and then she thought about asking Evie to take a break from parenting her half-demon children and sighed. "I can wait."

"Ready to go then?" Bev asked.

"I guess. Who all will be there?" Viv's stomach was tying itself in knots, and she tried to tell herself it was hunger and not nerves when contemplating seeing her super-hot, super demony, kind of ex. She smiled at Bev, then really noticed her for the first time that day. "You look amazing, Bev. What the hell? How do you do that?"

Bev's honey brown hair was swept back in waves down her back, her skin, untanned and light brown, was clear and glowing, and the generous curves she'd hated when she was a teen and grudgingly accepted as she crept towards thirty, were embraced by her clothes, falling perfectly on her body and enhancing her figure.

Bev blushed and smiled, then ran her hands down the coral, flowing tunic that was tight around her breasts and hit right at her hips. She was wearing a turquoise blazer, denim shorts, and chunky wedges with turquoise beads. "It's amazing what clothes that fit can do for a person's appearance and self-esteem."

"It's definitely working for you," Viv said. "You've always been a hottie, but somehow, you keep elevating your game. It's kind of unfair, you know, hoarding all the beauty in Eden Valley."

Bev blushed, and a grin spread across her face. "We all get some-thing, I guess. You got brains, an exciting lifestyle, a cool condo in the Fremont neighborhood, and a kick-ass figure that looks good in tight leather pants. Evie got the compassion, determination, and a hot man to father her kids. And I got eternal youth." She shrugged. "I also got a kid currently obsessed with fashion design and sewing."

"Holy crap! Shelby made all this?" Viv picked up the hem of Bev's shirt and crouched down to examine it. "This is some professional level fashion right here."

"I am definitely hashtag blessed," Bev said. "Most of the time. Now, ready to go? You can continue to praise my beauty and my kiddo's brains on the way there, if you want to."

VIV HUNCHED into the corner of the large, out of the way table and scowled at her sparkling water. Evie and Bev were chatting animatedly with Elle about something that'd happened at the fifth-grade graduation and talent show, yet another thing Viv had missed. Resentment curdled in her stomach and acid rose in her throat. Elle was the third Bev and Evie deserved. Someone who was there, who could hold sleepovers. A mom.

The anger she couldn't control anymore heated her blood until she felt like she was on fire. It took a minute of deep breathing trying to push everything back into the cold, smooth-walled cave, complete with deep, unfathomable lake where she kept her anger. If she was being honest with herself, which she tried not to be—there was a reason she quit therapy—she stuffed the rest of her big emotions into that nearly unreachable vault, too.

Evie reached out, grabbed her hand under the table and squeezed. The heat that'd been building faded, leaving her left shoulder last. She was used to that. The brand she'd gotten when she'd tumbled into hell's side entrance burned every time she let her emotions out.

"Are you...smoking?" Elle asked. A faint crinkle appeared between her black eyebrows, the only lines that marred her brown skin.

"I don't smoke," Viv retorted. It wasn't in her nature to be jealous. It didn't make sense. It was awesome Elle'd finally come out of the house and started parenting and making friends. It must have been so lonely... Nope. Not working. She couldn't replace envy with empathy. It was an ugly emotion, but everything about her was ugly lately.

"Your shoulder *is* smoking," Bev said. "And there's a hole in the shirt."

"Is that where your..." Evie paused and worried at her lower lip. "...tattoo is? It is, right?"

Bev was nodding before Viv could answer. "It is!" Bev turned to Elle. "Viv and I got matching ink last year. Kind of matching. Same day, same style, same place."

"I don't know what yours looks like, Sweet B, but I can verify that's where Viv is marked." Sam slid into the booth next to Elle and smirked at Viv. "It is smoking, though. You might want to let things out—or maybe have a glass of ice water."

The warmth that flooded Viv this time wasn't anger. At least not entirely. It was lust forward with hints of guilt, a little anger, and something else she steered away from before she could identify it.

"Hey ladies," Sam said. The smile on her face threatened to melt parts of Viv she didn't want melted, but it wasn't directed at her.

Ugh. More emotions she wasn't prepared for and that she'd spent the last year trying to pretend didn't exist. She closed her eyes and thought cool thoughts. Ice skating. Skiing. Snow shoeing. The heat— at least the angry heat—disappeared.

"Better," Evie whispered to Viv. "I'll let you know if it happens again." Evie squeezed Viv's hand again before letting go.

"I didn't know you had tattoos," Elle said. "Can I see?"

"No," Viv snapped at the same time Bev said, "Sure, but maybe not right now. Not sure the whole restaurant needs me to accidentally flash them trying to show off."

"Cool." Elle grinned. "Do you have one, too, Evie?"

"I do have a tattoo, but I didn't get mine with Bev and Viv, and I am definitely not showing anyone my tramp stamp." Evie leaned forward and cupped her chin in her hands. "Do you have any ink?"

Elle shook her head. "No, although now that I know about them, I think I might want one. They're kinda fun and sexy, right?"

"Super fun and sexy," Sam said.

Viv stood up, bumping her water glass and nearly tipping it over. "I'm going to the bathroom," she announced, louder than she'd intended.

"Want me to come with?" Bev asked.

"I think I can manage without a hand hold," Viv said back, her voice biting through the air hard enough to make Bev flinch. Dammit. She was being bitchy again. She sat back down and looked at Bev. "I'm sorry. I was being rude, and you didn't deserve that. I'm just a ball of emotions right now."

"I'm sure it doesn't help that Sam and I are here," Elle said. "We're the newcomers to the group, and you probably wanted to talk to your friends without virtual strangers listening in. If you want, we can head out." The look on her face was so genuinely kind and thoughtful, wide-eyed and sincere, that Viv felt the sweetness oozing over her and cutting through the bitterness.

"Oh, Viv and I aren't strangers," Sam said, her voice taking on a bit of Southern drawl.

"We're not much more than strangers," Viv retorted. "A couple months of barely leaving the bedroom isn't bosom buddy territory."

Sam's gaze dropped from Viv's face down to her chest, then she quirked an eyebrow and met Viv's eyes, a challenge in her own. "If you say so." Sam turned her attention back to Elle. "I can catalogue all of Viv's ink for you. And send you pics of mine, too. No secrets here, right, ladies?"

Evie stared at Sam, and Viv felt the steel in her eyes even though it wasn't directed at her. "Play nice, Sam. We're not here for chaos, and if you cause too much trouble, I'll ban you from holding Alex again."

"Again?" Viv blurted.

Sam rolled her eyes. "Last time she banned me, it was because I challenged someone to a drinking contest in her bar."

"No," Evie corrected. "It was because you pretended it was your first beer, acted tipsy, challenged a tourist to a tequila shot contest by throwing a couple hundred dollars on the bar. When you drank him under the table, you forced him to pay up and taunted him for losing to a 'girl.' And if that wasn't enough, when he tried to fight you, you let him."

"Oh no," Viv said. "That's…"

"Fun, right?" Sam said. "I know. I did not deserve a three-week ban."

"He and his friends broke a table and knocked over one of my servers coming after you. She could have been seriously hurt. It was reckless and stupid, and you deserved more than a three-week ban, but Luc talked me into being lenient, and Lily backed him up." Evie shrugged. "But when I conceded, it was under the condition that if you got carried away and tried to start fights or send nudes, I get to pick the sentence."

"She's a tyrant," Sam complained. "Evie doesn't know what fun is, but she has all the power because she gave birth to the cutest baby demon I've ever seen." She crossed her arms and pouted.

Evie's smile managed to look both smug and beatific. "Never underestimate the power of good genes on the mother's side."

Viv laughed, and it took her by such surprise that she nearly choked, then snorted as she tried to get herself under control. She was in danger of giggling if she couldn't pull herself together, but something about these women—even with the interlopers and without her standard brunch bloody Mary—was untying knots in her neck and shoulders with surprising speed.

"I hate to interrupt your bodily function fest, but it's time for you guys to order or get out," a bored voice interrupted.

Viv narrowed her eyes at their server. "Brandy. I can't believe you're still working here. I was sure you would've gotten fired by now."

Evie spoke up before Brandy could make the retort Viv saw slowly forming in her mind. "Biscuits and gravy, please."

Sam ordered a tall stack of pancakes, three eggs, and six sausages, along with a cup of coffee, black. Viv and Bev got their usuals—pancakes with extra syrup and a ham and cheese omelet.

"And what did you want, Kevin's mom?" Brandy asked. "Or are you just going to take what's not yours from someone else's plate."

"What the hell, Brandy?" Viv said. "Just let her order and get out of here. No one needs your pettiness today. I don't know what bone you have to pick with Elle, but give it a rest, will you?"

"She knows what she did," Brandy said. "She might fool all of you with her sweet and innocent look, but what's she been up to since she moved here? Why Eden Valley? Find out what she's hiding and then tell me she's worth defending."

"I'd like the Belgian waffle with blueberries and cream," Elle said, voice leveler than Viv was managing right now.

"Let me know if you need anything else, Aurielle," Brandy spat. "I'm sure that you can have anything of mine you'd like."

"Brandy, knock it off," Viv said. "You're being even more awful than usual. No one here wants anything of yours. If I recall correctly, that's usually the other way around, isn't it? You wanted Evie's ex, and you're welcome to him, but you went after another woman's husband. And you wanted more than Jer. You wanted Evie's whole life, everything she had and everything she never got. Isn't that why you had to fake your pregnancy twelve years ago? To trick Jer into marriage and to make Evie feel bad?"

Brandy threw her order pad at Viv, who for once had no idea that was coming and didn't have time to duck. Then Brandy burst into tears and ran out of the restaurant.

Viv's jaw dropped. She looked at Evie whose wide eyes indicated she was as shocked at Viv.

"Should I... Should I go after her?" Viv asked. "I was not prepared for that. Thirty years of her backstabbing snark, smugness, and weird intrusions into our lives after repeatedly claiming she wanted nothing to do with us inferior creatures did not lead me to believe I could make her cry by bringing up a lie she told more than a decade ago."

"Are you sure it was a lie?" Sam asked. She was staring at the door Brandy'd disappeared through, eyebrows furrowed.

"Yeah," Evie said, although she didn't sound certain. "She told me she was pregnant in front of Jer right before I found out I was pregnant with Lily. He was at least as surprised as I was—he'd always said he'd had a vasectomy. And then she and Jer had an epic fight, broke off their engagement, and she left town for a couple years, leaving her bar in his neglectful hands. It was being foreclosed on by the time she got back, and I picked it up for a pretty good price."

"What Evie isn't saying is that Brandy spent the year between getting caught in Jer's bed and leaving town after she admitted lying about her timely pregnancy being insufferably cruel to Evie." Viv's eyes narrowed. "But she was gone for almost two years... I guess she could've had a baby in that time. But why wouldn't she stay? Or at least come back with a kid she could hold over Evie's head?"

"If it wasn't Jer's..." Bev's voice trailed off.

"He never wanted kids," Evie admitted. "Maybe he told her he'd take her back if she didn't keep it?"

"But that still feels like something she'd talk about," Viv pointed out. "Brandy doesn't keep things bottled up. That's never been her style."

"And she's hated me since high school," Evie said. "I don't know why—we'd been friends, kind of, until we were sixteen—but after the summer before our junior year, she and Joanne Olson became bffs and that was it. They spent the last two years of high school playing mean-spirited pranks on us to get us into trouble."

"Still..." Sam said, tapping a finger on her lips. "There's something there that I don't understand." She shifted her attention back to the table and looked directly at Aurielle. "Do you know what she's talking about? What did she mean?"

Elle's brown skin had taken on an ashen cast, and her eyes were wide. Viv couldn't tell if she looked scared or about to cry.

"I don't know... I've never spoken to her other than to order food." Elle's eyes shifted to the left and down.

She was lying. Viv was certain. But why? That made even less sense than Brandy lying about lying.

"I guess we should let someone know our server ran off," Bev said, shifting the conversation back to the present. She grabbed the order pad that'd bounced off Viv and landed on the table. "At least I can turn in our order." She walked away.

Evie and Sam started an argument about how often Sam was

allowed to babysit her nieces—never, according to Evie. Viv kept her eyes on Elle. Maybe she was upset because Brandy had yelled. It sucked to be on the receiving end of unexpected vitriol. And if this wasn't the first time, that could explain the lie.

A premonition hit her, followed seconds later by a blinding headache. There was more to Elle than she was letting on. It wasn't the lie about Brandy. Or at least not entirely. It was all tied together, but the ends of the string were out of sight and out of reach. It didn't make sense and didn't resemble any of the flashes of insight she'd had over the last year.

"Too vague," Viv muttered, holding her head in her hands.

Gradually, the white light that had exploded across her vision receded, and even the sparkling auras in the periphery of her closed eyes disappeared. She identified the pressure on her head as hands holding her skull together and not her brain trying to explode.

"What?" she asked. It always took time for her brain and mouth to reconnect after an intense vision.

"Look at me, sweetheart," Sam crooned.

Viv blinked away the remaining haze and opened her eyes. Sam's dark amber eyes were inches away, brimming with worry. It was Sam's hands on her head, and waves of soothing coolness rippled out from the pressure.

"Are you okay?" Evie asked, peering over Sam's shoulder.

Viv thought about it for a moment, waiting for the headache that had disappeared as quickly as it'd started to return. "I think so?" Uncertainty colored her voice. Sam's closeness pressed against her, taking up more and more of her awareness the longer she knelt between Viv's legs. Viv looked at the demon in front of her, intending to tell her to back off, but her gaze stuck on Sam's lips. They were full and lush and fire-engine red today. And they could do things to Viv's body she hadn't dreamed possible. Viv leaned forward, drawn in like a tractor beam. Her breath hitched.

"Shameful!"

The voice behind Viv jolted her out of the spell cast by Sam's face. And for the first time since Bev and Evie had forced their way into her condo and dragged her back to Eden Valley, Viv didn't feel too much. The emotions receded and disappeared into the emptiness she'd been cultivating since she was eleven and told her mother she was going to marry a girl when she grew up. It wasn't the first time her mother's words had devastated her, but it was the first time she'd been made to feel that *she* was the problem and not something she'd done.

Viv jerked away from Sam's hands and pushed her chair back to put some distance between her and the demon. She whipped around, but not fast enough to miss the flash of hurt in Sam's eyes. One more person she'd disappointed. It might be time to keep score.

Viv stood up and regarded the woman, prematurely bent and lined, with the customary detachment she'd been practicing for over thirty years.

"Hello, Mother."

CHAPTER FOUR

"Hey," Sam said softly, sitting next to Viv on her bench. "Are you okay?"

Viv stared out over the lake. She couldn't look at Sam. Not now, not so soon after nearly losing control earlier.

"Fine." She might suck at feelings and relationships and standing up to her mother, but she knew how to chase someone out of her love life.

"Do you want to talk about anything?"

Viv felt Sam shift on the bench, moving closer. The heat from Sam's body warmed Viv's skin. It was one part a gift of her demon heritage and two parts the lust Viv couldn't quite dismiss.

"Nope." One-word answers were key.

"I don't mean about your mom, although I'd listen. I mean about whatever you saw right before she showed up. It looked intense—I haven't seen you like that before." Sam slipped an arm along the back of the bench.

"You haven't seen much of anything in the last year," Viv snapped. Oops. Broke the one-word rule.

Sam's shrug bumped her shoulder against Viv's. "That was your choice, not mine. I know what you're doing here. You're trying to pick a fight so I go away, and you can mope and replay your list of sins on a loop until you feel as bad as you think you deserve."

"I don't do that. I'm thinking." Viv slid down to the end of the bench and out from under Sam's arm. "And you're interrupting my alone time."

"Sweetheart, all you have is alone time. You push everyone away so hard that even your best friends have trouble infiltrating your walls. You need to let someone in. It doesn't have to be me, but you can't carry everything by yourself." She brushed her hand against Viv's shoulder. "You deserve happiness. You don't have to earn it. You don't need to wait for your mother's approval or to feel you've lived up to some imaginary milestone you've created for yourself based on your friends' lives. And the sooner you let yourself believe that, the sooner you can stop running away and start living your life."

Tears formed at the corners of Viv's eyes, and she turned to look at Sam, but the demon was already gone.

THERE WERE two trails around the lake. The first, the most popular one with tourists and anyone who preferred comfort to complication, was a graded dirt path, wide enough for three people to walk abreast, and had benches every quarter mile or so. It was twelve miles around the lake if you wanted a long but pleasant and easy hike. Informational signs about the history of Eden Valley and the Cascade Mountains dotted the trail, and even the hills were barely hilly.

The other trail was little more than a worn dirt path that only permitted passing if one person stepped off the trail. It was rooty, rocky, and deceptively steep in some places. The only people who used that one were trail runners in the early morning or late evening, and locals avoiding the crowds.

Viv was about three quarters of the way around the lake and was panting and sweating far more than she'd anticipated in the cool mountain air. The elevation didn't usually bother her, but she didn't usually do anything more active in Eden Valley than drink wine and sit on Evie's back porch.

"I am so stupid," she muttered to herself. She used to run six days a week between three and fifteen miles. Her secret hobby—one she'd never shared with Instagram or her bffs—was half marathons. But the solitude of running required too much time on her own with her thoughts. She needed more distraction, more noise. And two years off running meant she could no longer go for a spontaneous fifteen-mile trail run, especially when she was wearing the oversized shirt she'd borrowed from Bev—now with a scorch mark on the shoulder— leggings, and worn sneakers with too-thin socks. Blisters were forming on the balls of her feet, the backs of her heels, and in between her toes.

She clenched her teeth against the discomfort—no pain, no gain, right?—and kept moving forward. It was more of a shamble now than a run, but it was forward movement, and she had three miles to go to get back to Bev's. She slowed to a walk to catch her breath and looked down towards the lake. From the trail's vantage point, she could see the lower, wheelchair accessible trail as it wound around the swimming beach.

The beach was crowded, as it always was in late July. Hordes of tourists from Seattle, Portland, and Spokane descended on the mountain towns of the East Cascades every summer to beat the heat and spend some time in nature, and Eden Valley always got more than its share of summer people. But no matter how many signs locals posted along the beach and in the stores warning the tourists to stay out of the water, some people thought they knew better.

The lake was cold—even in late July—and had claimed a life every summer except for last year for as long as anyone could remember. Until last year, Viv had firmly believed that it was the cold and deceptive depths responsible for the drownings. But now, after Lily'd been pulled under last April when she fell overboard showing off while canoeing, there was no denying it anymore. Eden Lake was something more than a dangerous mountain lake.

Viv shook her head and started moving forward again. There

might be something in the lake, something hungry and a little angry, but it couldn't get her here, and there was no reason she needed to dwell on that now.

She stopped. Her gaze was pulled back to the lake and an over-whelming sense of wrongness overtook her. The vision of a child—not more than three or four—hit her. The baby was being pulled out like they were caught in an ocean riptide instead of wading in a mountain lake.

This time, there was no accompanying headache or flash of mind-numbing light. Viv scrambled down the trail, crossed the lower trail, and ran onto the beach. She scanned the shore, looking for the child she'd seen in her vision. A little kid in a ruffly polka-dotted pink swimsuit and a little sun bonnet tied under their chin toddled away from their parents, deep in conversation with each other, and towards the lake. Viv picked up speed. Every muscle was screaming, and she was sucking air.

The child hit the water. Two steps. Three. The water was up to their chest. The lake pulled back, exposing more shoreline—like a beach before a tsunami hits—and then surged forward.

Viv plunged into the water just as people started to scream. She grabbed the child, held them back, and stared into the dark, swirling lake. "You can't take anymore," she yelled. "You've had enough."

The pull on the child stopped so suddenly that Viv stumbled back-wards and landed on her butt in the sand, the child still in her arms. The kid started to struggle, and Viv turned to deposit them on the beach behind her, out of reach of the water.

"Mama mama mama!"

The parents rushed forward, and the father scooped the child up and held them close.

"I saw what you did," the mother said. "Thank you. You saved her."

Viv climbed to her feet. She was wet and covered in sand. "Just stay away from the water. Please. It's not safe."

The woman threw her arms around Viv, shocking her into returning the embrace. "Thank you."

Viv patted her back until the woman let go and turned all her attention to her child.

As soon as she had her breath back, Viv trudged back to the trail—the lower impact one this time—to finish her circuit of the lake and head back to Bev's.

VIV STEPPED out of the shower and wrapped one of Bev's luxuriously huge bath sheets around her body. Twenty minutes in the hot shower had done wonders for her aching muscles and the tension that kept building in her neck.

She walked into the guest room, now her room for the time being, and stopped, clutching the towel to her chest like a bad romance novel virgin on her pirate ship wedding night.

Sitting on the bed in a neat, solemn row were Lily, Shelby, and Kevin.

"What are you doing here? In my room? While I was showering?"

Lily rolled her eyes, something she'd been practicing on her mom for at least three years, but that Viv had seldom been subjected to. "Aunt Viv. You're not naked. We've all seen towels before."

Viv pursed her lips. This was not a situation she'd been prepared to handle, either by her mom-friends or by premonition. Getting a warning about this seemed a lot more useful than avoiding a spilled drink at a restaurant.

"I am willing to concede that not only is this not the first towel you've seen, it's not the first towel-clad post-shower person you've seen. However, you are in my room without my consent, and I feel very uncomfortable."

Shelby stood and grabbed her friends by their arms. "She's right. This is wicked inappropriate. We can tell her we need to talk and let her come to us."

Viv smiled. "That sounds amazing. Thank you, Shelby. I'll get dressed and meet you all in the living room in ten minutes?"

Kevin grimaced. "Not private enough."

"How is that not private enough?" Viv demanded. "There's no one else here but the four of us."

"Back garden. Ten minutes. Bring snacks." Kevin disappeared down the stairs, and after a backwards glance, Lily clattered after him.

"Aunt Bev's due home any minute, and technically she doesn't know we're here," Shelby said. "Lily and I said we were at Kevin's, and he said we were all at Lily's. It'd kind of suck to get caught. I've been a pretty bad kid this year, and I don't want Aunt Bev to be any madder at me than she already is."

"You're not a bad kid," Viv said automatically.

"Do you know what happened?" Shelby asked, one hand on the doorjamb. With her head tilted and her body half-poised to rush out of the room after her friends, she looked like she was hovering on the very last precipice of childhood.

"No. And I don't need to know. You're a good kid, Shel. We all have things we screw up, and if you think you screwed up, then you apologize and make amends. But screwing up doesn't make us bad. It makes us human." The words she'd intended to be well-meaning cliches for the twelve-year-old in front of her boomeranged back and socked her in the chest. "I've had a pretty terrible year myself and made some major mistakes. Do you think I'm a bad person?"

The pause that stretched out between them was long enough that Viv was getting nervous her life lesson was going to backfire on both of them.

Shelby finally exhaled a great puff of air. "No. You can't be a bad person or Aunt Bev and Aunt Evie wouldn't be friends with you."

"Back atcha, kiddo," Viv said. "Maybe we've made mistakes, but Bev still loves us, so we must be okay, right?"

Shelby giggled, and the years melted away until she looked like a kid again. "You're pretty ridiculous. But I love you anyway. Thanks for not being a jerk."

"Any time, kiddo."

Shelby stepped out of the room. "You'd better hurry. There's only a few minutes left of the ten Kevin gave you." She ran down the stairs and Viv heard the backdoor slam.

Viv set the timer on her phone for five minutes and dropped the towel.

KEVIN, Shelby, and Lily were sitting on the porch swing, each with a sweating glass of lemonade in hand, watching Viv with solemn, inscrutable expressions.

So far, no one had said anything. Viv was impatient and desperately wanted to prod them along so she could head to the living room, sit in front of an AC vent, and play mindless games on her phone while listening to the newest episode of her favorite true crime podcast. But she sensed they were deciding something, and that whatever they were deciding was more important than anything she could imagine. A jolt of knowing hit her, but like the one earlier, this one had no lasting effect.

She looked at Kevin. "This is about you, right?"

He looked up at her, his emerald green eyes startlingly bright against his light brown skin. He blinked, and they were brown again.

Something caught in Viv's throat. She'd seen eyes like that before…

"It's not what it seems," Lily said. Her bright smile sent rays of calm over Viv.

Viv's neck muscles started to relax, and her shoulder blades melted down her back. She shook herself and glared at Lily. "Liliana Grace, I have known you for eleven years, and you will not use your demon powers on me. Do it again, and I will—"

"What? Tell my dad? Tell Papa Abe?" Lily scoffed.

"No. I will tell your mother."

Lily gasped. "You can't tell Mom I'm abusing demon powers. That's not fair. You have to tell another demon. Those are the rules!"

"The rules you just made up," Viv said. "I might not have been around a lot in the last year, but I know you, and I know your mom. Don't even try me, Lily."

Lily crossed her arms. Her lower lip jutted out. "Fucking fine. But listen to Kevin anyway. All the way through before you judge."

Viv nodded. "Promise."

Kevin looked at his friends, and they nodded, encouragement evident in their eyes. He stood, looked at Viv, and said, "I'm the monster."

Viv took a step back, nearly losing her balance as the soft ground gave way beneath her. "Oh, no, honey. You're not a monster. I don't know what's happened, but I can tell you right now that no matter what it was, it doesn't make you a monster."

"I didn't say I was *a* monster. I said I was *the* monster." Kevin smiled, and his eyes flashed emerald again. Viv barely registered that, though. Her attention was stuck on his fangs. His teeth were elongating and developing points, the way she'd always assumed vampires would, but a second row of teeth joined them, then a third, and he opened his mouth until there was nothing to look at but his huge, gaping maw.

"Holy shit," Viv breathed. "You're the Eden Lake monster."

Kevin's mouth snapped shut with the clicking of teeth, and his jawline and eyes returned to his usual look. "I am. And I need help."

CHAPTER FIVE

V iv was in the kitchen refilling lemonades and rummaging through Bev's cupboards to find snacks for the three hungry tweens in the backyard. She shouldn't have retreated in the face of Kevin's revelation, but she needed a minute to think, to figure out how to handle this. She'd known Kevin since he was five and followed Lily home on the first day of kindergarten. He was a child. The drownings had been happening for at least a hundred years. And they'd been happening for the last eleven since he was…born.

"Aunt Viv!" Shelby yelled. "You should text Aunt Bev and ask her to fetch some ice cream before coming home. We finished Lily's stash today and will need more tomorrow. It's summer, and ice cream is required. She won't do it if I ask, but if you do…"

Viv's lips curled in a wry smile. She might be stymied by the news the kids had dropped on her, but their need for daily ice cream somehow restored normalcy to the afternoon.

"Bev. Have I ever told you how wonderful and selfless you are?" Viv texted her friend.

"Do you need something?" The reply was nearly instantaneous.

"If it's not too much trouble…"

Bev sent an eye rolling emoji. *"Just tell me, and if it's within my power, I will get it for you."*

"Ice cream sandwiches would be amazing. Maybe a half dozen?"

"..."

Viv stared at the phone for a second, then tucked it into her pocket, grabbed a box of popsicles and four glasses of lemonade, and headed to the back door. "Can someone get the door for me?"

Kevin hopped up and got the door, then took two of the glasses from her.

"Thank you." Viv smiled at him. He was a good kid. Always had been. There must be some kind of mistake.

Her phone text notification vibrated her pocket. Viv handed a glass of lemonade and the popsicles to Lily who grabbed the lone grape one and passed the box on to Shelby. Viv dropped into one of the Adirondack chairs facing the swing and set her glass down on the wide armrest before looking at her phone.

"I am deeply suspicious of your request, but your wish is my command. And if my child is there, tell her she is in big trouble when I get home. See you in 30."

"Ice cream is on the way," Viv said, looking at the kids—no, not kids. Not anymore. "And Shelby, Bev says you're in big trouble, but I think she was mostly kidding."

Shelby hunched into herself for a moment, and Viv struggled to identify the look on her face. Shame? Guilt? Fear?

"Are you okay, Shel?" Viv leaned forward and tried to get her niece to meet her gaze.

Shelby kept her eyes resolutely on her lap. "Today isn't about me." She elbowed Kevin lightly.

Now that they were ready and he'd dropped his monster bomb, Kevin seemed to be struggling to find the words he needed.

"Kevin, whatever you need to say here today, unless it presents an immediate danger to you or someone else, I will keep to myself until you decide I can share it." Viv's mouth was dry, and she took a gulp of her lemonade. Radiating calm and acceptance and love was not her area of expertise. Her method of aunting had always been to spoil, share silly inside jokes, and do her best to be the opposite of her mother.

Kevin took a deep breath and met Viv's eyes. "You saw my other face," he said, then paused as if waiting for confirmation.

Viv nodded. "I did. And I've seen your eyes before, in the lake and in a vision, but I don't understand."

"I don't know where to begin," he admitted, worrying at his lower lip. "It felt like I needed to tell someone—besides Lily and Shelby—but now I'm scared."

"Have you girls known for long?" Viv asked, hoping the question would give Kevin time to collect his thoughts and decide how he wanted to proceed.

Lily and Shelby exchanged a glance over Kevin's head, then nodded. "Since last summer," Lily said. "After Sprinkles rescued me from the lake."

"That was an accident!" Kevin said. "I didn't mean..."

Shelby patted his shoulder. "We know. You would never hurt either of us on purpose."

"I just... I get so hungry." Kevin looked at Viv through impossibly long eyelashes.

"You...eat people?" Viv kept her expression neutral, something only possible through years of talking to her mother and not wanting to let her know how much she was hurt. Ugh. That was twice in five minutes she'd thought of her mother. Inhale. Hold. Exhale.

"Not exactly. I mean, I know the teeth look scary, but those are mostly for fish." Kevin traced patterns in the condensation on his glass of lemonade, ignoring the orange popsicle melting in his other hand. "I do need people, though. But it's not their bodies. It's their life. I try to only take enough to survive. One a year is enough, especially now that I'm..." he gestured at his body. "But after almost taking Lily last year—I was hungry, and she was the first person in the lake in almost a year—I decided I needed to stop. Lily helped me find a way to get my energy without pulling anyone under. Little sips of life energy from a lot of people instead of gulps from one or two a year." He shuddered, and his eyes flashed green. "Today was an accident."

"Okay. This is a lot," Viv said. "And I have so many questions. I want to be open-minded, but to be completely honest, I'm struggling. This doesn't fall into the moral grey area I've accepted as my new normal after finding out Lily is a half demon and Evie and I have demon powers."

"Not to mention, you spent a lot of time smooching Aunt Sam," Lily pointed out. "She and Daddy are greyer than me and Alex. And you and Mommy are barely grey at all."

"And Papa Abe?" Viv asked, buying for time. This situation hadn't been in the fun aunt handbook.

"Oh, he's nowhere near grey," Lily said. "He's a King of Hell. He powers hell with the souls of the dead—they make everything go and keep him supplied with the most expensive of everything." She shrugged. "But he doesn't hurt people before they go to hell. Just has them sign binding contracts with almost zero loopholes."

"So not like me at all." Kevin sounded like he was on the verge of tears. His voice was thick, and he'd screwed his eyes closed. "I don't mean to. At least not anymore."

Shelby and Lily put their arms around him and circled in for a small group hug, shielding him from Viv's view and probably smearing their bodies and clothes with sticky, melting faux fruit.

"Okay," Viv said. "There's nothing we can do about the past, at least not now. Let's deal with the present and hopefully that'll help sort out the future." A flash hit her. Kevin, in the middle of the lake with his mouth wide and rows of fangs elongated, pulling everyone into the lake and swallowing them whole. It was immediately replaced with an image of Kevin, pale and thin, with his eyes closed under a white sheet Elle was pulling over his body to cover his face. A third image tumbled over the other two—Kevin, Lily, and Shelby on a raft in the middle of the lake, laughing. They looked at least five years older than they were right now.

"What did you see?" Lily asked. Her cool, slightly sticky hand pushed back Viv's hair from her sweat-dampened forehead. "Are you okay?"

Viv shook her head and grabbed her lemonade, taking a long

drink. "Too much, too many futures. That's never happened before. Usually, I get flashes of the immediate future. These were... I don't know when, but not imminent." Her stomach churned and a headache threatened.

"Can I help?" Lily asked.

"No, sweetheart, there's nothing you can do right now. I'll be fine. I just need a minute." Viv closed her eyes against the flashing lights and inhaled deeply.

"I can help, actually," Lily said. "But Mama says it's better to get consent, even when I'm having good intentions. Papa Abe says human consent is irrelevant. And Aunt Sam says as long as I'm doing no harm, it's better to help and ask for forgiveness after."

"How?" Viv asked, swallowing hard to keep her breakfast where it belonged.

"Can I show you?" Lily asked.

Viv felt Lily's hands hovering an inch above her face, and somehow the small space between them was cooler than the air surrounding them.

"Let her," Shelby said. "Lily's hands are magic."

"Okay," Viv said. She hated the idea of demon powers being used on her. She was still reeling from Evie breaking her own rules and using her demon-granted powers on Viv.

Lily's hands bridged the distance to Viv's head. They were cool against the heat of Viv's body, and like before, Viv's shoulders relaxed and the tension in her neck released, taking with it the brewing headache. Her nausea slowly subsided, and with it, the rising desire for a drink she hadn't wanted to admit to, even to herself.

"Better?" Lily asked.

"So much," Viv said. "You'll be able to make a fortune in college as a hangover cure-all. I can't believe that healing is a gift given to demons. It doesn't seem very hellish."

The light pressure of Lily's hands disappeared from Viv's face, and although she'd braced, the nausea and headache didn't return. When Viv opened her eyes, Lily was back in her spot on the end of the garden swing. It might be the lingering effects of the sudden-onset migraine, but it looked like Lily was glowing, just a bit.

"Healing is a great way to get people to trust you," Lily said. "And just about anything can be used for evil. It's less about ability or power, and even the intention behind it, and more about the impact it has and what you do with it. If I made you feel better and then offered to do it again next time if you did something for me, something that seemed little, but that each time was a bit more, that wouldn't be so great."

"When did you get to be so wise?" Viv asked, leaning back and taking a drink of her watery lemonade.

"The last year's been interesting," Lily said. "There are a lot of opinions about what I can do and what I should do, and I have to figure out the best way to wade through it on my own." She looked sideways at Kevin, who appeared to be trying to make himself disappear through willpower alone. "That's what I've been trying to tell Kevin, but he doesn't believe in moral grey areas, at least not when it comes to himself."

Lily and Shelby scooted closer to Kevin, knocking the slushy popsicles on the ground and once more cocooning him in their arms. It was clear that the girls felt very protective about their friend, and Viv wondered if the fact that she wasn't a parent was the reason they decided to trust her. She wouldn't have to worry about punishments for any broken rules, and since she'd already promised to keep it to herself unless someone was in immediate danger, she wouldn't even feel obligated to rat them out to their parents.

Shelby took up the narrative. "We don't know everything, but we know Kevin is old. Like really, really old. He was born with the lake, and for a long time, he was barely awake. The life force of the animals who lived in the lake or drank from it or swam in it sustained him. When colonizers showed up in the mountains, that's when he began to stir, and when Eden Valley was founded, the magic that came with the first settlers roused him. The years before that aren't very clear, but the last hundred and fifty are."

"What are you?" Viv asked. "I know that sounds rude, but you're not human."

"I'm human," Kevin protested. A green flash lit his eyes for a moment, but then he blinked and it was gone. "At least I am now."

Shelby leveled a stare at him, and he squirmed under her regard.

"I'm as human as Lily, anyway," he amended. "I'm eleven. I wanted to be born, to be human. To have all the things the people who'd fed me all these years had, the things they'd left behind, the things they missed most. I found a person who desperately wanted a baby and… I don't know how to explain it. I chose her to carry me, to be my mother." Kevin looked as uncomfortable as any eleven-year-old when discussing how babies were made.

Viv kept her jaw from dropping by great effort of will. Whoever Kevin's biological mother had been had experienced the first immaculate conception in over two thousand years. "You're adopted, though, right?" Viv asked, then clenched her teeth. She hoped this wasn't a huge revelation the way her parentage had been last year.

Kevin nodded. "The woman who carried me to life wasn't a very good person and had already decided not to keep me by the time I was born. I didn't know enough about people to understand all the nuances of human relationships. When I was born, Aurielle was waiting. She chose me, although for what purpose, I still don't know. She has been a very satisfactory mother, although it took her a while to adjust to it. She brought me back here. I don't think either of us can leave for long." He took a deep breath and uncurled like a new fern as the burden of his secret lifted and was shared.

"Why now?" Viv asked. "I mean, why are you talking to me about this now? I think I understand why *me*, but it's the why *now* I'm missing." She winced. She wasn't the best at being an authority figure or role model in the best of times, and this month—this year—had not been the best of times.

"I slipped today," Kevin said. "I almost took another life. I didn't mean to, but I wasn't paying attention. We were playing and it happened. I'm hungrier than I realized, and the fix Lily made for me is slipping. And then you saved us. The baby and me. I felt you, your fear." He licked his lips and his eyes flashed green again. He took a deep, shuddering breath. "And I'm scared." His lip trembled again, and he faded from monster to a child on the cusp of growing up.

Lily took his hand and looked at Viv. "We couldn't talk to our parents. They're weird about stuff like this. Mama and Aunt Bev would flip out, and we don't want to be separated. Elle is… We don't know what she is. And if we talked to Daddy or Papa Abe or Aunt Sam, it'd get back to Mama somehow. You're our trusted adult." She opened her eyes wide and projected waves of guilelessness and sincerity.

"Stop, Lily," Viv said. "You don't need to convince me to help or talk me into the reason why I'm the one you chose. I get it. But I don't know what to do."

Shelby pursed her mouth, then stuck her lower lip out in a half-pout. "I guess we shouldn't have expected you to do anything."

"Hey, hey, hey!" Viv held up her hands. "I didn't say I wouldn't, just that I need a moment to process everything. This is a lot all at once. I'm still grappling with Kevin's immaculate conception twelve years ago." A suspicion rose in Viv's mind, and this time she couldn't keep her mouth from dropping open. "Kevin, do you know who your biological mother is?"

"Not really. I could know if I wanted to, but it's never been important to me. She was a means to an end and wasn't suitable to be a permanent mother." He didn't look even remotely curious, but Viv's was off the charts.

She gathered her thoughts and was about to speak when a flash of intuition hit her—the third in as many hours. This one didn't leave her heaving and blind, though, so it was a win. Just like every other time she'd been home—back to Eden Valley—the visions were intensifying. The flashes of pain she got in Eden Valley were often sharp and excruciating—the pain seemed dependent on the seriousness of the vision—but it didn't last hours like it did in Seattle. But she knew that for as much as they seemed innocuous now, once she was back in Seattle, the pain would be debilitating. She was so afraid that she was going to get stuck here someday—the town might let her go eventually, but she wouldn't be able to walk through that door without destroying herself. She focused again and saw three sets of eyes looking at her expectantly. "Bev's gonna be home any second. If you kids don't want to get caught here, you'll need to make a run for it."

"What about your agreement to help us?" Lily asked.

The kids stood up and glanced around the backyard.

"Meet me at the Witch's clearing tomorrow after lunch," Viv said. "Hopefully I'll have a plan by then."

That must have been good enough because Lily and Kevin took off towards the back fence. Viv watched with interest—she hadn't known there was a gate there. They disappeared through a gap in the grape vines Viv hadn't noticed before. Shelby stood in the middle of the yard, shifting uncertainly from foot to foot.

"The glasses and popsicle wrappers," she said, looking more pinched and worried than any kid should.

"I'll take care of it," Viv promised. "See you at dinner."

Shelby turned and followed her friends through the gap in the vines.

THE FRONT DOOR slammed shut and keys clattered in the bowl on the end table near the front closet.

"Hey Bev!" Viv called out. "I'm in the kitchen! You better have my ice cream sandwiches."

Bev walked into the kitchen with a grocery bag overflowing with produce. "Your sandwiches are at the bottom. I don't know how Shelby got you to ask for them, but it's summer, so I'll allow it." She stopped unpacking the groceries and stared at Viv. "Are you... Are you doing dishes?"

"I know how to do dishes," Viv said. "I have lived alone for all of my adult life."

"I wasn't questioning your knowledge. I was questioning the need... I did dishes this morning before going to work." Bev narrowed her eyes. "Are you getting up to shenanigans with unruly children?"

Viv smiled at Bev. Too bad she didn't have Lily's ability to project feelings. "I know zero unruly children and would never perpetrate shenanigans with such children if I were to find any."

"Fine. I'll let it go. If they were with you, at least they are being supervised by a reliable adult. That's better than the trouble they get up to most of the time." Bev handed an ice cream sandwich to Viv, took one for herself, and put the rest in the freezer. "How was your day? Did you have a pleasant walk?"

"I'm still sorting out everything," Viv said. "A lot happened today. Well, not a lot, but what did happen was significant. I can't talk about all of it yet, but there is something I do want to talk about... Do you think Evie would mind if we descended on her tomorrow night to talk?"

Bev folded up her grocery bags and tucked them into the hall closet next to her purse. "Not at all. The kids are having a sleepover there tomorrow night—they do a lot of summer sleepovers and have been rotating houses. I think they're as good for the parents as for the kids. At least twice a month, it's blissfully silent here."

"Only twice a month? That doesn't seem like enough." Viv finished her ice cream sandwich and tossed the wrapper into the garbage.

"It'd be more if I could talk Shelby into doing a sleepover camp when Lily heads to her grandfather's for her demon summer camp. All the ones we found were full of nature, and apparently not the fun kind. Maybe next summer I can find her an art and design camp or something. They must exist, but I couldn't find them on short notice." Bev came back into the kitchen and poured herself a glass of water, downing it in three gulps.

"There are probably some in Seattle," Viv said. "It's never been on my radar, but I'm sure I can find out for you. And if it's not a sleep-away camp, Shelby can always stay with me for the duration."

"You'd let a child stay with you?" Bev asked, genuine shock widening her eyes. "I don't know if that's a good idea."

Viv crossed her arms across her chest to deflect the hurt she hadn't expected. "I know I've not proven very trustworthy lately, but I would never do anything to endanger Shelby or any of the kids."

Bev crossed the kitchen in three long steps and grabbed Viv's shoulders. "Genevieve Kane, don't even go there. I trust you with my life, with Shelby's life. The only life I don't always trust you with is your own. I am not worried about your ability to ensure Shelby is fed, clothed, cared for, and getting to and from camp. I am worried about what Shelby would do with that level of relative freedom. It's been a tough year for us both, and there were days I didn't think we'd get through intact. We did, we made it, and so far," Bev rapped her knuckles against the butcher block, "this summer is, if not easy, easier. I'm just afraid..."

Viv waited for Bev to finish her sentence, but when the silence stretched out, she prompted, "Afraid of what?"

The smile Bev wore now didn't make it to her eyes. She looked tired and sad. Viv kicked herself for not noticing sooner.

"Afraid of everything," Bev said. "Afraid of screwing up. Afraid of losing her. Afraid of losing you. I've never been so afraid as I have in the last year. Something changed for me after we got our fancy hell brands. I didn't get anything useful—if excruciating—just fear. I can't stop every worst-case scenario from playing through my head. Every day, millions of ways a person can die play through my head." She paced the kitchen, then opened the fridge and grabbed a bottle of sparkling mineral water. "Want one?"

Viv nodded and took the bottle Bev held out. "Shit, Bev. I didn't know."

Bev's mouth thinned into a narrow line. "How could you? I didn't tell you, and you weren't here to see what was going on for yourself. I didn't want to put more on you than you already had. Between the near-constant dread and nightmares and parenting an almost-teen who goes from loving and affectionate to angry and destructive in the blink of an eye, I'm tired. Since the moment I held her in my arms for the first time when Holly and Mom showed up with her—and left her with me for weeks at a time—I've wanted nothing more than to keep her safe forever. But if this last year has taught me anything, it's that I can't. Not now, when she's still a child, and probably never. I'm so scared all the time, Viv."

Sobs broke through her speech, and Viv stood to pull Bev into her arms. She patted her friend's head and murmured, "Shh," over and over while Bev cried herself out.

Movement at the kitchen door caught Viv's eye. Shelby was in the doorway, mirroring tears streaming down her face.

"Bev, Shelby's behind you. Why don't you guys talk. I'll take myself out for a bit. I might not want to, but I need to visit my mother. There are a few things of mine there, still, and I want them back—if she hasn't destroyed them yet." Viv spun Bev around and caught Shelby's eye. "I wish every day that I'd had a mother as loving, accepting, and understanding as either you or Evie. I've spent the last thirty years running from her and from myself. I'm gonna stop running away now. Boundaries instead of walls, strategic retreats, and all that."

Viv brushed by Shelby on her way out of the kitchen and dropped a kiss on top of the head that was quickly getting too high to kiss.

As she slipped out the front door, she heard Selby say, "You're the best mom I could've had. I love you."

CHAPTER SIX

Viv settled onto the low concert chair she'd borrowed from Bev's garage and cracked open a soda. She looked around the clearing—she'd spent countless hours here with Evie and Bev when she was growing up, but hadn't been back since the summer after they'd graduated high school. It looked almost exactly the same. The next generation had added their personalities in the strings of flags that decorated the trees that made up the perimeter. There was a string of skull and crossbones, one that was flags of the world, another of trans pride flags, and a fourth string in a pastel rainbow with writing on them. Viv stood and walked over to the flags.

"I am beautiful. I am safe." Each had a different affirmation on it. Viv read each of them and paused in front of the one with the most raggedy bottom and faded lettering. "I am strong. I deserve love. I am."

Viv returned to her chair. She'd hoped to have ideas and solutions, to walk in and be able to solve all the problems. But she wasn't any further along now than she'd been yesterday. She'd used this meeting and the imminent need to figure things out as an excuse to once more avoid visiting her mother. Instead, she'd parked herself in the diner and had a chocolate milkshake—her second ice cream treat of the day.

She'd been ravenous since getting back to Eden Valley, and she wasn't going to argue with her body. Not yet anyway.

Childish voices made their way towards her, and she scrambled to her feet. Not fast enough to avoid getting a face full of slobber as Sprinkles bounded into the clearing and made a beeline for Viv. She'd shed her socially acceptable shape and managed to get Viv with all three tongues before Lily made an appearance and called the hellhound back.

"Sorry, Aunt Viv. She gets so excited when she doesn't have to hide who she really is." Lily scratched the space between the ears on the head closest to her. "She's just such a good girl, yes she is." Lily made kissy noises at the dog, then jumped back, laughing, as Sprinkles tried to lick her face.

Kevin dropped to the ground in front of Viv's chair and crossed his legs. Shelby did the same, and after Sprinkles stopped panting happily and running around the clearing barking and almost dancing, Lily sprawled on the ground next to her friends with Sprinkles thumping down beside her with a puff of dust and grass pollen.

Viv sat again and suppressed a groan. Her thighs were not impressed with her today. Between the ill-advised run around the lake yesterday and the up and down from this too-low chair, they were reminding her none-too-gently that she was in her mid-forties.

"I don't really have anything else," Viv said. "I'm not equipped to handle supernatural problems like this. I know you don't want to talk to your parents, but I don't see another way to solve this." She turned to Kevin. "You didn't mention your father yesterday." Or ever, Viv thought to herself. She'd never even met the man, which was nearly impossible in Eden Valley.

"Oh. Right. Him." Kevin propped his elbows on his knees and lowered his chin into his hands. "He's not really..." He scratched his head. "He's not particularly useful without my mother to point him in the right direction."

"That's one of the reasons we were friends right away," Shelby said. "None of us had dads." She shrugged and turned her head away, but not before Viv saw her mouth tighten and hurt flash in her eyes.

"I never met my dad," Viv offered.

Lily cocked her head to one side. "Is that because he died?"

"No. He ran away when he found out my mom was pregnant with me. He never wanted to be a dad." She squashed down her own hurt just enough to not make a thing out of it, but not enough that the kids wouldn't see it. "You know what you all have, though, that not every kid has?"

"A giant hellhound named Sprinkles and cosmic powers?" Kevin asked, a sly smile creeping across his face.

"I don't have either of those things," Shelby protested, but she had an answering grin for Kevin. This was apparently not the first time they'd had those conversations. "And *you know* me and Aunt Bev skipped the line where they handed out magic powers."

"But Sprinkles belongs to all of us," Lily said. "Call her over and you'll see."

"Hey, Sprinkles, come here, girl," Shelby crooned.

Sprinkles, without even a glance at Lily lumbered up, trotted over to Shelby, and landed with a whump in her lap, rubbing her chin with one of the dog's huge heads and running a tongue from head number two up the side of Shelby's face.

"Now you try, Aunt Viv," Lily commanded.

Viv leaned down and clicked her tongue to draw Sprinkles' attention. "Hey girl, I've got scritches for two chins and extra dog treats later."

Sprinkles closed the eyes on the head looking at Viv. A second head looked at Lily, who shook her head slightly.

"Wow," Viv said. "That's amazing that you all have a great animal friend. I feel a lot safer now—as long as you never go anywhere without her."

"The only places she's not welcome are school and the public pool," Kevin said. "We could take her swimming in the lake, but that would stress people out too much."

Viv suppressed the urge to tell them to stay out of the lake. They were probably safer in the lake with Kevin and Sprinkles than anyone else.

"I did some research earlier while I was drinking my milkshake and didn't learn a ton. There's a lot out there on lake monsters, but at least ninety percent of it is on Nessie and giant eels and extinct dinosaurs, and the rest is a baseball team in Vermont. I do know what could happen if we don't act, and what will happen if we can figure this out. But I don't know how to get from point A to point B." Something Kevin had said the day before about his mother teased at Viv's mind, but she couldn't quite get a hold of it, and it didn't feel as important as everything else. Instead, she asked, "you said Aurielle chose you, but it sounded like you meant more than just adoption, and Lily said y'all didn't know *what* Aurielle is, not who. What did you mean?"

"She feels more like Daddy than you," Lily said. "But none of us can figure it out. Like, does she know who Kevin is, really? Is she a demon like Daddy?"

"Have you asked your dad what he thinks?" Viv asked. The mystery of Elle's origins receded like gently lapping waves sweeping it away. Its unimportance washed away her curiosity. She tried to hold on to it, but something else grabbed her questions and wrenched them away. It was always like this in Eden Valley, although she could never put her finger on what she'd forgotten and when.

"No, but I asked Aunt Sam. She said she didn't recognize Elle but that she didn't know every demon. Then she got a real weird look on her face, handed me the Coke she was drinking, and took off for two weeks." Lily smiled blissfully. "Coke is delicious, isn't it?"

Viv laughed. "I know for a fact your parents wouldn't be impressed with you downing a caffeinated, sugary soda."

"Sometimes discretion is the bigger part of... I don't remember the rest of it, but it means it's okay to keep a few secrets, right?" Lily asked.

The children were getting restless, and the afternoon sun was beginning to leisurely head west, lengthening the shadows.

"Secrets are okay as long as they're not going to hurt someone—or are about someone ignoring consent, or—"

"Aunt Viv," Shelby said. "We know about bad touch and sexual harassment and all that stuff. Lily just means little secrets, like having a Coke or exploring the abandoned mansion in the woods. Stuff like that."

Lily glared at Shelby. "Pretty sure that exploring abandoned buildings is not a little secret."

"I'll forget I heard that if you promise you're being careful and not taking stupid risks. I've been in there, too, although I'd forgotten it existed until you mentioned it."

"This town makes people forget," Kevin said. "It doesn't work as well on kids, though. I wonder if we'll forget when we're old too?"

Viv stood up and folded her chair. "When you call me old, that means you're itching to get out of here. Run. Play. Climb trees. Hit the vending machine outside the library and get yourself a couple caffeinated beverages. Just not diet." Viv handed out a handful of ones. "But if you get caught with Cokes, I'm gonna say I thought you'd buy root beer."

"Thanks, Aunt Viv!" Lily said, jumping up and grabbing the money. "You're the best." She threw her arms around Viv and hugged tight. Shelby and Kevin joined in the hug, and Sprinkles did her best to jump into it as well.

"Think about telling your folks," Viv said. "Or I can, if you'd rather. I know you're sleeping over at Lily's tonight. The *old* folks are hanging out on the deck to gossip and figure out some of our stuff." She tucked the chair under her arm and watched the kids scamper off without a response to her suggestion.

Viv took the path that would lead her closer to the water—it didn't seem as ominous now that she knew she was safe from the lake. But if Kevin was human now, he clearly wasn't diving in and grabbing people. He'd said he'd been playing with Lily and Shelby yesterday when he pulled the baby in by mistake, so he wasn't in the water. But if he wasn't grabbing people physically, then how did it work? And who'd sent the ripples out when she wished for waves the other day?

Each question asked spawned three more questions. Viv laughed and ignored the edge of hysteria that threatened to creep in. Maybe Kevin was a lake hydra in his original form.

ONCE MORE ON the bench she'd regarded as hers for almost as long as she'd lived in Eden Valley, Viv stared out over the lake. It was calm today, although she wondered if it had been earlier when Kevin had been so agitated. Did the lake reflect his moods, or did he reflect the lake's conditions? Would a windy night stir something angry and frenetic in Kevin...?

She breathed in deeply. It was easier to sit with her thoughts now than it had been in years. It shouldn't be. Being back was stirring up a lot of things she'd wanted to stay buried. Viv's complicated relationship with her mother that she'd never been able to sever, her smoldering feelings for Sam, and the demon-granted power that'd slowly been destroying her body and mind.

She paused, waiting for the headache or the urge for a drink to return. Neither did. Maybe that was the benefit of being home—no, not home. Home was Seattle. Eden Valley was her hometown, never home. It hadn't been since her mother had kicked her out the first time when she was fifteen and she'd stayed with Evie's family for three months until Gwen relented and let Viv come back.

"Hey, beautiful," Sam said, folding herself gracefully onto the bench next to Viv. "What's got you looking so serious?" She ran a finger lightly from the middle of Viv's forehead down to the tip of her nose and lingered there. "You've got a furrow just here."

Viv's breath hitched as the light touch ignited a spark in her chest. "How'd you find me?" Viv asked.

"You weren't at Bev's. You didn't answer your phone. And I know this is where you go to think—among other things." Sam smirked and heat flushed Viv's cheeks.

"I need to find a new retreat," Viv mumbled, not meeting Sam's eyes, afraid she'd see the burning intensity of the memory of what had happened the first time Viv had brought Sam here, and even more afraid she wouldn't. "Everyone knows to find me here."

"Everyone? Or just the people you trust?" Sam's finger left Viv's nose.

Viv's traitorous body tried to follow Sam's hand and reconnect.

Sam's finger drifted to Viv's shoulder and traced the seam of her bra strap, visible from underneath the narrow straps of her tank top. She trailed her fingers over Viv's shoulder blade and across the slightly raised skin the mark hell had left on her. It was half brand, half tattoo, and it didn't look like it had the night it'd appeared.

Somehow, the sensation of Sam's hands on her demon mark was even more erotic than the memory of Sam's lips on her... Viv gasped as Sam's body pressed up against her side, eliminating the space between them.

"We're good together," Sam whispered into Viv's ears, her warm breath raising the small hairs on the side of Viv's head. "I miss you." Her tongue darted out and traced the delicate shell of Viv's ear.

Viv bolted upright and away from the seductive demon. "Maybe we were good together for a minute last year, but there are reasons we walked away from each other. Reasons that haven't changed."

"We didn't walk away from each other," Sam said. She leaned back on the bench and crossed her legs. Today, she was wearing a yellow leather jacket over a black and silver corset top and a matching tight, short skirt. A skirt that wasn't concealing anything. Black boots with a low, chunky heel were laced up past Samiel's knees. "You walked away from me. From us. From Eden."

"What?" Viv jerked her eyes back to Sam's. She'd been caught at the edge where the black boots hit Sam's dark brown skin.

"You ended things. Don't spin the narrative that it was mutual. You left me." Sam sat forward and put both feet back on the ground, straightening her skirt.

"You refused to come to Seattle," Viv pointed out. "Just as much as I refused to stay here."

"But not for the same reasons," Sam countered. "I can't leave, not for long. The barrier is thinner here, and I am sustained, but if I spend any length of time in a place that is wholly in your world, I will weaken and fade. I need an Eden to exist."

"It's Eden Valley, not Eden, and I can't stay. Maybe this place sustains you, but it has the opposite effect on me. I hate it here. And I hate that it keeps pulling me in, pulling me back. Every day I spend here makes it harder to leave." Viv was nearly shouting by the end. It was the same argument they'd had a dozen times last summer when Viv had asked Sam to move in with her and the demon had refused. Except... "What do you mean the barrier is thinner, that this is *an* Eden?" Viv asked. "Last year you just said you needed to be here because of its proximity to hell; I thought you meant the hell mouth and the connection between Luc and Lily and your dad."

"Can't you feel it?" Sam asked. She stood up and brushed non-existent dirt off her backside. "The energy is different here."

Viv considered, then closed her eyes and breathed in deep. Nothing. She opened her eyes. "Maybe it's something mere mortals can't detect. Or maybe it's the repelling feeling that overtakes me every time I'm here."

"Is that this place? Or is that your mother?" Sam asked. She reached out a hand towards Viv but dropped it before making contact.

Maybe Viv was imagining things, but Sam looked almost sad.

"I think it's more likely that you're ascribing your feelings towards your mother to the entire town. If you dig deep, if you think about what draws you back, time after time, why you have a favorite bench, you might realize that this is more your home than anywhere else." Sam zipped her jacket up to just below her breasts and turned around. Before she disappeared around the bend of the trail, she paused and looked back. "You are worthy of love and happiness, no matter what bullshit your mother has spewed. Don't let her keep destroying your life."

Viv stared at the trail where Sam had disappeared. "That's not... That's not..." She couldn't finish her sentence. There were only so many lies you could tell yourself before trust was broken. Instead, she took the shortcut to the park and walked back to Bev's.

Tomorrow. Tomorrow, she'd visit her mother. It was time.

CHAPTER SEVEN

"S orry, sorry, sorry," Evie chanted as Viv walked into the house. Her brown hair was pulled back into a messy ponytail and Alex was strapped to her chest. "The older kids are still out walking Sprinkles, and the baby is fussy and awake; I meant to be ready by now."

"It's not a big deal," Viv said. "Bev is on her way, but she wasn't ready, either. I'll just show myself out to the porch."

Evie yanked open the fridge. "Lemonade? Sparkling water?"

"Is that the lemonade you wished for over a year ago?" Viv asked, peering into the fridge. It was stocked with fruits and veggies, a half-full bottle of rosé, cans of seltzer water, and a large pitcher of lemonade.

"It is," Evie admitted. "I guess there was more to my wish than I'd thought. I don't remember wanting lemonade for eternity, but here we are." She shrugged.

"Water is great—mineral if you have it, otherwise I'll take that lime-flavored one." She looked at Evie—her friend was more frazzled than she'd seen her in eleven years. Since last time she'd had a baby. "I can get it. Go, do what you need to do with the baby. If I see the older ones, I'll tell them it's getting dark, and they need to get their tween butts inside to start the sleep part of the sleepover."

Evie heaved a sigh and ran a hand through her hair, got it stuck, and yanked it out with a frustrated growl. "Thank you. I'll be right out. Probably."

Viv dug through the fridge until she found the sparkling mineral water she knew was in the back. She unscrewed the cap, grabbed a glass from the cupboard, and headed outside and settled into one of the Adirondack chairs Evie's dad James had made years ago. She poured the water into the glass and leaned back, letting the evening breeze carry the smell of pine and earth she could only get in these mountains tease her into relaxation. The feeling of rightness made the thoughts churning through her mind seem less terrifying. There would be a solution. There had to be. They had resources that most people wouldn't have—even if the kids were reluctant to tap into them.

A murmur of conversation drifted up from the shore. It seemed too quiet and subdued for it to be the kids, but Viv turned her attention that direction anyway.

Four shapes were silhouetted against the lake, the rays of the setting sun, interrupted by the jagged peaks of the Cascades creating long shadows. Their backs were to Viv, but three of the people were significantly shorter than the fourth, although they were no longer the roughly same height and shape of younger children. Shelby was stretching up in that gangly way adolescents do when parts of their bodies grow too fast for the rest to keep up. Lily hadn't started sprouting yet, and Kevin was smack dab in the middle. In fact, if Viv was a gambler, she'd take the bet that Kevin was fiftieth percentile in everything. Perfectly average. Not likely to draw any unwanted attention.

Viv couldn't make out the fourth person. There was something vaguely familiar about the shape, but she couldn't place it. Whoever it was, though, was clearly adult sized and not any of the kids' parents. She stood. She wasn't necessarily going to confront the stranger, but she wouldn't be a very responsible adult if she let three kids talk to them in the deepening twilight without at least finding out who they were talking to.

She walked down towards the lake, glass of water in hand. Viv made zero effort to stay silent—not that she could've been quiet even if she wanted to. Woods craft was not her strong suit. She'd always lagged behind on that skill during any of the outdoor camps she attended with her friends when she was the same age these kids were now.

She got within ten feet of them before anyone noticed her. Shelby was the first to see her, but the preteen didn't say anything. Her lips quirked up in a half smile, and she winked at Viv before turning her attention back to the other three.

"...tell anyone," the stranger said in a familiar voice that clicked the puzzle of his identity into place.

"Mat, what are you doing here?" she asked. Lily and Mat jumped and turned to face her. Lily looked guilty, Shelby was amused, and Kevin was...inscrutable. The only reaction Viv was really interested in, though, was Mat's. Her eyes bored into his, but the chaos demon, other than his initial startlement, didn't give anything away.

"Genevieve," he said. His lip curled as he looked down his nose at her. "I thought I felt an unpleasant aura on the wind."

Viv rolled her eyes. It might be almost dark, but she knew he'd see. "Kinda creepy, don't you think, lurking near your brother's house and talking to a group of children. Not a good look, Matrim."

Lily bristled and opened her mouth, presumably to protest being called a child, but before she could start a specious argument, Viv caught Shelby's eye and jerked her head back towards the house.

"Let's go, Lily," Shelby said, grabbing Lily's elbow and tugging her along. "I bet your mom has a bedtime treat for us."

"I doubt it," Lily scoffed. "Mom's no Grandma Hope, and she does not believe in bedtime snacks." She let herself be dragged along anyway, Kevin trailing silently behind.

"What do you want, *Kane?*" Mat asked. Other than the emphasis he placed on Viv's last name, his tone was bored. He shoved his hands in the pockets of his black jeans and looked at her with zero expression. "Are you here to destroy me?"

"What are you talking about?" Viv asked, thrown away from the questions she'd planned on asking. "Destroy you? Is that even possible? Why don't you tell me in great detail how you imagine I'd do that, and I'll ensure I never do." She pulled an imaginary notepad out of her pocket, licked the tip of her invisible pencil, and stood, poised to take notes.

"Hilarious, Kane," Mat said in a voice so dry Viv wished she was carrying moisturizer. "But you're right. It isn't possible for you to destroy me. I'm not as trusting and gullible as my sister. Your methods wouldn't work on me."

Viv bit her tongue before she could let a defensive jab out of her mouth. Starting an argument was probably exactly what he wanted—both because he loved chaos and because he knew what she was going to ask and didn't want to answer. "What were you talking to the kids about?" she asked instead.

Mat shrugged and slouched down a bit, rounding his shoulders and adopting a disaffected pose. Viv tried hard not to see the similarities between him and his twin. Every reminder of Sam was a bolt to the heart, and if anyone was going to be destroyed in the aftermath of their relationship, it was going to be Viv, not the nearly immortal demon.

"Just chatting," Mat said. "Lily's my niece, you know. I have at least as much claim to secret rendezvous in the woods as you do. Maybe more. I'm related by blood, after all. And I've been here the last year, unlike you."

Another bolt to the chest. He was full of them today. *That's because he's a literal chaos demon,* Viv told herself through clenched teeth. *You do not have to justify yourself to him.*

"Great. You've been around for a year, which doesn't negate the ten years I was here before you. You're a model uncle and brother. That didn't answer my question. What were you talking about? Whatever it was, it seemed like a topic that you didn't want me to hear. Between the way you jumped and the look of guilt on Lily's face, I'm gonna guess you don't want her parents to know, either. But, if you won't tell me, I'll let Evie know, and you can explain yourself to her."

The bored look slid off Mat's face for a second, and even though he schooled his expression again almost immediately, it wasn't fast enough. Viv saw the look of—not exactly fear, but—apprehension? Yeah, that was it.

Viv turned and walked away, slowly enough that Mat could catch up before she got close enough to be in earshot of the house. She knew he'd catch up and confess to avoid being the subject of Evie's wrath. He might be a demon who was old when the earth was young, but Evie was a mother, and she'd not only stood up to a King of Hell himself, she'd convinced Lucifer Morningstar to fold his clothes after millennia of never having to think about laundry. Evie might be human, but she was scary, especially if she thought there was a threat to one of her kids.

Viv walked slower and slower, but didn't hear anything behind her. When she was almost to the house, she turned and looked back. Mat had disappeared.

"Well, fuck," Viv said. She was pretty sure that meant they'd been talking about Kevin and his unique...situation, and if she told Evie and Luc he was having a twilight tête-à-tête with Lily and friends, she'd be his unwitting agent of chaos as well as breaking trust with Kevin. Mat knew she knew, and he was less interested in keeping confidences than in stirring the pot. She'd lost the upper hand the second she'd engaged and given him a choice instead of stating her intention to tell Evie he'd been having a chat with the kids.

"You sound a lot less mellow than you seemed when you first arrived."

Viv turned around and smiled at her best friend's fiancé. "Hey, Luc. The kids get in okay?"

He folded himself into the chair next to her, the glow from the kitchen window glinting honey gold in his deep brown eyes. "They're in and hounding Evie for snacks. I tried to intervene and send her out now that Alex is asleep, but she seems to believe that I would give in and hand out the brownies I know she made earlier and not get them to brush their teeth, put on pajamas, and head to bed to giggle and exchange confidences for the next three hours." He shrugged and grinned. "I feel betrayed by her lack of trust."

Viv smiled. "Tell me, Luc. What would you be doing right now if you were inside with three preteens convinced that if they ask in just the right way, they'll get a sweet treat before bed?"

Luc's grin widened. "Cutting up the brownies—ostensibly for you ladies—and 'accidentally' leaving three unattended while I went to another room for no reason at all. Might have put a gallon of milk and three glasses next to the brownies, too. Hard to say with me."

"That's what I would've done, too," Viv confessed. "I'm everyone's favorite aunt."

VIV LEANED back in her chair and peered towards the driveway. She was trying for subtlety, but when she glanced back at the other three women in the group, Evie was looking at her knowingly.

"It's a bummer Sam couldn't join us tonight," Evie said. "She said she had some business to attend to."

Viv jerked her attention away from the front of the house where her eyes had already wandered again and smiled tightly at Evie. "Oh, that's too bad," she said, then cringed. Even to herself, she knew that didn't sound casual.

"Did she say what the business was?" Elle asked, running her finger around the rim of her glass.

"Nope," Evie said. "Just business. Luc thinks she's probably running errands for her dad. She's not formally employed, but she does occasionally do some contract work for the acquisitions department."

Viv pursed her lips. They rarely talked about what Luc was, but she was almost positive Elle knew Lily was the granddaughter of a king of hell and Luc was named after the original fallen angel himself —Elle had been at Lily's birthday party when Lily'd conjured her lake monster vision and hadn't acted the least surprised to see a three-headed hellhound. "Why so cagey, Evie?"

Evie tilted her head and worried at her lower lip. "Habit, I guess. With Luc's return and the rumors spread about Lily's tenth birthday party, there were a lot of questions about him and his family. So I fudge the truth a little. I don't actually lie, though."

"She's almost as good as her soon-to-be father-in-law," Bev said. "But as far as everyone in town believes, Papa Abe is the CEO of a company with vague goals whose primary motivation is in acquisitions and mergers. He doesn't do hostile takeovers; he hinges his success on ensuring that all acquisitions are willing to be acquired. And Sam and Mat are both in acquisitions."

Viv took in the information and digested it. Acquisitions. For hell. That had to be buying souls. Her girlfriend—*ex*-girlfriend—was the devil people made deals with. "No hostile takeovers?"

Evie refilled everyone's lemonade glasses before she answered. "Luc says that not all the Kings make deals. Some rely more on temptation...snake in the garden type stuff. But Abe's kingdom is run entirely off people who agree to it. Sam finds people who are willing to trade and draws up the contracts. Mat is in 'accounts receivable.'"

"Ten years of gratification and then they go to hell?" Viv asked.

"Not everything on television is true," Evie said. "The amount of time agreed upon varies, but for most people, they get the rest of their lives. Just sometimes, the things they ask for—like insta-fame or insta-wealth—shorten their lives. You can do a lot of stupid things with too much money or too many people fawning over you."

"What's Luc's role?" Viv asked. The sick feeling was back. She should know this. Luc had been back for over a year. She'd spent a lot of time with Sam, and although there hadn't been a ton of talking, "Tell me about your job" was usually towards the top of the topics of conversation list.

"Legal," Bev said. "Contract review. After Sam or someone else in her division draws up the contract, they're sent to Luc for review to ensure the only loopholes benefit Abaddon."

Revulsion crawled over Viv's skin. This was...not okay. "And he's okay with that? You're all okay with that?"

"It's the way of the world," Elle said. She was fidgeting in her chair.

Viv watched Elle scuff her feet against the deck. There were dots to connect. Puzzle pieces that almost fit together. And still, Viv couldn't figure this woman out. She wasn't quite human according to what the kids got from Sam, but she wasn't a demon, either.

"I don't know if I am," Evie said. "But I don't think I can change it. And at least there isn't any subterfuge. They don't find desperate people and promise love or cancer cures, holding happiness over people's heads in exchange for eternal damnation. They find people who are already greedy or cruel and offer them the push they need. The folks who likely would've ended up in hell anyway, just via another route."

"What about collateral damage?" Viv demanded.

"If an innocent is killed due to a contract with hell, they aren't sent to hell unless they've also signed a contract," Elle said. "It's not a free-for-all, and there isn't free rein to do whatever they want. There are rules. Regulations—more than are necessary—but hell has a lot of lawyers. Enforcement."

"How do you know all this? And why do you seem so okay with it?" Viv asked. "I know you're hiding something, something that's going to end up biting us all in the ass, but I can't figure out what it is."

"I listen," Elle said, not meeting anyone's gaze. "And what I'm hearing from you right now is that you'd rather I wasn't here." She stood up, nodded at Evie and Bev. "Thanks for inviting me. It's my turn to host the kids' next sleepover, so I'll call to set up the dates and details." She walked off the porch and towards the lake, then disappeared into the trees when she hit the trail.

"You were rude," Evie chastised.

"But there is something," Bev said. "She's great, and I'm so glad she came out of the house and started interacting with people. It makes me feel a lot better about Kevin's well-being, and it's nice to know there's nothing to worry about if the girls go to his house. But something isn't quite right." She shifted in her chair to stare at the place where Elle'd disappeared, then grinned. "I'm sure we'll find out eventually. No one can keep secrets from Evie indefinitely."

Evie tapped her chin with one finger. "I've asked Luc and Sam about her, but they've got nothing. I want to talk to her husband, but the few times I've seen him outside the house, he's with Elle, and barely responds to any attempts at conversation."

"What's his name again?" Viv asked, tapping her chin. "I know I've heard it before, but not enough for it to make an impression."

"Brandon Jones, but Elle usually calls him Brand," Bev replied.

"He's hot enough to be a brand," Evie said. "I get why she might have stayed inside for years once Kevin started school and they had some alone time."

"I feel weird gossiping about our friend," Bev said. "It makes me feel...dirty. Can we talk about something else? How's Lily doing with her 'other' classes?"

"Mind if I join you?" Luc asked, walking out onto the porch with a plate of brownies and a short glass with an inch or so of dark liquid that glinted amber in the porch light. "Say the word if you want me to go. I'll leave the brownies and go watch the documentary I'm in the middle of."

"Real Housewives is not a documentary," Evie said, plucking a brownie from the top of the pile.

"It's a glimpse into the lives of actual human beings," Luc said, setting the plate down between Viv and Bev. "I have years of catching up to do—I seldom took the opportunity to consume your media and culture on previous visits."

"If letting you hang out will keep you from reality tv, I am AOK with you staying," Viv said. She eyed the brownies. Chocolate wasn't her favorite, but Evie's brownies were usually amazing. She grabbed a brownie and took a bite. Good decision.

"What were you all talking about?" Luc asked. He sat down in the chair Elle had vacated earlier and leaned back, taking a sip of his Scotch.

"You know. Lady stuff," Bev said. "Periods and shopping and our continuous love for the color pink."

Luc nodded. "Makes sense. I've learned all about women in the last documentary I watched."

"It was the Bachelor," Evie said. "I need to find him something better to watch, but he insists he's not a reality show addict, merely a student of the human condition."

Viv snorted. "You're fooling no one," she said to Luc. "Hide your predilections under the veneer of 'learning' as much as you want. We know the truth. And speaking of truth, have you branched into the vintage 'documentaries?' Survivor, Road Rules, Real World?"

"Not yet," Luc said. "I want to learn about your music and dance, next."

Viv took another bite of her brownie and watched as Luc and Evie bickered light-heartedly about his reality tv obsession, and Bev tossed out suggestions to further his studies. Movement from the upstairs hall window caught her eye. She stared, trying to figure out if it was a wayward child spying on them or a trick of the light.

A flashlight blinked on and lit up Kevin's face, making him look like a malevolent specter from a horror movie. He crooked a finger at her, inviting her in. Viv shrieked in surprise, then tried to choke it down when Kevin's expression changed into a very human adolescent showing of exasperation.

"Are you okay?" Evie asked. "You look like you've seen a ghost." She turned to Luc. "Are there ghosts? Please tell me my house isn't haunted."

"There aren't any dead here," Bev said absently. "Only the lake feels like a grave."

"What now?" Evie asked. "What do you mean?"

Bev shook her head. "Sorry. I don't know where that came from. Too many paranormal mystery shows, probably. I have my own documentaries queued up."

Viv pursed her lips at her friend. Was everyone hiding something?

She looked back up at the window, but it was empty now. "I need to use the restroom," she announced. "I think I saw a bat or something and it startled me, and if there's one thing we all know about being startled during perimenopause, it's that certain muscles lose their grip on reality."

"I've had two kids, and I'm quickly approaching forty-five," Evie said, flapping her hand towards the house. "I get you."

Viv walked into the house and headed to the guest bathroom near the stairs. Kevin was sitting on the bottom step in his pajamas. Viv squinted her eyes at him. "Are those...sharks...on your pjs?"

Kevin rolled his eyes. "They were a birthday present. Shelby and Lily think they're hilarious, so I wear them to every sleepover. The one time I forgot, they made me call Elle and have her bring them over."

"You call your mother Elle?" Viv asked. "You didn't before."

"Sometimes I do. When I'm tired and forget. I wanted to talk to you about my problem, though, and not my mother. Mat has offered to help, but I don't know if he really wants to help, or he wants to watch things go wrong."

"Did you tell him what was happening, who you are?" Viv leaned back against the wall.

Kevin nodded. "Last year, after I accidentally almost took Lily and her grandpa. He asked me at the party—he was already suspicious. Everyone else was so focused on Lily that no one was looking at me. Except him. I thought he might be like Luc and confided in him. And now, he's... I don't know the right word but making me tell him stuff or he'll tell Luc and Evie that it was me who pulled Lily into the lake."

"He's blackmailing you?" Viv said. "I mean, I know he's a chaos demon, but blackmailing children seems extreme, even for him."

"He says it's okay since I'm not a real child." Kevin rubbed his eyes. "That's almost true. I'm very old, but also only eleven."

"What do you want me to do?" Viv asked. "I don't know how to help you. This is so far beyond my area of expertise. I'm trying to come up with ideas, and I'm so grateful y'all trusted me with this huge secret, but this is so far beyond my knowledge and abilities."

"It's not, though," Kevin said. "If you'd just let go, you'd be able to see the answer. I know it. I can't see what you do, but I know it's there. In your head." He tapped the side of his head in emphasis.

"I don't have control over the visions, if that's what you're implying," Viv said.

"Maybe don't try to be in control so much?" Kevin suggested. His shoulders slumped. "I'm running out of time. I'm so hungry all the time, and there are days I can barely keep up with Lily and Shelby. I'm tireder than I knew was possible."

"I need to talk to Evie and Bev," Viv said. "I need to be able to tell them what's going on."

"I don't want to lose my friends." Kevin's lower lip trembled, and he suddenly looked much younger than his eleven plus a few thousand years.

"You will either way," Viv pointed out. "At least this way, there's a chance. You may have to decide, though… Do you want to be human? Grow up, live your life, and die? Or do you want to hold on to the lake?" She pinched the bridge of her nose and braced herself for a stab of pain. That one had come out of nowhere.

Kevin sat up straight. "Was that a vision?"

"I don't know," Viv said, relaxing a bit as the anticipated pain didn't arrive. "I guess so. Kind of." She pushed herself off the wall and stood up straight. "You need to go back to bed, and I need permission to talk to my friends about you."

"Which friends?" Kevin demanded. "I need names."

"Evie and Bev, of course," Viv said. Then she considered. "And probably Sam and Elle, if it comes down to it."

"I don't know what my mother knows, although since our legal connection was not an accident, she probably knows more than she's ever admitted to," Kevin mused. "That one's easy. And Sam might already know if Mat told her. It's the others I'm afraid of."

"I'll let you sleep on it," Viv said. "But you need to decide. Like you said, you're running out of time."

Kevin flashed a tight-lipped smile, then stood and ran back up the stairs. Viv headed into the bathroom—she hadn't been lying about the effects of being startled on her middle-aged bladder.

When she emerged, Evie was waiting for her. "You were gone a long time. Just checking on you."

Viv suppressed an eye roll. It was good to have friends who cared. Even if they were sometimes suspicious and nosy. "Kevin was on the stairs, so we talked for a few minutes, then I sent him to bed. He was having trouble sleeping."

Evie narrowed her eyes, then nodded.

"I know I've given you reason to mistrust me," Viv said. "But I need you to take a step back. I'm not going to go on a bender in your house. Or at all. Being back here, where it all started, is working. I'm not getting the blinding pain with most visions, and even when I do, it disappears almost immediately. I have no need to self-medicate since the one thing I was trying to medicate away has disappeared."

"I'm not sure that's how it works," Evie said doubtfully.

"I promise to talk to you and Bev if I need to, if it gets too hard to bear without help. Please, though. Trust me."

"You're right," Evie said, pulling Viv in for a hug. "And I'm sorry."

"I love you, Evie," Viv said into her shorter friend's hair. "And I will need you tomorrow. I'm finally facing the music and visiting my mother."

"Oooh," Evie said as she let go of Viv and took a step back. "I'll bake cookies. Do you need someone to go with you?"

Viv considered. She desperately didn't want to go alone but felt like she needed to. Something important was going to happen, and it would only happen if she went by herself. "No. I have to do this myself."

CHAPTER EIGHT

Viv followed the same path Elle had taken when she left after reassuring Bev she didn't need an escort, convinced Luc not to drive her back to Bev's, and let Evie take up the argument when Viv snagged her jacket and walked off the porch towards the lake.

She had every intention of going straight back to Bev's—just the long way 'round, which was safer when traveling by foot. But the moonlight sparkling on the water drew her attention, and she stopped and stared. Even though the lake was dangerous—had always been dangerous—it had also been her refuge.

"Hey, Viv, it's Sam." The demon's voice floated towards her from around the bend of the trail behind her.

Viv suppressed her startle reflex and turned around to watch Sam walk towards her. "You just don't give up, do you? How'd you find me anyway?"

"Bev told me, over Evie's and Luc's protests. I came to apologize. What I said earlier was uncalled for and cruel. I never knew my mother, not really, and have little emotional attachment to my father. My upbringing was nothing like yours, and familial bonds in hell have a lot less innate strength than those of humans here on earth. I shouldn't have been impatient with you and your complicated relationship with your mother. It is difficult to understand maintaining ties with someone who only hurts and never heals, but then—" she shrugged and took a step closer to Viv "—I still talk to my twin, so I have no room to judge."

"It's okay. You're right. I give her too much power; I always have. I can't pretend that being here hasn't helped mitigate the effects of the visions. But I also can't rid myself of the roiling ball of fear and dread that are always present when I'm in Eden Valley. Maybe it's my mother. Maybe it's this town, the lake… Whatever magic exists that makes me forget why I want to leave. But as much as I'm relieved the visions are easier to bear, I'm still not sure I can stay." Viv turned back to the lake and took a deep breath. "I'm going to see my mother tomorrow. I don't know what I'm going to say, but I have to say something. This has gone on long enough. Too long. I can't stay here, though. Not as long as she's here."

Sam moved, and Viv caught the motion out of the corner of her eye. She pivoted to face Sam, who was affecting a wider legged stance, almost bow-legged in appearance. She held her hand up to the space in front of her forehead, tipped an imaginary hat, and drawled, "Are you saying this town ain't big enough for the both of you?"

Viv burst into laughter, and a second later, Sam joined her.

"Stop!" Viv said. "I have to stop laughing, or we'll both regret it."

"You bet your boots I'll stop," Sam said. "I'm your huckleberry."

Viv leaned against a nearby tree and wiped the tears streaming down her face. "Are you watching every western-themed movie in existence?" she asked.

"Someone has to interrupt Luc's documentary viewing," Sam said. "And I like cowboy movies. The only issue I have is there are way too many men. Women would be much better in almost every role, and they're a lot easier on the eyes than all those old, craggy faced white dudes."

"Sam Elliot's mustache, though," Viv said. "You have to give the mustache a pass."

Sam pursed her lips and considered. "Fine. The mustache can stay."

She held out a hand to Viv, and they walked in silence to the path that brought them into town through the park.

The streetlights illuminated the mostly dark storefronts, and the raucous noise from Eden Valley's two bars floated down the street, competing for prominence. Sam stopped suddenly and spun around, facing Viv but not letting go of her hand. Sam tugged her forward hard enough that Viv stumbled into Sam's waiting arms.

Viv sucked in a deep breath to slow her racing heartbeat and cool the heat that burned through the chill of the mountain lake breeze, but instead of dampening the flames, she breathed in the scent of vanilla and blackberries and warm, rich earth... Sam's scent.

"Sam," she started, moving her head so she could make eye contact with the demon. Instead, her gaze snagged on Sam's lips—always Sam's lips. She threw caution to the wind, lowered her head, and kissed her. She knew the romance books always said there was a pause, a hesitation, the tantalizing hint of skin against skin before delving deeper, but she couldn't go slow, couldn't pretend to tease. Viv pressed her lips against Sam's, tongue eagerly seeking entrance, and once more inhaled the scent that was so uniquely Sam.

Viv's hands cradled Sam's head, and she pulled back and down, tilting the shorter woman's face upwards.

After a brief pause, Sam responding in kind, entwining her arms around Viv's waist.

For a moment, everything was perfect. The moon, the night, the lake... And most definitely the kiss.

When they broke apart, gasping, Viv looked down at Sam and smiled. "Guess I'm not over you at all."

"Can't say I'm complaining, little lady," Sam answered. She ran a hand over the curve of Viv's hip, then up, skimming her waist and brushing the side of her breast. "I'd be tickled pink if you'd join me in my bunk."

Viv laughed again. Sam's words had broken the spell cast in the summer heat, and given her the space to think clearly, even with fingers still lingering on the swell of her breast. "I'll need to text Bev and let her know," Viv said. "But I think we could work something out."

"I missed you," Sam said, suddenly serious. She pulled her hand back from the teasing position where she'd let it rest and cupped Viv's face in her hands. "After more years than I can count of spending time with humans, wrangling over the smallest details to ensure their desires are met and paid for, it never occurred to me I would ever have more than a fleeting desire, and for anything other than the pleasure of the moment."

"Mat said I destroyed you," Viv said. She flicked her glance away from Sam's face and looked past her into the darkness of the trees. Something moved. A pinprick of light flashed and disappeared. A trick of the light. Or dark. Moonlight and water could create odd reflections. She pulled her attention back to Sam.

"You didn't destroy me," Sam said. "I was incredibly sad, bordering on broken-hearted, when you went back to Seattle, but not destroyed. I might like you—quite a lot—but I'm still a woman, and strong enough to survive a breakup, no matter how devastating." She paused and narrowed her eyes. "When did you see Mat? He's not supposed to be here."

"Earlier this evening. He was talking to the kids—he's been doing that a lot, I think—and I interrupted. He's trying to stir something up, make a bad situation worse. And he's angry with me for what I did to you." Viv glanced back into the trees again as another flash of light caught her attention.

"He has no right," Sam retorted. "No right to be here when Luc has banished him from Eden Valley. And certainly no right to speak on my behalf, to be angry when I'm not."

"People don't always make logical decisions when someone they love has been hurt," Viv said. "I'd be selling Tennessee ham from a roadside stand if anyone touched Evie or Bev or the kids." There was a long silence, and Viv forced herself to meet Sam's eyes, even though she was afraid of what she'd see there. "Or you."

Sam smiled, and for a second, it felt like the sun had risen at midnight—warmth and light suffused Viv's body, and she stepped back into Sam's arms and out of the yellow patch of the nearest streetlight.

This time, the demon twined her arms around Viv's neck and pulled her down for a passionate kiss that left them both gasping.

"Wanna get out of here?" Sam asked. "I've been staying in Bev's rental cabin, so we'd have some privacy."

Viv nodded, unable to form coherent thoughts.

"STOP!" A bright light erupted, cutting through the shadow of the park's trees, and highlighting the women.

Viv threw her arm up to shield her eyes and blinked against her temporary blindness. A sick, familiar feeling formed in her chest. She might not be able to see who was wielding the spotlight, but she'd know that voice anymore. She wanted to curl up into invisibility, to hide herself behind Sam, to run away. Instead, she started laughing, notes of hysteria coloring her voice. "Guess this time it's actually true that I've been tempted by the devil."

Guenevere Kane lowered the industrial flashlight enough that Viv could stop shielding her eyes.

"What are you doing here, Guenevere?" Sam asked, tone hard and biting. She kept her arms around Viv's neck.

"I am rooting out evil, wherever it hides, with the light and truth of Jesus Christ," Gwen said. "The unrighteous will not inherit the kingdom of God, fornicators, homosexuals, and sodomites—all are sinning, and all are condemned to hell. I will save this town by any means necessary. I will save Genevieve, even though she is my curse for stepping into sin in the first place."

Viv stepped out of Sam's arms, and the sick feeling she always got in her mother's presence solidified into a spiky ball of ice cold enough to burn.

"What do you mean, I'm your curse?" Viv asked.

"Don't engage," Sam said. "She's trying to throw you off balance, make you feel small enough that you'll listen, take heed of what she's saying, and internalize her hate and make it your own."

"Don't listen to that temptress," Gwen commanded. "She has already fallen into the pit. You can still be saved. Renounce her, renounce your sinful lifestyle, and come home. If you pray for forgiveness, you can one day bask in the glory." Gwen had her hands raised above her head in the parody of a tent revival preacher, bobbing the flashlight's beam across the trees, the street, and Viv's face.

"Mother, stop," Viv said. She held out her hands and took another step away from Sam. "It's time for you to go home. I'll stop by tomorrow, and we can talk about this."

"You're going to 'talk' to her? After she's followed you around and yelled at you, called you unclean?" Sam's eyebrows attempted to disappear into her hairline as she crossed her arms in front of her chest. "Leave her. Come back to my cabin, and I'll help you forget."

Viv looked between her mother and Sam, then shook her head. "I can't. I need to resolve this—" she gestured at her mother "—before I can move forward."

Sam dropped her arms to her side and sighed. "Of course. Let me know when you hit that resolution. I'm going home, and I'm definitely not holding my breath." She walked off the sidewalk and down the street towards the barely visible beach. When Sam was almost out of view, black and gold wings erupted from her back. She crouched low, then launched herself into the sky.

Viv stared after her, regret trying to wash away the shroud of shame still hanging over her. She took a step towards the lake, but before her feet left the sidewalk, Gwen shrieked.

"The devil has been vanquished! You have your chance at redemption!" She shone her flashlight into the sky, trying to find Sam's silhouette against the darkness.

Viv closed her eyes for a moment. Sam was right. There would be no chance at reconciliation, at coming together and making her mother let go of the deep, poisonous anger that colored every interaction they had.

"Mother," Viv said softly, pulling the older woman's attention back to her. "What did you mean 'I'm your curse'?"

"The punishment for sinning," Gwen said. The casual surprise in her tone rocked Viv back on her feet. "I sinned, first by not saving my family from the devil's grasp, and then with your father, and God punished me by taking him and leaving you."

"He didn't die," Viv said. "He left when he I was born."

"Who told you that?" Gwen asked. She swept the flashlight's beam across the ground and stepped back until she was illuminated by a streetlight. Her face was twisted, adding age and emphasizing her bitterness. "Was it Hope? She always wanted what was mine. My sister preferred her, and Greg wanted her, too. I abased myself to keep him, and what did I get out of it? Nothing. Just you." Gwen paced, her voice quieter. She pointed the flashlight at Viv again with a smile that was the very opposite of comforting. "You preferred her too, didn't you? No matter how I tried to lift you up into the light, you kept slinking back into the dark." The steel edge and lack of inflection in Gwen's voice changed Viv's mother from hysterical crackpot into something more sinister.

Viv flinched at the memories of how her mother tried to "lift her into the light," and her back hit the wrought-iron fence separating the sidewalk from the park. Even now, in her mid-forties, Gwen could still make her feel afraid.

Viv took a deep breath. "You should go home now. I'm going back to Bev's. I'll see you in the morning." Viv sprinted down the sidewalk, took a turn to the left, and jogged back to Bev's, not stopping until she was safely inside behind a locked door.

CHAPTER NINE

Viv stood on the front porch of her childhood home, frozen in indecision. The crunch of gravel behind her made her wheel around. The pressure on her chest multiplied, and the air whooshed out of her lungs as the beating of her heart overtook everything else in her chest cavity.

Sam was behind her at the edge of the gravel and flagstone path that led from the sidewalk to the door. "I thought I'd check to see if you wanted any support," she said. "I can go with you, if you want."

Viv shook her head. "I need to do this alone."

"Why?" Sam's blunt question made Viv take a step back.

"Because that's what adults do. They step up to their problems and take care of them. I am a strong, independent woman, and I can do this." Viv tried to meet Sam's eyes but fell short and stared at the shorter woman's shoulder instead.

"I'm not human, and I haven't spent much time in your world, but I know that's not true. Being a strong, independent woman means asking for help when you need it and not being too stubborn to accept it when freely offered." Sam set a hand on her hip and rolled her shoulders up for a second before straightening and firming up her posture. "I want to help you, with your mom, with the headaches and your precognition, and out of your clothes."

Viv shook her head, even as her pulse jumped at Sam's last words.

"I won't offer again," Sam said. "If you change your mind, you'll have to ask." She turned as if to walk away, then looked back at Viv.

Viv closed her eyes. A sad smile crept across her face. Help was always conditional and asking for it made a person vulnerable. She couldn't even bare herself like that for Evie and Bev. There's no way she could trust Sam. A summer fling, no matter how much tension still pulled them together, wasn't enough.

When she opened her eyes again, Sam was gone.

"Story of the last year," she said. Then, squaring her shoulders and metaphorically girding her loins, she walked up to the front door and knocked.

Viv stood in the middle of the living room. Her shoulders had rolled up around her ears, and she was hunched in an effort to conceal how much taller she was, a habit she'd developed to placate the much shorter Gwen when Viv had surpassed her mother's height at age twelve. Viv concentrated on a rip in the wallpaper above her mother's head. The wallpaper was white with burnt orange, avocado green, and harvest yellow flowers in varying sizes scattered randomly across it like the seventies had projectile vomited on the wall. The wallpaper and the small rip at the seam near the ceiling had been there as long as she could remember and fit with the decor in the rest of the house.

"Are you listening to me?" her mother yelled.

Viv forced herself to look at her mother. "I hear you, but I wasn't listening." She flinched in anticipation of her mother's certain anger. She drew in another breath and added, "Although I'm sure I can figure out which of your three scripts you were berating me with. It was either a rant about my lack of faith and refusal to attend the church of your choice, a screed about how leaving Eden Valley has deprived me of a husband and you of your rightful grandchildren and now it's all too late and you'll die alone and angry and it's all my fault, or—and this is where I'd put my money—more homophobic bullshit. I've heard that one so many times in the last thirty years, I could probably recite it along with you. I'm evil, unnatural, a sinner, in league with the devil, and if I'd stayed in the Valley and attended church and married a man twenty years too old for me and popped out a litter, I wouldn't be on the fast track to hell right now."

Gwen's jaw dropped a moment, but then she threw her shoulders back and said in the quiet voice that meant the yelling was over and the real verbal abuse was about to start, "Don't you talk to me with that kind of language. You may not like me, but I am your mother, this is my house, and you will respect me."

Viv laughed. "You're three for four. I don't respect you and haven't for a very long time. Any hope you had of earning my respect died when you met with Pastor Olson when I was in high school and asked him for advice and prayer because I wasn't straight. Asked him, might I add, not in the privacy of his church office, but on his front porch where his daughter Joanne was serving the iced tea. It was one thing to castigate me in private for my sexual orientation, but Joanne nearly ruined my life."

"You're exaggerating," Gwen said, her voice dripping with condescension and a sneer cutting a gash in her face. "The only one who ruined your life is you."

"I'm not here to argue with you," Viv said. "I trusted you when I was a child, but you aren't worth me trying anymore. You're a bitter woman who's lost whatever ability to be nice you might've been born with. You can't polish yourself up with Jesus, no matter how hard you try. I am here to get the few things I've left, and then I'm leaving. I'll be blocking your number. Don't call. Don't write. Don't drag my friends into this by attempting to send messages through them." She turned and walked through the house, noting for the last time the purple shag carpet, avocado appliances in the kitchen, and abundance of popcorn ceilings and wood paneling.

When she opened the door to her childhood room—the place she'd crashed every time she'd visited Eden Valley for the last twenty-five years out of guilt and misplaced obligation—the scent of mildew hit her. The banker boxes holding her childhood memorabilia that'd been stacked in the closet had been pulled out and placed underneath the large, open window. The cardboard was wet and dissolving around yearbooks, photo albums, newspaper clippings, academic awards, and the roses from the first girl she'd kissed—they'd been carefully pressed and dried and hidden, along with a letter that ached with teenage forbidden love in…

A noise behind her had Viv whirling around. "Where is it?" she demanded.

"Where's what?" Gwen asked, her innocent tone belied by the smirk that still scarred her face.

"My Bible," Viv said.

"You mean Grace's bible, the one I gave you when you were born?" Gwen asked. "The Bible that belonged to my poor, dead, damned sister. The one you hollowed out and hid the signs of your perversion in?"

"The letters?" Viv asked, although she knew the truth already.

"Burned. Along with the photos of you with that Jezebel and all those dirty books." Gwen cast her eyes downward and affected a pious demeanor. "I blame myself, of course. I should've kept you home as soon as I knew you were starting down the pathway with the devil on your shoulder. You shouldn't have been allowed to read those books or hang out with people who lead you astray and supported your descent." She glanced back up and nearly glowed with self-righteous smugness.

"It's fine," Viv said. "If they'd meant that much to me, I would've taken them with me. I do appreciate that you moved all my things under an open window—wet yearbook is the best memorabilia. This room reeks of mold and mildew. You should get that taken care of before it makes you sick." She looked around the room. There was nothing left. Everything she'd left was gone, except for the things her mother had ruined. "This makes it easier, actually. Since I have nothing left to carry out, I guess I can leave the baggage I'm dragging."

She pushed past her mother and walked to the front door without looking around. "Goodbye."

The screen door slammed shut behind her, punctuating her mother's command. "Get back in here, Genevieve Kane. If you walk away now, don't ever ask to come back."

"That's the idea," Viv said, likely too quietly for her mother to hear over the sound of her own impotent anger.

She kept walking, though the town, past Bev's house, and found herself standing in front of the cabin Sam had said she was renting.

Viv felt lighter than she had in years and everything she'd been pushing away started crashing forward.

"I've been an idiot," she said, then for the second time that morning, knocked on a door while struggling to breathe.

While she waited for Sam to answer the door, she mentally wrote and rewrote the script of what she was going to say. Starting with a mild grovel seemed appropriate, followed by a heartfelt feelings dump interspersed with suggestive comments.

Viv glanced down at her outfit. Luc had picked up everything she'd needed, and she hadn't even blushed when he'd handed her a suitcase of her underwear, in addition to other things. She was no longer stuck wearing the same two outfits interspersed with Bev's too short and too big clothes. She was wearing skinny jeans, a tight ribbed tank top, a fitted hoodie, and her leather ass-kicking boots. She pursed her lips and pulled the zipper of the hoodie down to just below her breasts, then leaned forward and shimmied enough to make her cleavage more prominent. Satisfied that she was as seductive as possible with limited time and resources, she leaned back, shifting her balance, and knocked again.

When no one came to the door, Viv deflated. Of course Sam wasn't here. It was Monday and she likely didn't hang out waiting for people to stop by. After a couple more minutes, Viv pulled out her phone and texted.

Hey. It's Viv. I stopped by your place, but you're not here. Got time for a coffee and a chat?

Viv stuck her phone back into the hoodie pocket and walked back towards Main Street. She was almost to the coffee shop when her phone beeped.

This number has been disconnected and is no longer in service. Please try again.

Viv put the phone back in her pocket, walked into the coffee shop and ordered an iced Americano with room. After doctoring her coffee, she walked down the street sipping her beverage. She hadn't realized how much she'd counted on the demon waiting for her. They were supposed to figure out Kevin's problem, figure out Viv's problem, celebrate with champagne and sex, and live happily ever after in Viv's Seattle condo.

Viv drained her coffee, tossed it in a nearby trashcan, and tried to figure out what to do. Bev was at work. The kids were at swimming lessons every morning this week, so she couldn't find Kevin and drill him on his monstrous origins as a productive distraction, and Evie'd mentioned taking Alex to the pediatrician today for shots and her six-month checkup.

That left... No one. There was nobody else in this town she'd had more than passing conversations with in the last twenty years.

"Hey... Are you okay?"

Viv looked up from her examination of the sidewalk in front of the park entrance. Elle was standing in front of her with a large bottle of mineral water. She was wearing a large straw hat with a floppy brim and a pink ribbon with tiny white polka dots. Her dark brown skin was set off with a yellow sundress and matching yellow flats.

"You look amazing," Viv said while she tried to come up with a better answer to Elle's question.

"Thank you," Elle said. "I hadn't realized how much I would enjoy fashion when I came here. But it's fun, isn't it?" She smoothed her fingers over her waist and down the skirt.

Viv almost let it go... It wasn't important. But there'd been so much unsaid, so many things glossed over in the interest of more pressing things. And now, the pressing thing was Viv's slowly cracking heart, and she needed something else—anything else—to latch onto now. "What do you mean 'when you came here'? Eden Valley is not a fashion hotspot. More the opposite, really."

Elle's eyes shifted to the left in what Viv was quickly learning was her tell. Elle was about to prevaricate.

"Don't," Viv said. "If you don't want to, or *can't*, tell me, just say that. Don't change the subject or redirect or lie. I know there's something weird about you. I don't think it's bad weird, but let's not pretend you're on the up and up."

"I have no idea what you're talking about," Elle said stiffly, shoulders setting firmly.

"I think I know why you avoided making friends—or even talking to anyone—for so long," Viv said. "You're a terrible liar."

"I am not!" Elle said. Her hands snapped to her hips and a flash of anger lit her eyes. "I'm one of the best. That's why I was chosen."

"Mmhmm. Chosen for what, Elle?" Viv narrowed her eyes.

Elle's eyes darted around as she looked everywhere but at Viv. "I can't…"

"We all have secrets," Viv said. "You know mine—all of ours. We're trustworthy. Or at least Evie and Bev are. I realize you and I aren't friends, and you have no reason to trust me. But don't leave Evie and Bev in the dark. They deserve a friend who can be honest with them."

Elle stopped fidgeting and stared at Viv. "You deserve that, too. And although we don't know each other well, I know how highly Evie and Bev regard you, which is enough for me. It's not a lack of trust that keeps me quiet—it's so much more."

"You need to tell someone," Viv said. "Burdens shared and all…"

"Do you believe in angels?" Elle asked.

Viv blinked. "I think I got whiplash from that complete one-eighty. What do you mean?"

"Do you believe in angels?" Elle repeated.

Viv considered. "I've never really thought about it much. I know there are demons, and logically that makes me feel there must be angels. But does that then imply the existence of the Christian god? I can't believe then. There's no world in which my mother's faith is valid."

"Let's walk to the park," Elle said, touching Viv's elbow and jolting her out of the theological rabbit hole her brain was deep diving into. "If I'm going to trust you, you should be sitting down."

Viv let Elle lead her to the park. They found a bench away from the play structure that offered a glimpse of the lake between the trees. Viv watched Elle sit and shift until she could see the lake and Viv at the same time. Something on Elle's face—the serious intensity and the pinched look around her eyes, too unlined to be the same age as Viv—raised the hairs on the back of Viv's neck. She was almost positive she was going to regret pushing Elle into sharing confidences. Sitting and stewing in her own disappointment and self-recrimination over screwing things up with Sam was looking more and more the better option.

"I'm an angel," Elle said.

Viv stared at her, words short-circuiting in her brain. "You're an angel," she said. "Of course. Where there are demons there are angels. Are you here for Lily? Is that why you suddenly started being social and infiltrated yourself into our lives? You had your adopted monster spying on Lily so you'd know…"

"Adopted monster?" Elle asked. "Why would you call him that?"

"Don't try to distract me now." Viv shoved a finger in Elle's face. "Are you here to hurt my friends?"

"No! Of course not. I would never hurt anyone." She paused and seemed to reconsider. "I guess that's not completely true. But I am not here for your friends and their children."

"Why are you here then? What other reason would an angel have for being in Eden… Oh. The lake. You're here because of—"

"Kind of. It's complicated." Elle shrugged and glanced out at the lake again.

"Is that how you know so much about hell's contracts and contract enforcement?" Viv asked. The puzzle pieces were finally starting to snap together.

"Yeah," Elle's shoulders released away from her ears. "There's more, but I think you're right. This is stuff I should share with everyone, and I'm not sure I want to say it more than once."

"Brunch?" Viv asked.

Elle's smile didn't quite reach her eyes. "I might lose my nerve by Saturday. Is there such a thing as emergency brunch?"

"I'll have to check with Bev. She's the only one currently tied to a day job schedule, and she'd mentioned she'd used up most of her time off in the last year." Viv pulled her phone out of her pocket and composed the group text.

Hey. Emergency brunch needed per Elle's request. Any way we can all make that work tomorrow?

Evie's answer was almost instantaneous. *I can do whenever as long as I can bring Alex. But Wednesday would work better if it's a baby-free affair. Will the emergency hold?*

Bev's answer was a little slower, although the three dots signifying that she was considering an answer.

Elle produced her phone from… Honestly, Viv wasn't sure where it'd come from, but decided this wasn't the biggest reveal of the day.

It's not really an emergency. But I do want to talk to you both, with or without baby.

Bev's reply finally came in, and Viv swore she could hear the apology lacing Bev's words. *I really can't. I want to, but…* The text ended with a shrug emoji followed by a bank.

Viv looked at Elle who was worrying at her lower lip and staring at the phone.

What about an early dinner? We can call it happy hour instead of the early bird special, Viv typed. As soon as she hit send, she looked up to watch Elle's face. A smile bloomed across her face along with an expression of naked relief.

I can do either today or tomorrow, no babies required, Evie said. *Wednesday, Luc leaves for Seattle again after lunch.*

I'm free, as long as Kevin can hang out with Lily at your place under adult supervision, Elle answered.

Bev's reply was quicker this time. *Meet at 5:30? And I'll send Shel over, too, Evie if that's ok?*

They're all still here anyway. I'll let them know they'll be staying for dinner. And another night? Evie said.

If you don't mind, I'm sure the kids would love it, Bev said.

Elle sent a thumbs up emoji.

See you all in a few hours. Viv shoved her phone back in her pocket and offered a smile to Elle, whose phone was no longer visible. "I'm heading back to Bev's for lunch and a nap. See you later?"

Elle nodded and stood. "I'd meant to comfort you—you looked lost and alone when I spotted you. I'm sorry I let this carry me away. Are you okay?"

"Not yet," Viv said. "But I'm not ready to talk about it. Maybe after your big reveal later?"

"Feel free to steal my thunder whenever," Elle said. "See you later."

Viv watched her walk away. She'd thought Eden Valley was out of surprises, but somehow there was an endless supply. After a deep breath, she turned around and headed out of the park. Just as she stepped out from under the tree cover, she was knocked backwards with the image of Elle hovering over the lake, silver wings spread wide and pointing a pair of impossibly large scissors at Bev, who was cowering on the shore.

When the vision faded, Viv was on the ground covered in dust and surrounded by concerned park goers.

"Migraine," she gasped out. "Sorry."

"Do you need help back to Bev's?" a vaguely familiar voice asked.

Viv blinked a couple times, trying to clear the flashes of light obscuring her vision. "Colin?"

Evie's bar manager stood in front of her with a hand out. Viv let him pull her to her feet. "An escort would be great," she said. "I'm still a little wobbly." For the second time that day, she let someone lead her through the park's front gate.

CHAPTER TEN

V iv slid into the booth at Ambrosia and looked around. She was the first one there, and that unprecedented event needed celebrating. She heard the server approach and turned to order. "I'll have a water and a glass of bubbles."

"Sure you should be drinking alone?" Brandy's voice was coldly amused, a nice change from the sneering meanness she usually expressed.

Viv looked at her. "I'm sorry for hurting your feelings last weekend. I didn't know I'd strike a nerve—I was just trying to protect my friends. My friends, who will be here soon, so I won't be drinking alone. If you'd rather not wait on me, I get it—and can order at the bar. But if you're going to be our server, please let's be courteous. I want a glass of the house sparkling wine, a glass of still water, and an order of the happy hour nachos."

"You didn't hurt my feelings," Brandy scoffed. "There is nothing you could say that would matter enough to me. I'll put your order in." She whirled around and stomped away.

A couple minutes later, a different server dropped off Viv's beverages. She took a sip of the wine, paused to enjoy the play of bubbles over her tongue, then swallowed and waited. She wasn't sure what she was waiting for. An insatiable need to gulp the rest of the glass and order another? The drinks police to show up, sirens blaring, to take it away? The bleakness that accompanied her post vision headaches when she smothered them with alcohol?

The headache she'd gotten earlier when leaving the park had slowly dissipated over the course of the afternoon. She'd treated it with several glasses of water, some aspirin, and throwing herself into her work. She'd only lost one client when she announced she needed a couple weeks off due to a sudden illness, and she was easing back in to get ahead of the work she'd promised to resume next week. By the time she'd sent off a draft design to one of her oldest clients, the headache was gone.

She took another sip of wine, then switched to water. Everything seemed okay, but she didn't want to push it, especially knowing she'd have to defend herself to her friends.

"What's the emergency?" Evie said, sliding into the booth. Her gaze snagged on the bubbles in front of Viv, and she froze. "What happened? Are you okay? Was it your mom?" The glass of wine disappeared.

"Hey! That was rude." Viv glared at her friend. "The emergency isn't mine, it's Elle's. My mother was awful, but I think I closed that door forever. I had a vision several hours ago, it was intense, but the pain and despair are already gone. I am trying a glass of wine here, in public, with my girls. So back off and give it back."

Evie set her mouth in a stubborn line. Viv knew that look well. Evie was as easy going as all get out—until she wasn't. She was getting ready to dig in her heels. Viv braced herself. Then Evie's expression softened, and she drew a deep breath.

"I'm sorry." The wine appeared in the place it'd disappeared from. "You're a grown ass adult, and I'm treating you like a child. Your choices are your own, and I don't want to lose your trust by not trusting."

"Thank you." Viv took another sip of the wine and then looked at Evie suspiciously. "This isn't what I was drinking before. This isn't Washington sparkling wine—it's champagne."

Evie grinned sheepishly. "I didn't know what you were drinking, so I guessed. Oops."

"I'm not complaining. This is amazing. I hope this glass is depriving someone awful of something they probably don't really appreciate anyway." Viv took another sip and reveled in the fresh biscuity taste. "I love bubbles so very much."

Evie smiled. "I do worry about my accidental supernatural shoplifting...I hope I'm not stealing from anyone. I don't mind taking things from the man, but don't want to be screwing with people's lives. Like, what if the person whose champagne that was saved for years for that bottle to celebrate and now they can't? Luc keeps saying I'm not stealing as much as creating, but I don't know... Sometimes it just feels wrong."

"What do you want?" Brandy demanded of Evie, sparking Viv from delving into the philosophical supernatural guilt that had plagued Evie since she started exhibiting her magical wish fulfillment skills last year.

"A glass of the rosé please and an order of happy hour nachos." Evie said. Neither her gaze nor her voice wavered, but Viv saw the tension in her jaw.

"I already ordered the nachos," Viv said.

"We're gonna need two," Evie said. "I'm starving."

"Might want to slow down on the nachos," Brandy said, dropping her eyes down to stare at Evie's midsection.

"What is wrong with you?" Viv exclaimed. "Do you even hear yourself? There is nothing okay about the way you talk to Evie. Whatever your problem is, now's the time to get over it. It's up to you whether or not you can drop whatever grudges you've been harboring for the last twenty-five years, but you are not going to talk to her—or anyone—like that again. Grow the hell up, Brandy." Viv leaned back in the booth and held Brandy's gaze until the other woman dropped her eyes, mumbled something about getting Evie's wine, and walked off.

"Wow!" Evie said. "I don't know if I'm wow-ing you or her, but wow. That was...a lot. She always knows just what I'm feeling insecure about and manages to poke it with a sharp stick." She grimaced.

"I'm not losing the baby weight nearly as fast this time, which is perfectly normal and not something to be stressed about at all, but I am struggling a bit."

"Maybe her superpower is knowing how to be the worst possible person at any given time?" Viv suggested. "She made a snide remark about me drinking when I ordered."

"She makes the same comment to me every time Luc and I stop in for a glass of wine." Evie laughed, then grimaced. "What if you're right? We can't let her talk to Bev."

"Why? Bev is the most self-assured, confident person I know. There is literally nothing Brandy could say that would shake her." Viv tilted her head to consider. "Except…"

"Shelby," Evie finished. "And it's been a tough year for them. When she brings my wine, I'll order for Elle and Bev."

Elle and Bev showed up at almost the same time as the two orders of nachos and glasses of local chardonnay.

Bev looked at Viv's glass—still more than half full—and opened her mouth. She closed it abruptly and glared at Evie.

"It's handled," Evie said. "And that's not why we're here." She shifted in the booth and looked at Elle. "What's the emergency?"

Elle took a deep breath and a deeper gulp of wine, glanced at Viv, then said, "I'm an angel."

Viv watched her friends take that in. Bev's eyebrows slanted into a vee. Evie nodded.

"That makes sense," Evie said. "Now that you say it, it's kinda obvious. I can't believe I didn't pick up on that earlier."

"What?" Viv said. "This makes sense? It's obvious? How?"

Evie smiled. "When I'm near her, she makes me feel kinda the same as I feel near Luc, but different."

"I hope different," Elle said. "You're attractive, but not really my type."

A burst of laughter escaped Viv before she could tamp it down.

Bev asked, "What kind? The stereotypical Christian angel with fluffy wings and a harp and a halo? Something older? Are you ranked? Why are you here?"

Elle's eyes widened and she leaned back. "Oh. Um. I didn't think you'd believe me."

Evie snorted. "Honey, I'm engaged to a demon. I've been to hell. My daughter has a three-headed hellhound that sleeps at the foot of her bed every night."

Viv heard the subtle threat woven into Evie's acceptance. She and her family were off limits and more than capable of defending themselves against any angelic interference.

"I should have known you wouldn't argue," Elle said ruefully. "It's just, when I first arrived, I tried to tell people, and they were...less than kind. I find most people aren't believers. And the ones who are, well, let's just say they aren't believing in the right things."

Bev tapped the table. "Do you want me to repeat my questions?"

"No. I think I've got them down." She took a deep breath. "Most of us manifest forms that match the expectations that centuries of belief have created. My true form is older, though. I don't know how to describe it, exactly. But if you've seen Lucifer or Samiel take their true forms—not just wings attached to their human façades—you'll have a better idea of what I am."

Evie leaned forward and cupped her chin in her hand. "I haven't seen that," she said. "Guess Luc and I have our next date night planned." She looked at Viv. "You?"

Viv shook her head mutely and tried not to think about Sam's wings and the warmth that threatened to flood her body at the picture forming in her mind.

"Okay, well—it's not as pretty as how we're imagined. More... ancient. We're not fluffy guardian angels. We're warriors. Made for war. Those of us who are guardians don't guard people from paper cuts or plane crashes. We guard things more important." Elle paused and took a sip of a wine.

"More important than people's lives?" Bev said. "That's...not cool."

"How old are you, Bev?" Elle asked.

"Forty-four."

"And when your child is frustrated with a school assignment or some rule of yours that she doesn't like, how does that rate on the scale of what you find important?"

Viv watched the dots connect on Bev's face. Her friend didn't say anything, though.

"I'm older than anyone you've ever met. Older than the demons you dance with here, older than Abaddon who styles himself a king of hell, and older than the one who begat him. I was old when the Morningstar, in a fit of youthful pique, led the rebellion on heaven. It is difficult for me to place the lives of individuals I don't know ahead of the things we guard."

While she was speaking, Elle's face changed. She was still recognizable, but it was harder to look at her. Viv's eyes started watering.

"Turn it down," Evie snapped. "People are starting to look at you. And don't try to intimidate us. We might not be as old as you, but you can't tell me you don't understand the type of love and compassion Bev's talking about. We still don't know who you are and why you moved here, but I've seen the maternal tenderness in your eyes when you look at Kevin."

Viv, strengthened by her knowledge of Kevin's and Evie's indomitable spirits looked Elle directly in the face. "I know now why the angels in the bible always started every visitation with 'don't be afraid.' You're scary, but not nearly as scary as you think you are. Why don't we skip the rest of Bev's questions and move to the last—the one you wouldn't answer earlier when I asked. Why are you here?" Viv thrust her chin out in challenge.

Elle sighed and the lines of her face softened. "Apologies. I have only been here for twelve years, and I am still adjusting. It's been six thousand years since I last walked this earth. To answer your question, the reason I'm here now is as a protector."

"What are you protecting?" Viv asked. The answer wasn't obvious to her even with what she knew about Kevin.

"And what are you protecting it from?" Evie asked.

Elle held out her arms. "I'm protecting this. Eden Valley. The world." She paused a moment, then added one more word. "Kevin."

Viv wiped the last of the cheese and guacamole off her fingers and regarded the nacho plates still heaped high with naked chips. "I love nachos, but I wish they came on trays instead of plates. More toppings, fewer chips. No one in the history of the world has ever said, 'These are fine, but I'd prefer more chips and less cheese.'"

"Actually, that's not true," Elle corrected. "On April 27, 1984, William Hansen of Shakopee, Minnesota expressed that exact sentiment, adding that the guacamole was too spicy. He was immediately shunned by his family and friends and eventually run out of town and forced to take refuge in an abandoned cabin in Northern Michigan where he eventually died."

Viv stared at Elle—was this some random angel power, or was she joking? The hint of a smile finally playing around the edges of Elle's lips gave it away. "Oh my god," Viv said. "You almost had me for a second. That was hilarious."

Elle's smile widened. "Humor is the hardest thing about living as a human. Angels don't spend a lot of time joking, but people spend a lot of time trying to figure out what makes their friends laugh. I watched a lot of your media to learn jokes, but I think it's subtler than that."

Evie shook her head. "You should get together with Luc and Sam so you can take turns picking the 'documentaries' to learn about being human."

"Do they watch the Bachelor?" Elle asked, eyes widening. "That's my favorite way to learn about your mating rituals."

Viv opened her mouth, reconsidered, and snapped it closed.

"You seem to have mastered our 'mating rituals.'" Bev made air quotes. "Your husband is really hot. And... Actually, I don't know anything else about him, so my judgment is purely superficial. Does he know you're an angel?"

"Angel?" Brandy scoffed and dropped the check on the table. "There's nothing angelic about *Aurielle*."

Another piece of the puzzle snapped into place in Viv's mind.

"Kevin is your biological kid," Viv blurted. "You really were pregnant all those years ago."

"But Jer had a vasectomy," Evie said. "How…"

"Didn't you say he accused her of cheating?" Bev asked. "Maybe he has super sperm that snuck on through."

Viv turned her attention back to Brandy who was frozen in place, a look of abject misery on her face. Elle was similarly still, but her expression was unreadable.

"Sorry," Viv said. "We shouldn't be speculating about your life like this. No matter what history exists, this is rude."

Brandy jolted into motion. "Whatever. Just ask your *angelic* friend how that adoption went down. And don't talk to me anymore." She turned and stalked away.

"We never talk to her if we don't have to." Viv's eyebrows drew down in a vee as she stared after Brandy.

"Wow," Evie whispered. "I feel kinda bad. I really never believed her."

"There is nothing about her story that is your fault, Evie," Bev pointed out. "She's had zero reason to continue her catty campaign of pettiness for the last twelve years, and that certainly doesn't explain the fifteen years before she got pregnant. I wouldn't waste too many tears on her."

Viv looked at Elle. "You knew when you moved here that Brandy was from here, that Kevin was conceived here, right?" She was being very careful to skirt around Kevin's immaculate conception.

Elle nodded. "I needed to be here, and I needed the child. I did not expect Brandy to return to this town after the adoption was complete, but I'd underestimated Eden Valley's pull on those who belong to the town."

"Did you…" Viv chose her words carefully. "…force the adoption?"

"Yes. Of course," Elle said. "It was necessary."

Evie and Bev recoiled in unison. "That is not okay," Evie said. "You can't just take people's babies."

Elle licked her lips. "I don't know how to explain in a way that you will understand, but please believe me. This is for the best."

"I'm going to need a minute," Bev said. She stood and dropped a couple twenties on the table. "I'm going to swing by home, change out of my business casual, and go check on Shelby."

Elle nodded. The confidence with which she'd admitted—no, stated—she'd forced Brandy to give Kevin up for adoption was starting to crumble. "Okay. I'll see you later?"

Bev didn't answer, just flashed a tight grin and left.

"I need to get back home. It's about time to top Alex up." She stood and looked at Elle. "I'm not as upset as Bev. I'm engaged to a demon, my future father-in-law is a king of hell, and my children are literal hellspawn. I get expediency. But this is hitting hard right now. I can't stop thinking about losing my kids like this, then being forced to see them every day, knowing I can't tell them who I am and feeling an ache in my chest where I hold my love for them. Brandy isn't my favorite person but losing a kid shouldn't happen to anyone." Evie started towards the door. "Stop by later for another glass of wine and an explanation, if you have one."

Viv and Elle were alone at the table. Elle stared at Viv, a stricken look in her eyes. "I thought… I don't know what I thought."

"I understand why you did what you did. It was the right choice. Brandy wouldn't have been able to parent Kevin. But wouldn't it have been kinder to wipe her memory? Or rearrange it so she remembered giving Kevin up for adoption, willingly and happily, but not to whom?" Viv took a sip of her now room temperature champagne.

"I tried," Elle admitted. "She'd done all the paperwork to place him for adoption. I just…nudged things a bit to expedite the process. There was an arrangement made, and I was only one part of it. She would've gone on with her life, not really remembering any of the details of the adoption and how things happened if she hadn't returned to Eden Valley. This valley is great at erasing difficult memories formed here, but it also excels at restoring memories altered elsewhere."

"Kevin came to me," Viv said. "I didn't want to betray his confidence, but you know why he's here, don't you?"

Elle nodded. "He told you?"

"A bit. I don't want to go into all the details—he was adamant that he wasn't ready for me to discuss this with adults—but it's time to force the issue." Viv grabbed the cash Bev had left and shoved it in her pocket. "I'll pay the check, then we're going to Evie's. First, we'll talk to Kevin, then we'll have a full meeting—kids, adults, demons, angels, and monsters."

CHAPTER ELEVEN

Viv and Elle walked up the long driveway, skirted around the house, and headed into the woods.

"Are you sure?" Elle asked. "They won't be at the house?"

"Trust me," Viv said. "They won't come in until it's dark or they're hungry. I grew up here... Mostly. Evie, Bev, and I spent most of our free time out here. It's just close enough to hear people yelling your name to come inside, and far enough away to be private." She walked the worn pathway through the trees, continuing the conversation with Elle. She didn't want to surprise the kids. "Do you have an extended family on paper?" Viv asked. "I've never met anyone who was completely new. And is Brandon someone you found here to support your family façade, or is he an angel, too?"

"So many questions," Elle murmured. "It's hard after keeping everyone at bay for so long, at protecting our secret, to think about giving even more away." She trailed into silence.

Viv stepped on a dry twig, making it crack loudly.

"Why are you being so noisy?" Elle asked.

"I know you're stalling, but I'll answer anyway," Viv said with a grin. "Not only is it uncool to give the aura of eavesdropping, surprising an adolescent half-demon and her hellhound is never wise."

"Ah. That makes sense." Elle nodded, considering. "Humans' need for privacy was unexpected. Angels have very little privacy, nor do we desire it."

"For someone who has no desire for privacy, you certainly are reticent when it comes to your secrets," Viv observed.

"Privacy isn't the same thing as guarding secrets," Elle countered.

"What do you call ten years of never having more than a two-minute surface conversation with anyone in town? Guarding not only your secrets—which I will admit, are too heavy for most people—but yourself. Not making friends, never socializing, not even attending school events." Viv pushed some branches aside rustling the needles of the conifer.

"You may have a point," Elle conceded. "How did you learn to protect the privacy of the children? Is this something all humans know?"

"I learned everything I know about approaching the witch's clearing from Hope, Evie's mom and all-around fantastic person. She let us know she trusted us until we gave her reason not to. I spent a lot of time here growing up." Viv's tone became wistful as the memories of endless summer days on the beach with Evie and Bev swirled up. "My mom either didn't know or didn't care when I didn't come home for days and weeks at a time, and Hope and James always welcomed and treated me like one of their own."

"Did you and your mother develop a better relationship when you grew up? I don't think I've seen her more than a couple times—I drove her home at Lily's tenth birthday party after her grandfather made his appearance. She didn't say much to me, just asked if I believed in God."

Viv snorted. "You haven't answered a lot of questions about god and Jesus and Abrahamic mythology, but based on the look on your face, you were able to reassure her soundly on that matter."

"There's a lot more to it than what you'll learn in church—there's a lot out there that's misinterpreted or wrong. Religion has almost zero resemblance to the reality of the situation. There's too much black and white and not nearly enough appreciation to the full spectrum of the mortal experience." Elle spread her hands wide. "It's less black, white, and those shades of grey—of which there are way more than fifty, by the way. You've seen the effects of light through a prism. The visible light spectrum is a small part of the electromagnetic spectrum, right?"

"If you say so," Viv said. "It's been a hot minute since I spent any time studying science."

"It's fascinating the way humans developed the language and tools to understand what should be ineffable," Elle said. "I've read everything I could get my hands on. Quantum mechanics and theoretical physics are especially captivating. It's fun to read about black holes and the backdoors from such a...*young*...perspective."

Viv was saved from having to respond to Elle's implication that the most advanced sciences Viv could think of were barely scratching the surface of cosmic knowledge by the trees thinning out into the natural clearing that had been used as a hideout, reading nook, teenage escape, and, as of a year ago, demon summoning.

As Viv had predicted, the kids were in the clearing, sitting on low lawn chairs and looking altogether way too innocent and still for preteens. But as long as there weren't any signs of real trouble or Ouija boards in sight, she'd let them have their secrets.

"Hey," Viv said. "It's time to decide, Kevin."

Kevin didn't look at Viv. His stare was fixed on the woman slightly behind her.

"Aurielle? I mean Mom?" He winced at his mistake. "Why are you here?" He switched his focus to Viv. "Did you tell her?"

"Nope. I told you I wouldn't. But Elle was confiding some things about her background, and it became evident that I know who you are... I confirmed that we've talked, but not about what. But you need to share what you know. We're going to be stronger together." Viv dropped to the ground and crossed her legs. The part of her that was forty-four winced at the sudden movement, but the muscle memory of the hundreds and thousands of times she'd done the same movement here guided her down gracefully. Whether she'd be able to get back up was a different story.

Elle sank to the ground next to Viv. "Kevin. If you have a secret that threatens this town, I need to know. I have asked very few questions and excused much of your actions here as growing pains, but I cannot much longer. I don't know what kind of deal you made, what you promised Her in exchange for a guardian with a blind eye, but even Her grace only goes so far. Whatever it was, the terms are up."

Green flashed in Kevin's eyes, and his tight grin revealed teeth pointier than Viv was comfortable with. Unlike the other times he'd let his monster shine through, this time it didn't disappear back into the eleven-year-old Viv had known since he was five. The planes of his face hardened and became more angular, his ears shrunk and elongated, and his skin, tanned brown from a summer of spending most waking hours outside, took a greyish cast. Viv suppressed the shudder that threatened.

"I didn't realize that your God already had the showdown She wanted, rendering Her tolerance null and void." Kevin didn't sound like a child anymore, and that was even scarier than his algae-stained teeth. "I wasn't expecting it for at least another ten years."

"Events moved more quickly than anticipated," Elle said. "I was not given advance warning, but I did hear what happened. A grey angel and several true oracles intervened where they had not been invited and forced Her to accept an indefinite truce with the High King of Hell." She sounded more pissed off than anything, and the tightness in her face reinforced her anger.

Viv had to physically prevent her jaw from dropping. Everything was too vague for her liking, although she probably didn't want to know more if she was honest with herself, but the revelation that there was a high king of hell hadn't reached her, and that made her wonder if Evie knew. She opened her mouth to ask some questions, then snapped it closed again when she realized she didn't know where to start.

Kevin crossed one leg over the other and steepled his hands like a tiny Bond villain. He just needed a cat to complete the look. "If a decision was not reached and no victory was won, my deal should still be in effect. The agreement was I would be allowed to exist here, under your *adult supervision*, until the war between heaven and hell was won—at least this iteration."

A chill snaked up Viv's spine, and from the looks on Lily's and Shelby's faces, they were feeling at least as much trepidation as Viv was. This debate between these two—Viv didn't know how to refer to them, not people for sure, maybe ancient entities?—was unequal parts fascinating and terrifying.

Elle and Kevin backed down simultaneously, as if they'd suddenly remembered they had an audience.

Kevin's visage lost its predatory cast and blurred for a moment before returning to the innocent face of an eleven-year-old still holding on to the last of his baby-fat. "My apologies," he said stiffly. "My…mother…and I apparently have some disagreements as to her role in my life that have yet to be resolved."

"You're talking like a weirdo grownup again," Shelby said. "You'll make people pay attention if you do that." Out of everyone, she looked the least perturbed.

Lily cleared her throat, commanding everyone's attention. "It's getting dark, and we'll get shouted in soon if we don't show up." Viv could almost hear the eye roll in her voice. "Kevin, just tell her what's going on. If she's been covering for you so far, she might be willing to keep doing it. It's like when Avery cheated off you last year, and when you didn't tell on her, she kept cheating, and pretty soon you couldn't tell because you'd let her do it so many times it was almost like you didn't care."

Kevin's shoulders slumped, and he looked at Shelby. "You too?"

"Duh. It's only what I've been telling you to do for a whole year." Shelby crossed her arms and her eyes and stuck her tongue out at Kevin.

"Fine. I guess there's nothing else we can do now." He looked at Elle. "I can no longer control the hunger. My control is wavering—I almost took a child last week. Viv saved them, but it was close. I didn't mean to, but I am unable to feed as deeply as a human, and it's beginning to show." He stood up and held his arms out. "My clothes you bought me at the beginning of fourth grade are too big now. I think I'm dying, and soon my body will take over and do whatever it needs to do to survive."

Elle narrowed her eyes. "When's the last time you fed?"

"Two summers ago. I've been surviving on the residual energy that exists in the lake." He hung his head a bit. "I've been skimming life energy off tourists in town, but even with Lily's help it's not easy, and it's not enough. I'm so hungry." The emerald eyes and greenish teeth flashed for a second.

"What exactly are you asking?" Elle flowed to her feet even more gracefully than she'd sat down.

"I don't know." Kevin said. His lower lip trembled, driving home the fact that although he was ancient, he was inhabiting the body of a child. "I don't know how to fix it without messing up everything. I want to stay here, keep my friends, go to school. I don't want to die." Tears dropped from the corners of his eyes, and before they hit the ground, Lily and Shelby were on either side of him and wrapping him in a hug.

"You will not die," Lily said fiercely. "If I have to, I'll make Papa Abe fix it. He owes me one."

Viv made a mental note to follow up on that before Lily headed back to Abe's again.

"I don't know if he can help," Kevin said. "I don't know if Aurielle can, either. I'm not part of heaven or hell. I'm…here."

Viv creaked to her feet, pretending her knees weren't groaning in protest, and put her hands on her lower back to stretch. "There's nothing we can decide right now that we can't discuss at the house. I'm getting cold, you kids are probably hungry, and it's almost dark."

"We will go back first," Elle said. "So you can have your privacy and secret conversations without us overhearing. But we will be waiting." She walked out of the clearing without a backward glance forcing Viv to scramble to catch up.

Viv regarded her mineral water and wished she could conjure up a milkshake. She'd do about anything for a mint chocolate chip shake right about now. Instead, she sipped her water and turned her thoughts around, looking for solutions or plans or anything relevant.

"Penny for your thoughts?" Evie asked, slipping onto the porch swing next to Viv.

"Mostly wishing I could wish a mint chocolate chip milkshake into existence," Viv said. "My other thoughts will have to wait."

"You can ask for stuff like that, you know. It's not weird or awkward. Unless you're Lily who asks for the most ridiculous things —like a life-sized trebuchet, or C4, or a broken grand piano." She shook her head. "Her father has decided that Mythbusters was an appropriate 'documentary' to watch with her as a father daughter bonding experience. They've certainly bonded, but her thirst for destruction was ignited." Evie wrinkled her nose up and down, and a mint chocolate chip milkshake—complete with whipped cream, a cherry, and a straw—appeared in her hand.

"Love the Bewitched throwback. Thank you." Viv accepted the shake and took a long drink. "This is perfect."

"Since it's just you and me until Elle and Bev show up and Luc finishes feeding the monsters and getting the youngest one to bed, wanna tell me how this morning went?" Evie leaned into the corner of the swing and turned enough to look at Viv directly.

Viv thought back over the day that already seemed interminably long. "This morning?" The devastation she'd felt when her text to Sam was bounced back reverberated in her rib cage, causing her to hunch over.

"That bad?" Evie asked, putting her arm around Viv and pulling her close. "Do you want to talk about it? Do you want me to go tell her off? Or, better yet, do you want me to tell my mom to give Gwen a call and give her a piece of her mind? I know she's wanted to for at least thirty years but held back because she was afraid it'd end up making things worse for you."

Oh. Right. All the way to the beginning of the day.

Viv laughed, and even to her own ears it sounded hollow and humorless. "It was even worse than anticipated. She was awful. I knew I was a disappointment to her, but I didn't realize how much she resented me, resented your mom, and sincerely believes I am a curse from her god—an unwanted consolation prize for losing her beloved but damned sister and my father with whom she sinned, further cementing my 'living curse' status." Viv shrugged and tried to keep the hurt she hadn't yet let herself feel out of her voice.

"I'm nearly speechless," Evie said. "I knew she was bad. I knew she was disappointed in you because she cares more about what angry tv pastors say than the evidence in front of her that you're actually pretty great. But I had no idea her resentment went so deep. I can't imagine Lily or Alex ever doing anything or being anyone that would make me feel that way." Evie took a deep breath. "I feel like I've spent most of the last couple weeks apologizing to you, but I'm sorry. I tried to include your mom in our lives. She was your mother, and that made her an honorary, if awful, aunt. The kind that everyone dreads seeing at family dinners, but no one knows how to disinvite. I should've asked you earlier, supported you more. I messed up."

Viv leaned her head into Evie's shoulder. "No, you didn't. If you'd asked earlier, I would've said that continuing to invite her was fine. Better than fine. I used to think she was redeemable, if only she'd open her eyes. And maybe she still will, but it's not up to me to make her see."

Evie dropped a kiss on Viv's head. "I'm really proud of you. I know that sounds kind of condescending, but I am. We grew up together, but I still can't imagine the kind of strength it took to walk away from her and tell her you're done with her."

"She made it infinitely easier by burning half the stuff I'd left behind and setting the rest in front of an open window—all spring, based on the smell. There was nothing. No yearbooks. No teenage love letters. None of the romance novels I devoured on the sly." Viv's voice hitched. "I didn't expect it to hurt this much. She's been cruel to me for thirty years, and it's still hard to walk away."

"There's got to be so much tied to that relationship," Evie said. "Years of guilt and internalized criticism. Even before you came out and she started calling you an abomination, she wasn't kind. I don't remember hearing her ever say anything nice to you. An A- meant your grades weren't good enough, your body wasn't shaped right, you weighed too much… How much of your high school overachievement was an attempt to make her proud? And how much of the sheer amount of time you've spent exercising as an adult was to keep your body in the shape your mother wanted?"

"I'm going to need a lot of therapy," Viv said. "Ugh. I bet therapists love it when you show up with Mommy issues." She laughed, and this time there was a hint of humor in it. "Thank you, Evie. For being my refuge when I was growing up—and always. I owe your parents a thank you note. Probably more, but I can't conceive of a gift that is good enough to adequately express my gratitude."

"They don't need a gift, and you know that. But maybe you should take that trip to visit them you've been promising since they moved to Hawaii." Evie bumped Viv gently with her shoulder.

"Girls' trip?" Viv asked.

"Girls' trip," Evie confirmed.

"I don't know where we're going, but I want in," Bev said coming up the path.

"Is it time?" Elle asked from behind Bev.

Bev jumped and looked around, then straightened up and exhaled with a huff. "Elle."

The women joined Evie and Viv on the porch, and Luc came out and claimed the last chair.

"What's up?" Bev asked.

Viv looked around towards the screen door. Three sets of eyes stared back. Viv crooked her finger, and the kids spilled out the door in a fluid heap as Sprinkles bowled through them trying to get a strike in hellhound bowling.

"I thought you'd all retired to Lily's room for giggling and pretending to be asleep every time you hear footsteps on the stairs," Luc said, fixing them with a stern look.

"I know you're not mad, Daddy," Lily said. "When you're angry, it starts to smell like rotten eggs, and when you're really really mad, you smoke and your eyes glow."

Luc shrugged. "I have to work on my tells," he said. "The kids have already figured me out."

"They need to be here," Viv said. "The rest of the story is theirs. Well, Kevin's mostly, but Shelby and Lily are part of it now, too."

The three children stood, suddenly the center of attention of five adults, and looked like they were suddenly feeling the pressure of the spotlight. Sprinkles pushed her way to the front and stood between the two groups.

"Why don't I grab more chairs," Bev said. "It'll be a lot less intimidating if you can sit instead of standing in front of us like naughty children being dressed down by teachers."

Three answering relieved smiles followed and while they waited for Bev and Luc to return with the chairs, Viv squashed down the trepidation rising when she thought about what was going to happen next.

"Well, that was a lot," Luc said.

"I cannot believe you've kept this from me for a year," Evie said. She was not looking at Kevin, and Viv could feel the tension in her body. "You nearly *drowned* and now you're telling me that boy, the boy that I've let spend countless hours here, that I've fed, that I've treated like my own child, is responsible?" Her voice was rising, and if she'd been a demon, Viv knew that they'd all be gagging on the stench of sulphur and cowering before her. As it was, she was probably at least as scary as Luc was when he was angry—not that Viv had ever seen him that mad.

"Mama," Lily said in a placating voice that Viv recognized from her childhood when Evie'd tried to talk *her* mother out of whatever had happened to upset Hope. "I didn't drown, and as soon as Kevin realized what he was doing, he stopped so Sprinkles could bring me back. He felt really bad, and I didn't want you to be mad at him. It was an accident. You always said accidents happen, and you won't be mad if it was really, truly not on purpose." Lily's eyes widened as she looked at her mother from behind her impossibly thick lashes.

"Don't throw my words back at me," Evie said. "You're eleven, and it's much too soon to be taunting me." As she spoke, her anger almost visibly dissipated. Lily got up and threw her arms around her mother, crowding her gangly body onto Evie's lap and elbowing Viv in the boob in the process.

"Oof, Lily," Viv said. "Elbows!"

"Sorry, Aunt Viv." Lily turned her wide-eyed innocence toward Viv.

"Don't even try it, child," Viv said dryly. "I know all your tricks—I watched your mother perfect them thirty years ago."

Pain hit, blinding strobe lights taking over her vision while the sounds around her multiplied and magnified, overlapping each other until she was drowning in a cacophony of creaks, concerned voices, the wind through the trees, and Sprinkles' enthusiastic barks.

In front of her, a tableau unfolded: the lake, churning and inky with a whirlpool forming in the center. Dark clouds roiled over the lake, blocking the light from the full moon and stars unfettered by light pollution. A figure thrashing half in and half out of the water drew her attention. The second she wanted to look closer, her vision zoomed in until the figure's face was visible through the soft-focus Viv was used to in her psychic flashes. She bit back an exclamation of surprise. It was her. She was looking at herself struggling in the water, a look of terror altering her features, but not enough to be unrecognizable. Her hair was longer and the lines on her face she'd come to accept—if a bit grudgingly—were gone. But it was her. She'd looked at that face every day in the mirror for the last forty-odd years, and there was no mistaking it.

The vision disappeared as suddenly as it had come on, and Viv's awareness returned with the same quickness. She was on the deck curled into a fetal position. Evie was on the ground next to her, holding her up. When Viv slowly straightened into an upright sitting position, she saw Bev and Luc between her and the kids, talking quietly to them and shielding them from her. Elle was sitting exactly where she'd been before, an awed expression on her face.

"What?" she croaked, then grimaced. Her throat was too dry to speak.

A glass of water appeared in front of her, and she gulped it gratefully.

"What happened?" she asked as soon as the sticky sand feeling disappeared.

"I thought you were having a seizure," Evie said. "I haven't seen you have a premonition like this before. Is this common?"

Viv shook her head and tried to stand. Her legs wobbled at the slightest pressure. She closed her eyes and huffed. "Can you help me up? I'm shaky."

"Of course," Evie said. She stood and held out an arm. She and Viv clasped each other's forearms, and Viv let herself be hauled to her feet.

She collapsed gracelessly into the swing and took another long drink of her water. She was halfway through her second glass before she realized she wasn't in pain. There was no nausea. No excruciating headache. No lingering vertigo or tinnitus. "I feel fine?"

"You're probably going to have bruised knees," Bev said, returning to her seat and taking Viv's hand.

"Won't be the first time," Evie said.

"Evelyn Addams," Bev gasped. "There are children present."

"What did you mean?" Lily asked. "Why is Aunt Bev freaking out?"

"I went to church a lot as a kid," Viv said. "And we did a lot of kneeling while the pastor told us how we were all going to hell." She laughed. "Guess he was right in my case. I kinda want a t-shirt. 'I've been to hell and back, and all I got was psychic abilities and a demon niece.'"

"Not sure that's going to catch on for mass merchandising," Bev said. "Nice save, by the way."

Viv flashed her friends a lopsided grin. "I'm even quicker on my feet than off them."

"Stop!" Bev said, laughing. "I know Evie's mom spent our teen years scandalizing us, but we should wait until we don't have to explain every double entendre before making them."

"What's a double entendre?" Lily asked. "Is that slang for boobs? Like if you have nice carnage?"

"Carnage?" Evie asked, her face mirroring the confusion Viv felt.

"Yeah. Carnage. You know…" Lily pushed the flat planes of her chest together creating a gap in her tank top.

"Cleavage," Bev said. "Carnage is what's on the battlefield after a war."

"I know that," Lily said scornfully. "I just thought they were the same word with different meanings. We learned about them in school. Homophones."

"It makes sense, though," Shelby offered. "Wars were fought and lost over the beauty of Helen of Troy, so maybe her boobs were the scene of carnage."

"What do you let these kids read?" Viv asked. "Send them to me, and we'll consume more wholesome stuff like Stephen King and Michael Bay movies." She saw Kevin behind his friends, and knew they were trying to hide him while he struggled with control.

"I'm sorry," he said. "I've hurt too many people. I need to make it right." He turned and ran towards the lake.

"Kevin!" Shelby screamed, chasing after him, Lily on her heels.

The lake was churning. Waves crashed to shore, and black clouds lit only by flashes of eerie lightning swirled low over the water. Viv was on her feet and down the steps almost as fast as the kids and slightly ahead of Bev and Evie.

A crack behind her caused Viv to stumble and look back. Luc stood on the deck, glowing infernal red, his eyes lighting up the night and wings stretching out on either side of him before he launched himself into the air and flew over them.

Viv resumed her breakneck run to the lake and skidded to a stop at the end of the dock behind Lily and Shelby. Kevin had hit the water and kept running across the surface. Maybe that was a gift given to all products of immaculate conception? Viv tamped down that thought before she could make an inappropriate Jesus joke in the middle of a crisis.

When Kevin reached the center of the lake, a huge maelstrom formed, and he swirled down as if he'd stepped onto a spiral escalator.

Luc dove down like an eagle after prey, but the maelstrom disappeared before he hit the water, and he corrected to skim the surface and return to the sky. He did a slow circle around and then flew back to land on the dock behind Evie and Bev.

Elle joined them. "What has he done?" she whispered. "Is he gone? I'm not ready for him to be gone." Her voice broke and turned into a sob. She pushed her way to the front of the dock, sliding between Lily and Shelby. They mirrored equal expressions of shock and grief.

Elle turned around first. A single tear trailed down her cheek. "It is a surprise, that's all," she said stiffly. "I was not expecting my assignment to end so soon, but what with events in the west failing to find a balance between good and evil, allowing the space between to rise to prominence, and my son—" she choked for a second, then steadied her voice "—my charge leaving before the end of his contract, I find myself at a bit of a loss."

"It's okay to be sad," Shelby said, slipping an arm around Elle's waist. "Even if you don't know why. I've been sad my whole life even though my life is pretty great. I'm gonna cry so hard later, but right now I can't."

Lily stood on Elle's other side and reached for her hand. "I know you're not Kevin's mom, but you are, you know? He loves you. And you love him." Lily's shoulders shook and she started crying. "He's just a big stupid head. He was supposed to stay so we could fix it. I'm so mad at him."

Evie crouched behind Lily and pulled her gently back until Lily spun around and threw herself into her mother's arms, body wracked with sobs.

Viv stared out into the lake, still churning with angry waves and topped with greenish black clouds lit by the constant play of thunderless lightning. "I saw this, but there's more." She didn't want to tell anyone the rest of her vision. That she was supposed to be the one in the lake, fighting for her life...or had she been fighting for the opposite? "It's not over yet," she said.

CHAPTER TWELVE

Seven people stood at the end of the dock and stared out over the stormy water. The place where the whirlpool had appeared looked no different than any other part of the lake.

"Did you see Kevin disappearing?" Evie asked.

Viv winced. "No. It was someone else."

"Maybe when Kevin went in, he took the place of whoever else was going to be there?" Bev suggested hesitantly. She took a deep breath that caught halfway in.

"Maybe," Viv said doubtfully. She hadn't seen Kevin disappear, but something about this didn't feel finished. "The storm isn't over yet." She waited for the pull of the lake, the pull Evie'd felt when she'd tried to throw herself in to find Lily last year. But nothing whispered to her; she didn't feel drawn any more than usual. She worried at her lower lip, trying to ignore the grief that surrounded her. The girls and Elle were led back to the house by Bev and Evie who Viv knew were keeping it together because they had to—it was the part of being a parent Viv was most certain she couldn't handle.

"What do you know?" Luc asked, stepping forward to stand by her side.

"I don't know," Viv ground out. "Something isn't right. This isn't what I saw."

"Do your visions always come true?" he asked.

"Yes. Down to the detail. The only time they ever change is if I change it. A server in a Seattle bar tripped with a tray full of empty glasses. I saw the tray landing on me, a rain of broken glass covering me. I moved, and the tray fell into the space I'd vacated. But if I don't move, don't change it, it always happens. I didn't do anything this time. It's not over. I'm positive."

Luc nodded and crossed his arms. His wings flared behind them. "If you're certain, I'm certain. I will stand vigil with you until you are ready to walk away."

Viv looked up at him. "You'd do that based on my word alone?"

"I've seen your brand—you bear the mark of Ipos. But more importantly, I have seen *you*. Not just from Evie's eyes before you protest she's biased. I have seen you. I saw you volunteer to go into hell to find my daughter. I heard you call yourself expendable, and I know you meant it. You would give all of yourself to the people that you love, and you never expect the same back. You are true, and I do not doubt either your word or your visions."

Viv didn't know what to say. No one had ever expressed so much faith in her. Well, if she was completely honest with herself, no one but Bev and Evie, but did they even count? They were her best friends, and best friends were notoriously blind when it came to the faults of those they loved. They'd been overlooking her weaknesses for decades, there was no reason to believe their opinions of her were anything more than the rose-colored glasses years of friendship provided.

"You're worth it, you know," Luc said. "Evie loves you, and she doesn't love blindly. She knows your faults and knows your virtues, and her scales weigh in your favor. She has included your mother in events for years because she thought that would make things easier for you. Lily called your mother Nana Gwen because Evie made that effort and encouraged the relationship. She was wrong to do so, but she did it for love." His wings waved in the breeze behind them, fanning Viv's back and raising goosebumps.

"What's your point?" Viv asked. She took a half-step forward, her toes inching over the edge of the slippery deck.

"My point is that you need to start regarding yourself as well as your friends regard you. They are neither blind nor stupid, and you need to step into yourself. You are smart—brilliant, if my fiancée is to be believed—resourceful, beautiful beyond measure according to my sister, and powerful. Hell pulled you in and marked you, and what you got in return is almost too much for any human to handle, but you're still here, more than a year later, and not even leveled by what you saw tonight. That makes you strong, stronger even than many demons I know. So act it. Tell me what you saw and why you're still afraid."

"How do you know I'm afraid?" Viv challenged. She didn't like what Luc was throwing at her but didn't know how to refute any of his logic.

"I'm not mortal, and I can smell your fear. It's one of the less desirable demon gifts." He shrugged. "I will find a way to work this to my advantage eventually. But ethically of course."

"Of course," Viv murmured. "I know you, as a demon lawyer responsible for looking for loopholes in the contracts mortals sign agreeing to consign their souls to an eternity of suffering in hell, look for integrity in all things first."

"I'm so glad we understand each other."

They stood side by side in silence, watching the lake. The localized storm neither escalated nor diminished. The waves in the center of the lake stopped. A perfect circle of impossibly still water formed.

Viv's mouth opened into an "O" that unintentionally mimicked what she was seeing. She glanced at Luc—was she hallucinating? Had the visions finally driven her mad?

But no, Luc was staring with wary shock. His eyes widened and Viv looked back, even though she really, really didn't want to see what Eden Lake was going to do next.

Viv and Luc were no longer alone on the dock. Bev had stumbled out the door and down to the edge of the dock, pushing past Luc and Viv, arms crossed over her stomach and sweat standing out on her face. The rest of the inside crew had followed her out.

"Bev?" Viv asked when Bev didn't say anything. She reached out towards her friend, intending to push a strand of sweat-soaked hair back from where it clung to her cheek.

"Don't touch her," Shelby commanded. "It hurts her to be touched when she's…" Shelby shrugged as her voice trailed off.

Evie looked at Shelby who grimaced and averted her eyes. "Is this a regular occurrence?" she asked in full-on mom voice.

"I can't talk about it," Shelby said. "Look!" She pointed at the black mirror that was the center of Eden Lake.

"Don't think that trick will work on me, young lady," Evie said.

"No, really," Luc said. "Look." He turned slightly and stretched out his wings behind him.

The still water was no longer still. It now swirled in a counter-clockwise direction. Slowly at first, then picking up speed and momentum.

"It's going the wrong direction," Viv said. "Water turns clockwise in the northern hemisphere."

The water abruptly stopped moving, then started spinning in the opposite direction, and Viv's stomach clenched. Somehow that was scarier than anything else that'd happened tonight, and based on Evie's gasp of shock and horror, Viv wasn't the only one who felt that way.

"What is going on?" Lily asked, standing on tiptoe and attempting to peer over her mother's head, something that was almost possible.

"Back to the house, Lily," Evie snapped. "You too, Shelby. I don't know what's happening, but I need you both off this dock and away from the lake."

"The dead are rising," Bev and Shelby said in unison.

Ice gripped Viv's spine and traveled throughout her body, raising goosebumps and causing her to shiver.

Elle, who'd been silent until this point, said, "There are no dead in the lake. You must be wrong."

"The dead are rising," Bev and Shelby said again.

Viv watched the whirlpool with renewed horror. Something appeared in the center slowly swirling upwards; it was a head. As it moved further up, it was apparent that it was an entire person. As their feet broke the surface of the water, it abruptly stopped churning and returned to the normal, relatively placid surface the mountain lake usually exhibited. The figure sank down to their waist and started thrashing.

"But...that's not me," Viv said. Everything else looked the same, but that wasn't her. Was it? Was she already dead and watching from shore? She didn't believe in ghosts, but if she had suddenly become one, she'd have to rethink her stance on this point.

"Of course it's not you," Evie said. "Why would it be?"

Luc launched himself into the air, but before he could pull the figure out of the water—was it Kevin?—someone else was there. A dark shape with glittering black wings, almost too big to be real, swooped down over the water, snagged the figure, and flew up again. Luc started to follow, but turned to glance at the shore, and whatever he saw ended his chase and brought him back to the dock.

The four women at the end of the dock stared out over the water watching Luc wing his way back. Bev sagged against Viv who put an arm around her friend to hold her up. Cold sweat had drenched Bev's body, and her clothes were soaked through.

"Sorry sorry," Bev said, pushing herself upright. After she stopped swaying, Viv let go and took a step back.

"Are you okay?" Viv asked. "What happened?"

Luc landed on the dock and tucked his wings behind him. "Shelby fainted."

Evie turned around and dropped to her knees next to Shelby's prone form. The girl had dropped to the dock so quietly no one had heard a sound.

"She'll be okay in a couple minutes," Bev said. "But we should get her inside and warm. And me, too. I need dry clothes and a cup of tea."

"Why didn't you say something, Lily?" Evie asked, slipping an arm around Bev.

"It never lasts very long, and she's usually embarrassed." Lily shrugged. "I knew she wouldn't want you to see, and I was hoping she'd wake up before you did. And she would've if Daddy hadn't decided to come back instead of finding out what flew out of the lake." She glared at her father.

"I will accept the blame for this." Luc picked Shelby up and flew her to the house.

Bev went more slowly, supported by Evie and Lily. Viv stayed on the dock staring at the place where someone had come out of the water, someone not her. Other than the two details that varied from her vision, it'd been exactly as it'd happened.

"I assumed I was drowning, but I didn't see it. It could've been an opposite drowning, and I didn't have enough context," Viv said. She shoved her hands in her pockets and hunched her shoulders.

"You said that earlier," Elle said.

Viv jumped and shrieked.

"Sorry," Elle said. "I thought you knew I was here." She stepped forward to stand next to Viv. "Is that what you saw in your vision? You in the water?"

"I thought so, but my visions always come true, and that clearly wasn't me." Viv tapped her chin with one finger and looked up at the sky. "I didn't see that last part, either. Who was that?"

Elle ignored Viv's last question. "Are you sure you didn't see Kevin go into the water?"

"No. My vision started after that, when the second whirlpool formed. I don't understand. Aaargh!" She yelled her frustration into the sky. "Usually my visions are informative—giving me a warning, allowing me to be prepared and sometimes to change things. This, though... It's not quite right."

The dark shape that'd snatched the person out of the water appeared in the sky as the clouds disappeared, once more allowing the night sky to take prominence. It dove towards them, and Viv ducked instinctively. It landed on the ground between Viv and Elle and the house, back to the women on the dock. Horns curved and spiraled up from the sides of the figure's head, and its huge wingspan was almost impossibly wide. The wings were black feathers with thin stripes of gold that shimmered in the starlight interrupting the darkness.

Someone dropped to the ground in front of the figure—too big to be Kevin.

The wings shimmered and shrank rapidly, the horns following suit, until they were gone and what was left in its place was a familiar head of black, tight curls, skin-tight black pants, and a bright yellow leather jacket.

"Sam?" Viv asked.

The demon turned around. Sam stared at Viv, then back at the body at her feet. "How?" Her voice trailed off after the initial question.

Viv walked forward, trailed by Elle. Sam stepped out of the way, allowing Viv to get a good look at the figure at her feet. The woman was unconscious, but even with her eyes closed, her face was unmistakable.

"That's me?" Viv asked. She crouched down and looked closer. The hair was longer and the face younger. From this close, Viv was able to spot the small differences. This woman didn't have pierced ears, much less the multiple piercings Viv sported. Her hair was dark brown, and not Viv's natural black hair currently streaked with rapidly fading blue and pink and sporting grey roots. An idle thought that she should ask Evie to wish the bleach and dye out of her hair until she was ready to keep up with her hair again floated through her mind.

"It's not me," Viv said. "But we could almost be twins. Identical cousins." She smothered a burst of inappropriate laughter.

The woman opened her eyes—they were bright blue. They widened as she looked at Viv's face, mere inches from her own, then she screamed and went limp.

"I think she fainted again," Viv said. She stood. Elle and Sam were standing a couple feet away.

"I don't understand what's going on," Elle said. "I don't like this feeling."

"She's not you," Sam said. "I thought..."

Viv tilted her head. "You thought that was me? That I was drowning?"

Sam nodded. "I was on my way back to my cabin when the storm started. When I saw her," Sam thrust her chin towards the woman on the ground. "She looked like you. I should've known it wasn't you. The hair is wrong, and she doesn't look as old as you."

"Thanks," Viv said dryly.

"You're welcome," Sam said. "But who is she?"

"Whoever she is, we should get her up to the house and get her warm and dry. And maybe someone who isn't me should be the next person she sees."

Sam picked her up effortlessly—it's good to be a demon—and carried her to Evie's house.

Viv started to follow, then looked back at Elle "Are you coming?"

"I'm not ready yet. I want to stay a while longer. Just in case…" She didn't finish her sentence, but she didn't need to.

"Don't stay too long. You might be an angel, but it's still cold out here now that the storm's cleared."

Elle nodded but didn't look at Viv. Instead, she walked back to the end of the long dock and stared into the lake.

Viv squared her shoulders and went back up to the house. Her shoulders were hunched with exhaustion—it'd been the longest day—and she didn't want to deal with this new mystery, but it didn't look like she had any choice.

CHAPTER THIRTEEN

Viv stood in the back of the room, out of eyesight of the stranger on Evie's couch, while Evie and Bev fussed over the woman who, other than her continued unconsciousness, seemed perfectly healthy.

Luc tiptoed down the stairs and back into the living room. "Shelby and Lily, despite their protests that they couldn't sleep and wouldn't even try, fell asleep within five minutes of turning on the spring rain white noise track. I left their door open, so we'd hear if either of them woke up, but for now, they're out."

"Good," Evie said, tucking a blanket around the woman and turning on the fire. "It's been an exhausting day, both physically and emotionally, and they'll need their rest. I don't know what's going to happen over the next few days in regard to Kevin, and they'll need all their strength." For a moment, her face crumpled, and Viv saw the same despair and fear she'd seen on Evie's face last year before they'd marched into hell to get Lily back after she'd been kidnapped by her grandfather.

"Evie?" Viv asked. "Do you need anything? A break? A drink?" Evie looked over at Viv, and the horror in her eyes softened.

"No, but thank you. This feels too much like what I went through with Lily. I know I was angry with Kevin, and by extension Elle, but I can't imagine how she feels right now." She looked around the room. "Where is she? Did she go home?"

"She said she wanted to stay by the lake and watch," Viv said. "Just in case."

"She shouldn't be alone," Evie said, pushing herself to her feet.

"I'll go," Sam said, the shadow she'd become detaching from the wall.

"Should I?" Viv asked.

"Nah, I'll be back in a bit. Stay here… Don't you want to find out who your doppelgänger is?" Sam exited the room with a swish that sounded like feathers against the wall.

Viv knew it was neither the time nor the place, but she couldn't help staring after Sam and imagining being wrapped in those wings, shielded from the world. Oh, and they were naked. Viv pursed her lips. She was going to have to apologize. Maybe even grovel. She'd definitely messed up.

The woman on the couch stirred and drew the attention of everyone in the room.

She opened her eyes and looked around. Viv shifted far enough around the edge of the room that she wasn't visible to the stranger.

The woman sat up and looked around. "What am I doing here?" she asked. "Who are you? Where's Hope? Is she here?"

Evie scrunched up her face and regarded the woman. "You know where you are? You know my… You know Hope?"

"Are you friends of hers? You kind of look like her… But I would've known if she had friends visiting, wouldn't I?" The woman tried to push herself to her feet but fell back against the couch. "What is going on? This isn't the right furniture."

"Why don't you have a cup of tea and tell us who you are and what you remember before waking up here," Evie said, handing her a steaming cup of what smelled like mint tea.

"Where?" The woman looked around, took a deep breath, and closed her eyes, taking a sip of her tea. "Okay. Why not? The last thing I remember is cold, but not fear. There was darkness, but it was peaceful. It washed away the memories of…" Her face crumpled and she cried, shoulders heaving with silent sobs.

Evie took the cup of tea and handed it to Bev, then sat next to the woman and put an arm around her. "Shhh… We'll figure this out. What's your name?"

Through her sobs, Viv heard her say, "Grace. Grace Kane."

For a moment, Viv thought she was going to join the throngs of folks who'd fainted that evening. She walked forward into the room and stared at the woman who'd just proclaimed she was Viv's aunt, the aunt she'd only found out existed last year because she'd thrown herself into the lake fifty years ago.

"You can't be Grace," Viv said.

"Look at her though," Bev said. "You guys could be twins. It makes sense. Kind of."

"Eden Valley sense," Viv agreed. She walked forward and crouched in front of Grace. "There's no real easy way to say this, so it's probably good you're still sitting down. It's been fifty years since you walked into the lake and disappeared. My name is Genevieve Kane—I'm Gwen's daughter."

Evie laughed awkwardly. "And I'm Evelyn Grace Addams. Hope and James's daughter. My mom named me after you. I live here now with my daughters and my fiancé."

Grace didn't say anything, just placed her head in her hands and rocked back and forth slowly.

"I THINK WE BROKE HER," Bev murmured to Viv. They'd retreated to the kitchen, leaving Evie and Luc to talk Grace through what was likely the first of many shocks after Grace had refused to open her eyes as long as Viv was in the room.

"I think we broke me," Viv replied. "It's been a lot of week. I was not prepared for the level of weird Eden Valley was going to bring."

"Is this why you didn't want to come back?" Bev asked. She opened the fridge and grabbed a couple mineral waters from where they hid behind the large pitcher of lemonade.

"Does that pitcher ever get washed?" Viv asked twisting the cap off her water and tossing it into the nearby garbage can.

"Every once in a while, it'll allow itself to be emptied and cleaned, but no matter where she puts it away, it's always full again in a few minutes. I think it might be self-cleaning, though. It's always sparkling and doesn't even hold fingerprints." Bev perched on one of the high barstools at the counter. "But you didn't answer the question."

"It's a complicated answer," Viv said. "I'm not sure where to start or where it ends. I can say that my avoidance of Eden Valley had very little to do—at least not consciously—with this kind of weird, though. You know why I left and why I never wanted to come back. You and Evie were my only anchors here...if you two had left town, I would've left it in my rearview."

"I'm sorry," Bev said, reaching out and grabbing Viv's hand. "I never wanted to be an anchor."

Viv replayed what she'd just said and winced. "Anchors are pretty awesome, Bev. Without them, ships would just drift out to sea. You and Evie never drag me down, just help me weather the storms."

"Aww..." Bev pulled Viv in for a tight hug.

Something clenched in Viv's chest. This. Friendship. This is what she'd lost sight of. She'd been paying lip-service to the idea of bffs for years, and that had been a mistake. She tightened her arms around Bev and closed her eyes.

"Thank you, Bev. For never giving up on me." Viv sniffled. "Dammit. I can't believe you made me cry."

"That's what friends are for." Bev let go of Viv and returned to her barstool. She wiped a finger under each eye, catching the tears before they could drag her mascara down her face. "I do have a question, though. You said that Evie and I *were* your only anchors here, not that we *are.* That, to me, implies there might be an additional anchor." She propped her chin on her hands, rested her elbows on the counter, and fluttered her eyelashes. "Wanna tell me about it?"

Viv laughed. "Slip of the tongue, Beverly. I meant you, Evie, and the kids, *obviously*."

"Mmhmmmm… It's pretty disappointing to hear lies like that drop from your lips. They might buy you a one-way ticket to hell. I'll have to see if I know anyone free to *take you*." Bev leered at Viv.

"Oh my god, Bev. You are being ridiculous, and I have no idea what you're talking about. I do not lie. I am a paragon of virtue."

Bev snorted. "A paragon of what?"

Viv flicked the moisture the sweating bottle had left on her fingers, hitting Bev in the face with the drops. "Since we're on the subject of things people said earlier, tell me more about the dead rising?"

Bev's lost every trace of humor and her face flattened into an expressionless mask. "I don't want to talk about it."

"Shelby said the same thing. You guys were in creepy unison—like a weird Greek chorus." Viv leaned forward forcing Bev to meet her eyes. "And when Shelby passed out, the way you and Lily talked about it made it sound like this wasn't the first time. What's going on?"

Bev squirmed under Viv's gaze. "It isn't important. Well, it's not important now. There are too many things going on more important than my mental health."

"There are a lot of important, life changing, town destroying things going on right now," Viv agreed. She leaned back releasing Bev from her gaze.

Bev's shoulders started to relax, and her jaw followed suit.

"But your mental health is as important as anything else, and this isn't something you should have to bear alone, especially if it's impacting Shelby, too. What's up?" Viv paused to give Bev time to reply, but after a beat, she said, "It's not because you're my friend—or at least not *only* because you're my friend. I'll drop it if you want me to —for now, anyway. But whatever's going on with you is happening alongside all this other weird stuff, and I have a feeling—*fuck*, more than a feeling—it's crucial."

Bev heaved a sigh and glanced towards the living room. "Why don't you peek in on your aunt and see if she's still needing time away from your face; I'll meet you outside. I want to check on Shelby and make sure she's okay and asleep. I don't want her to overhear."

"Sure thing." Viv slid off the stool. "Take your time. Within reason. If you're more than five minutes, I'll come looking for you."

"Pinky swear." Bev held out her little finger, and Viv hooked it with her own.

"Love you like whoa, Bev," Viv said. "Five minutes."

THE SKY HAD a light cloud cover. Not enough to completely obscure the light of the moon, but without the Milky Way casting its light over the Valley, it was almost impossible to see to the end of the dock. There were still two figures down there—Elle and Sam. An angel and a demon keeping vigil for a prehistoric monster.

"It's the beginning of a joke," Viv said.

"What is?" Bev asked, settling into the Adirondack chair next to Viv's.

Viv pointed with her chin. "The angel and the demon down there waiting for the Eden Lake monster to surface. I know it's not super funny, but I gotta find the humor where I can."

"I get that," Bev said. She inhaled deeply. "This is super hard for me, and I just need to say it. Shelby and I have both been diagnosed with schizoaffective disorder. Shelby spent some time in an inpatient facility earlier this year, and I guess it's inherited? We've both been hallucinating, and she has really struggled as she's dancing around puberty, and we fight with the insurance company to authorize puberty blockers for her. The diagnosis doesn't feel right, and this doctor makes me feel uncomfortable, but that could just be the crazy talking, you know?"

"Look me straight in the face, Beverly Hill. I am not a psychiatrist, or a therapist, or any kind of mental health professional. But I do know one thing—if your shrink is making you uncomfortable, get a new one. I know that's easier said than done, but you shouldn't be second guessing your instincts."

"I agree, kind of. But what if…"

"What if what?" Viv demanded. "If he's right, and you and Shel both have schizophrenia, then what do you lose by getting a second opinion? What's Shelby's psychiatrist say?"

"It's the same one," Bev said. "And he's not a psychiatrist, but he is an MD and was instrumental in helping Shelby find the right meds to keep her stable after her suicide attempt last winter."

Viv pushed down her instinctive reaction to demand why she hadn't been told. Not only did she have a decent idea why, this was definitely not the right time to center her hurt feelings. "Shit, Bev. I'm sorry. I wish I had better words, but right now I don't. I do, however, think you and Shelby need to see new and different doctors. Probably someone who specializes in mental illnesses. This isn't something to mess around with." She reached out and took Bev's hand.

Bev sighed. "I know you're right, but it's so much work, you know? He's the only mental health professional in town, and we waited months to get on his schedule. If we want to switch, we'll have to drive to Chelan and fight with my insurance company. Again. I can't yank Shelby out of anything right now."

"I'm not suggesting you salt the earth, just that you start looking. I know I won't be able to do too much because of HIPAA, but I will do whatever I can to help. I can research providers who accept your insurance and find out if they're taking new patients and what their waitlists are. More and more are doing online or phone appointments after an initial intake, so it might not be too onerous, schedule-wise, after the first visit or two." Viv paused for a moment then added tentatively, "Have you thought that maybe it's not mental illness as much as something that happened due to your hell brand?"

"No!" Bev said. "Yours hit right away. I don't think it would've waited almost a year to show up, and in such a creepy way."

"Hear me out, and if you still think there's no way when I'm done, I'll drop it." She took a sip as she waited for Bev to nod. When she got the non-verbal consent, she continued. "Earlier today, you spoke of the dead rising. Is that what it always is? Something to do with the dead?"

Bev nodded slightly but didn't comment.

"When we walked through hell to retrieve Lily, you said you could hear voices crying out in pain or something. I remember because I told you were basically a brown robe and a light saber away from Obi Wan mourning Alderaan." She paused and looked at Bev.

"So?" She didn't look argumentative, only confused.

Viv plowed forward. "So, who's in hell crying out in pain?"

This time, Bev did make the connection. "The dead. Oh wow. Oh. Wow."

Viv grimaced. Suggesting to someone that maybe they weren't mentally ill, they just hadn't tried *believing* hard enough that the dead were trying to make contact violated everything she believed about accepting mental illness and the medical treatments for it. Maybe she should suggest yoga and essential oils next. "I'm saying I'll help you both find psychiatrists in Chelan or Spokane or Seattle who work with your insurance and schedules who can give second opinions. Hearing voices is often a sign of mental illness, but what about blinding visions that I believe give me glimpses of the future? I think everything's all tangled up. Shelby would be struggling with or without the auditory hallucinations. She's twelve and trans in a small town that, no matter how accepting, still has plenty of people like my mother. But if the voices are real, then maybe there's a better treatment for her depression. I'm not trying to suggest that you and Shelby are fine, and she should go off her meds. I'm so glad she has you to advocate for her and be there for her when her life gets hard."

"I know," Bev said. "And I'm not going to flush all the meds down the toilet tomorrow or anything. But I am going to get those second opinions and be a little more open to the thought of something supernatural, as ridiculous as that sounds."

"Have you talked to Evie and Luc about this?" Viv asked. "They might know something. Earlier, Luc said I had Ipos's mark, whoever that is, and that's why he trusts my visions. He might know what's up with you, too, based on your one-of-a-kind tattoo."

"I haven't. When it started getting real weird, Evie was very pregnant, and I didn't want to make things all about me. There was enough at that point with Shelby struggling so hard and me helpless to make it better. I just…" Bev smiled at Viv with sadness and grief that was heartbreaking.

"We both need a few lessons in self-esteem, don't we?" Viv tipped her face up at the sky and closed her eyes. Seeing Bev say the same things Viv had been feeling about herself was the kind of real talk she hadn't been expecting. It made her doubt the reliability of her own self-identified shortcomings. "I'm here for you, you know that. And so is Evie. You should talk to her about it."

"I will. I promise. But only if we can stop talking about it now." Bev settled beside Viv.

"I love misty evenings," Viv said.

"Me, too. It feels so fresh, like I'm being renewed." Bev took a deep breath and exhaled. To Viv, it sounded like Bev had let go of everything that had been weighing her down.

Viv opened her eyes and glanced at Bev. "Is that how you stay so young? Rain magic?"

"It's served me better than sun worship. I was slathering myself in sunscreen before it was a song while the rest of you had the Coppertone baby as goals." Bev grinned at her friend. "I guess if you want to call that magic, you can."

"Kevin!"

Viv and Bev were on their feet and running towards the dock before Elle finished screaming.

"What is it? What's wrong?" Viv gasped as she skidded to a stop on the wet wood and narrowly avoided sliding into Sam.

"Look," Sam said, pointing out towards the center of the lake.

Viv peered through the misty darkness. The surface of the lake was still, a black mirror marked only by the changes of texture where it lapped against the shoreline and the island in the…

"There's an island," Bev said. "An island in the middle of the lake. I know I said I might be crazy, but I don't think I would've forgotten an entire island, right?"

"The island is new," Sam said. "And I don't understand." Her voice was full of chagrin.

Viv rubbed her eyes then refocused on the middle of the lake. "Yep. Island. What the hell?"

"Hell had nothing to do with this," Sam said. "I don't understand."

"You already said that," Bev noted. "Maybe instead of trying to understand you could do a little flyby and see what's up?"

Sam didn't answer, but she stepped sideways and snapped out her wings. She was airborne in seconds.

Viv watched her fly away, then looked at Elle. "You yelled Kevin. Why? Did he make the island?"

"I don't know," Elle whispered. "For a moment, I thought it was, but..." Her voice trailed off.

Bev slipped an arm around Elle's shoulders, and they watched the dark figure that was Sam wing her way to the island. She circled the island, then dove lower and disappeared into the trees.

Seconds later, she reemerged and flew back towards shore. She was carrying something. Sam flew over the women on the dock and landed at the end where it touched solid ground, then lowered her burden to the ground.

"Kevin?" Elle said hesitantly.

"I think so," Sam replied. "He's alive, but not. That doesn't make any sense, and I'm not a doctor, but he doesn't feel quite right."

Elle ran towards him and dropped to her knees next to the prone body of the monster she called her son.

CHAPTER FOURTEEN

Viv rubbed her eyes and looked at her watch as she walked down the driveway towards the main road. It was just after three in the morning, and she'd been up for nearly twenty-four hours, not counting her brief nap after bumping into Elle yesterday afternoon. Too much had happened in the last not-quite-a-day, and it felt like time had stretched unnaturally to accommodate everything.

Evie had offered everyone beds for the evening, but even with her spacious house, there weren't enough bedrooms for five extra people without doubling up. Sam had declined the offer and taken off twenty minutes ago—before Viv had the opportunity to delve more deeply into the moment she was sure they'd shared earlier and ask about the phone thing. Grace was asleep in Hope and James's old room. Bev took the pullout couch; Elle took the bed in the remaining guest room, and Kevin was still unconscious on the trundle next to the bed.

She should've asked Bev for her car keys before leaving; the walk was only about a mile—shorter than taking the lake trail and, at this time of night, probably as safe—but she was exhausted and wobbly.

A noise behind her made her jump, and she almost tumbled off the shoulder into the steep ditch.

"Need a ride?" Sam asked, stepping forward and grabbing Viv's arm to steady her while she regained her balance.

Viv looked around. "You're not driving," she pointed out.

"Don't need one." Sam's wings unfolded and spread wide. "What do you say?"

Exhaustion and curiosity warred with lingering hurt and a misplaced urge for independence. Exhaustion won. "I'd love one."

Sam opened her arms, and Viv stepped into them, closing her eyes and relishing the feeling of being held tightly. She was so tired, but the sensation of leaving the ground and her stomach behind woke her up. Sam tilted forward about forty-five degrees, leaving Viv half-reclined and her legs were dangling down awkwardly.

"Wrap your legs around mine," Sam said, her breath tickling Viv's ear.

Viv suppressed the involuntary shiver she told herself was more the cool night air than banked lust and did as instructed. Her body was molded against Sam's, and this time there was no pretending the feelings awakening in her body had anything to do with the ambient temperature.

She opened her eyes and peered up into the sky in the space between Sam's wing and her neck. The cloud cover from earlier had dissipated, and the moon and stars were again bright enough to see by. The view and the sensation of floating in air under a gravity blanket lent a dreamlike quality to the early morning. "I love the moon. People think it's constantly changing, but they're wrong. The moon is constant, it's only the way we perceive it that changes."

"Untangle your legs," Sam said.

A pang of disappointment caught in Viv's chest, but she did as Sam had instructed. Sam returned them to a vertical position, and moments later, Viv's feet touched the ground.

Sam held her while she accustomed herself once more to the ground under her feet, and when she felt confident she wouldn't tip over, Viv stepped backwards and away from the heat of the demon she definitely wasn't in love with.

Sam's wings pushed backwards, but before they disappeared, Viv asked, "Can I touch them?"

"They're very sensitive," Sam said. She didn't finish folding them back into the space where she hid them from the mortal world.

"Oh. Okay." Viv pulled back the hand that was reaching out to stroke the length of one of the shimmery black feathers. "I don't want to hurt you."

"I don't mean that kind of sensitive," Sam said. "But I don't want you to inadvertently start anything that you're too tired or not ready to finish. However, if you want to tomorrow after you've slept for at least ten hours, we can resume this discussion."

Desire tried to rise sluggishly but couldn't break through the bone-tiredness that was dragging her eyelids down over the contacts that were burning in her eyes—rebelling from having to work too long.

"Do you need help inside?" Sam asked. "I can walk you in."

"I'll be fine," Viv said. Her voice sounded like it was reaching her from far away and through several fathoms.

"I'll at least get you to the front door and make sure you make it inside," Sam said. She lifted Viv into her arms, cradled her against her body, and carried her the few feet to Bev's door.

"Thank you," Viv mumbled. She typed in the code to disable the lock. The numbers blurred, and it took three tries before she got it right.

Sam let go of her and stepped back. "Sleep well, Genevieve. I'll see you tomorrow."

The door closed behind her. Viv took off her shoes and dragged herself upstairs, stopped in the bathroom long enough to remove her contacts and pee, then fell into bed still clothed, eyes closing before her head even hit the pillow.

CHAPTER FIFTEEN

I t was well past ten before Viv walked into Evie's kitchen. Bev was already gone—she'd stopped at home for a quick shower and change of clothes before going to work. She'd also left a note for Viv, telling her Evie had invited her to brunch and asking her to keep an eye on Shelby today until Bev got off work. Sam's phone was still saying it was disconnected, reminding Viv she hadn't asked about it yesterday. But since Sam was as likely to show up here as anywhere, Viv had pushed her feelings aside in favor of breakfast.

"Hey!" Viv grabbed a strip of bacon off the plate in the middle of the table.

"No. Bad Aunt Viv." Lily bopped Viv on the head with an empty paper towel tube. "No bacon unless you've washed your hands and grabbed a plate."

Viv took a bite of the bacon and crossed her eyes at Lily who giggled. "My apologies, Liliana. Thank you for reminding me of my table manners."

"Lily!" Evie called from the kitchen. "Be polite to your Aunt Viv and get her a plate."

"If I can't snatch bacon from the plate, no one gets to," Lily proclaimed as she headed into the kitchen. She returned a minute later with a large plate stacked with French toast. "Sit and eat. Shelby will be down soon, and Daddy is walking Alex."

"He's not *walking* Alex," Evie said laughing. "He's on a walk with Alex."

"My way is funnier," Lily said.

"What about Kevin and Elle?" Viv asked, munching on the purloined bacon.

"They left super early," Evie said. "I heard them leave when I was feeding Alex, so about six, I think."

"I can't believe Kevin came back and no one woke us up," Lily huffed. "He's our best friend, and we were so scared."

"You and Shelby needed your sleep," Viv said. "I'm a little jealous, honestly. I slept until nine and I'm still exhausted."

"Do you want me to get you some coffee?" Evie asked. She looked away from the stove for a moment.

"I'll get it," Lily said. "You're busy doing very important things. Like making me more food." Lily filled a cup from the coffee maker and topped it up with cream before handing it to Viv. Then she snatched a piece of bacon from the table and shoved the whole thing in her mouth before winking at Viv.

"Bacon thief!" Viv said. "Bacon thief in the house! But don't worry, I'm on the case." She dashed around the table towards Lily, who took off shrieking into the living room.

"Stop thief!" Viv yelled.

"Or what?" Lily shouted back. "You can't have it back, that bacon is long gone." She hit the tile that led into the hallway between the kitchen and utility area and skidded on her socks into the back door.

"Lily, Viv, if you don't knock it off, someone's going to get hurt," Evie warned.

"Sorry, Mom," Lily said, sounding anything but contrite.

"Sorry, Mom," Viv echoed, sharing a conspiratorial wink with Lily.

"Lily, why don't you grab the berries and whipped cream from the fridge and put them on the table. Viv, can you get napkins and silverware? Then you should sit down and eat before your breakfast gets cold."

VIV WAS HALFWAY through her breakfast and was listening to Shelby and Lily try to outdo each other with the worst jokes they'd ever heard, looking for something that would make Evie crack a smile. Viv hid her grin; she could see the corners of Evie's mouth twitching and knew she was mere seconds from giving in and laughing.

A throat clearing from the doorway interrupted the latest joke about cyclops and drew everyone's attention away from the food.

Grace stood in the doorway. She'd showered and changed into a borrowed maxi dress. The emerald fabric draped over her figure. Now that it was light and the shock was starting to wear off, it was easier to see the differences between Viv and Grace. They were both tall with nearly the same color hair and similar features, but that's where the similarities ended. Grace was slimmer through the hips and had a smaller chest. Where Viv's jawline was strong, Grace's was soft. The differences were subtle, but as soon as you noticed them, you couldn't unsee them.

"Hi," Viv said. "Are you okay?" She clenched her teeth and closed her eyes. "Sorry. I just meant… I don't know what I meant."

"Would you like some breakfast?" Evie asked, pulling out the chair next to her. "We have French toast, bacon, and fruit, but if you'd rather have something else, I can get that for you." She glanced at the empty plate that had been stacked high with French toast and winced.

"French toast is fine, if it's not too much trouble," Grace said. She sat down and loaded her plate with berries, then speared them, one at a time, and ate them without looking at anyone else at the table.

"Not at all!" Evie went into the kitchen and returned moments later with a plate stacked high. Viv narrowed her eyes. Definitely wish toast. She caught Evie's eyes. Her friend shrugged and looked a little sheepish, then set the plate on the table, close enough to Grace that she could grab what she wanted without asking.

"Girls," Evie said. "Why don't you two clear your plates, brush your teeth, then take Sprinkles for a walk."

"Moooo-om! You didn't say the new houseguest looked just like

Aunt Viv!" Lily said. "You always make us leave just before things get interesting."

Shelby didn't say anything, just stared with narrowed eyes at Grace.

"I will fill you in later," Evie promised.

SHELBY PICKED up her plate and headed towards the kitchen. "I can explain, Lily. C'mon…"

Lily pouted, then stood up. "Fine. I know when I'm not wanted. C'mon, Shelby." She snapped her fingers. "Sprinkles! Walksies!"

"Teeth and clean clothes first," Evie said.

"Okay, Mom," Lily said. She grabbed her breakfast dishes and followed Shelby into the kitchen. Seconds after the clatter of dishes hitting the sink, the door slammed shut.

Evie shook her head. "Those girls are going to be riddled with cavities by the time they're teens. I do not understand the resistance to good dental hygiene."

When Grace finished eating and folded her hands in her lap. "I'm sorry," she said softly. "I don't understand what's going on, and I don't know what to do."

"Of course you don't," Evie said. "I can't even begin to imagine what you're going through—what you've been through."

"Me, neither," Grace admitted. "I don't remember anything. My baby…" She stopped and took a deep breath. "Me neither."

Luc looked at Evie and she nodded back at him. He stood up and left the room, taking Alex with him. He returned without the baby but with a laptop.

Luc, who'd been doing something on his laptop, turned it around. "Grace, we thought maybe talking to someone you knew before might help. This is a computer, and we're going to do a video phone call. I know it's weird, but I promise I'm not kidding."

Grace leaned forward, and for the first time since Sam had pulled her out of the lake, she looked more curious than confused. "Wow. Very Science Fiction. Cool."

Luc clicked the camera app and selected the contact at the top of the list.

"Evelyn, you'd better have an excellent reason for that demon of yours to text me at six in the morning telling me to prep for a Face-Time..." Luc rotated the laptop, putting Grace into focus. Hope stopped talking and stared. "Genevieve?"

Viv stood and crouched behind Grace so Hope could see them side by side. "Not me."

"Oh my god," Hope whispered. "Grace, is that really you?"

Grace nodded, eyes bright with tears. "Can she hear me?" she asked.

"I can hear you, Gracie. I... How?"

It was the first time Viv had ever seen Hope Addams at a loss for words.

"I don't know," Grace said. "I was sleeping, and then I woke up in the middle of the lake. A demon, but a female one, not like Quinn—" her voice broke, but she pulled herself together quickly and continued "—pulled me out. I don't understand. You look just the same, but not. You're—"

"Old?" Hope asked, her regular dry tone reasserting itself. "It's okay, you can say it. I'm in my seventies now. But you, you look just the same as last time I saw you." Hope turned her head, and the frame was filled with her thick, white braid. "James! Come here!"

Viv sat next to Grace as they waited for James to appear on screen. Out of the corner of her eye, she saw Evie and Luc having a brief but heated, based on Evie's wild gesticulations, conversation. Whatever they'd disagreed on resolved for the moment, Luc stepped out of the room, pulling his cell phone out of his pocket.

"What?" James asked.

"It's Grace. She's here. Alive!" Hope's voice vibrated with awe and emotion.

You're kidding!" James's face filled the screen as he peered into the webcam. "How?"

"That's what I asked," Hope said. "But so far, there haven't been any real answers."

"The only answer we have right now is 'I don't know.' It happened yesterday." Viv stood up and went back to her chair.

"Everything is a little overwhelming right now," Evie added. "We thought a familiar face might make things easier for Grace. There's a lot to adjust to."

The side door near the kitchen banged open.

"You are not going to believe it!" Shelby yelled. "There's a whole frickin' island in the middle of the lake!"

Lily was hot on her heels. "It's true. It's a real island with tall trees and everything."

"Oh. Right," Viv said. "Last night was chaotic and Kevin's appearance drove everything else out of my mind. Kevin appeared with the island—on it, actually." She grimaced. There was so much more, but she didn't want to talk about Sam yet, and didn't want to spill Bev's story without permission. "Sorry. I was just so exhausted."

Viv watched Evie's head swing back and forth between the kids and Grace.

"Go check it out," Hope said. "Your father and I will stay with Grace. We have a lot of catching up to do."

Evie, Luc, and Viv followed Lily and Shelby outside and were on the porch before it hit Viv. "Your mother just told us what to do and we did it. Her powers work, even from Hawaii."

Evie laughed. "She told me she'd stay with Grace. Through the computer. A machine that bears no resemblance to the last computer Grace probably heard of." She shook her head. "I just hope I'm that powerful someday."

"You are," Luc said. "I finally understand why your demon powers manifested the way they did—it's a literal interpretation of the gift your mother has. You can't tell me she doesn't get everything she wants. We're fortunate she uses her powers for good."

"But does she?" Lily asked. Her voice rang with melodramatic portend.

"She does," Shelby said. She bumped into her friend lightly, and they laughed.

"Alas, her powers are like mine in that they only extend to what people are actually willing to do. Otherwise Lily would be much, much better with her dental hygiene." Evie grinned at her daughter who rolled her eyes at her mother.

"I brush my teeth," Lily retorted.

"You do now—" Evie and Luc stopped walking and stared out over the lake.

Viv turned and looked as well. The island was even eerier in the daylight than it had been at night. It was a jagged, near circular—at least as far as she could tell with this limited view—chunk of land with trees tall enough to rival the famous redwoods in northern California. The tops of the trees were crowned with clouds, and the mist floated down to the ground in waves and ribbons, softening the island and giving the impression that it was a gateway to faery. It pulled at her. She'd spent a lot of her childhood jumping into closets looking for Narnia, looking for mushroom circles in the woods to stand in and cross her fingers, and setting traps for the tooth fairy, planning a campaign of extortion and maybe bribery for a ride back to their home. Not satisfied with the number of teeth she'd lost, she started paying her friends and classmates at school for theirs, too.

When her mother had found her box of teeth, she'd been appalled —rightfully so, even a broken clock was right twice a day—and tossed the teeth, much to Viv's distress. She'd also accused Viv of witchcraft and subjected her to extra church services, twice daily devotions, and a week of bread and water to "cast the devil out by starving him."

"Viv, are you okay?" Evie asked. She put a hand on Viv's arm.

Viv shrieked and jumped about a foot away. Her heart pounded and she gasped for air.

"What's wrong? Are you having a vision? Are you sick?" The questions poured out of Evie. She was ready to jump into battle, no matter what she needed to do.

"Don't touch her," Shelby said. "Just give her space. I think she's having a panic attack." The twelve-year-old pulled a chair across the porch and positioned it behind Viv. "Aunt Viv, if you want to sit down, there's a chair behind you. I'll get you a glass of water."

"Taken care of," Evie said. She had a glass of sparkling water in her hand.

Viv registered all this, but it felt like she was watching a movie of her panic—one of the old ones on a reel projection with crackling light at the edges and the weird accompanying sound of the film traveling through the reel. She sat down, tried to slow her breathing, and when the chest pain dissipated, she took the glass of water and drank deeply.

"Sorry sorry sorry," she said, head down. Now that the panic was receding, shame was creeping forward to take its place. Viv took a deep breath. It always amazed her how her brain could drive to the worst nightmares, even when her thoughts started somewhere completely innocuous. She pursed her lips and looked at the island. Or at least completely different, if not innocuous. "I don't know what happened."

Shelby moved to stand next to her and said, so quietly Viv was sure no one else could hear her, "Trauma response. Your startle reflex is heightened, likely due to stress or having to revisit the place where your trauma happened."

Viv was so startled by Shelby's sudden metamorphosis from preteen to college psych major that it jolted her back to the present. She looked down at Shelby and opened her mouth.

Shelby jumped in before Viv could say anything. "You would not believe how much my shrink likes to go on and on about PTSD. It's so boring." She grinned, crossed her eyes, and stuck out her tongue, transforming her back into a child.

Viv grabbed Shelby's hand and squeezed gently. "Thank you."

Shelby shrugged, squeezed back, and then stepped forward and returned to Lily's side.

"Do you want to talk about it now, or shove it aside and revisit later?" Evie asked. She'd pulled a chair up next to Viv and was probably resisting the urge to slip an arm around her friend.

"Later. Definitely later. Let's stare at the island instead." The burning in her chest was all that remained of the panic that had leapt to the forefront at Evie's touch, and she was eager to douse it with anything else, even that something else was a mysterious island that had shown up, fully formed and too large for the surrounding landscape, in the middle of the night.

The screen door opened behind them, and Viv jumped. Her heart was racing even though she'd identified the sound as soon as it happened. Dammit. *Trauma response. Nothing to fear. Except angels, demons, ancient lake monsters, and a mysterious island.*

"I want to go home," Grace announced. "I want to see Gwen."

Viv's shoulders slumped, and her chin met her chest. She saw the look Evie directed at her and knew what she was about to offer; she had to head her off at the pass. Grace was family, and Viv owed it to her to be the one to take her to the home she hadn't seen in fifty years. Viv gave herself one more moment, then straightened up. She could do this. "I'll take you."

CHAPTER SIXTEEN

For the second time in two days, Viv stood in front of her mother's house trying to build up her courage. It was easier today, probably because she was doing this for someone else.

"Is something wrong?" Grace asked. She'd showered and swept her hair back into a long braid. With Grace's hair pulled back and Viv's styled—her hair was all she had for armor today—Grace's resemblance to Viv was pushed to the forefront.

Viv hesitated, trying to decide how much to say. She opted for gentle diplomacy. "My mother and I don't have the best relationship. I think your disappearance was very traumatic for her, and she never quite recovered. It's possible my resemblance to you was too much."

Grace tilted her head and regarded the house in front of them. "That sounds unfair. You're her child."

Viv shook her head. "Let's just go in and get this over with." She led Grace up the path and knocked, then moved over to let Grace stand in the doorway. She didn't want herself to be the first person her mother saw when she opened the door.

The door swung open, leaving only the screen door as a barrier between Gwen and the younger sister she'd thought was dead for the last forty years.

"Genevieve? What kind of games are you playing?" She started closing the door. "I told you yesterday that if you walked out, you couldn't come back."

Viv moved to stand next to Grace.

"Hi, Gwennie," Grace said. "I'm home."

Viv stood in the doorway of her mother's sitting room. Viv hadn't been allowed in this room growing up—her mother always said it was reserved for adults—and she'd only seen it a handful of times since.

A large, dirty fireplace with unused rotting logs piled in it took up one exterior facing wall—Viv had never seen in lit, and as far as she knew, it hadn't been touched in over fifty years. Wood paneled walls and gold and brown shag carpet along with the windows covered with dark brown curtains gave it an oppressive aura. The flickering light from the yellow bulbs in the chandelier-like light fixture hanging low reflected off the plastic covers perfectly molded to the furniture.

Grace, after a quick look around with widened eyes, sat gingerly on the plastic covered wingback chair. Gwen took a seat across from her on the matching chair, leaving the loveseat for Viv. She chose to stand out of the way, hoping that her presence would go unnoticed and not bring any of Gwen's legendary wrath down on her sister.

The silence in the room was threatening to out-oppress the dark, musty gloom that pervaded. Viv was almost ready to break her pledge to herself to remain silent and had pushed herself off the wall she'd been leaning against when Gwen finally spoke, the first words she'd said since Grace had introduced herself.

"Is this a sick joke? Have you been in hiding all these years and just now came back to taunt me?" Gwen was visibly vibrating, and for the first time in a very long while, Viv almost felt sorry for her.

"No. Of course not. That would be horrific, and I would never do something like that." Grace's tone was soothing, calmer than Viv could've been in the same situation.

Ha. The same situation. Like there was any such thing. Two pairs of eyes turned towards Viv as she barked out a laugh, and the twin motion showed a resemblance that had hitherto been invisible, making it obvious Gwen and Grace were related.

Grace turned back to her sister. "I don't know what happened. I don't understand it. But I wanted to see you—needed to see you. You're my sister, and other than the niece I'd never met before, you're the only family I have left. You took care of me when we were growing up while mom and dad worked and were my rock when they died. I've been back in this world for twelve hours, most of which I spent in denial or asleep. Please, Gwennie." Grace held out her hands to her sister, but when Gwen looked at them the same way she'd regard a snake that'd slithered into her house, Grace withdrew her hands and folded in on herself just a little.

"I don't know what kind of game you're playing, but you're not my sister. My sister was a sinner—she got pregnant out of wedlock and when the devil she consorted with stole her child, she committed suicide, condemning her soul to hell. You look like Grace, and you sound like her, but if you're here and not burning in hell where you belong, you can't be my sister." Gwen's face, which had shown some emotion when Grace had walked back into her life, froze again. Her eyes were hard as diamonds, and the orange glow of the light flickered off them, making them look like they held the hell flames to which she was so willing to condemn her sister.

Grace's face fell and her shoulders slumped. "I thought you'd be happy to see me. This is all the family we have left." Her gesture encompassed the room.

"I have no family." Gwen's back was poker straight, and she scooted to the edge of the chair. "I am alone, as I always have been. The only difference between now and fifty years ago is that I have no illusions to the contrary."

"But we were always together, always family," Grace said. Her eyes were shining bright with tears. "And your daughter…"

"Your family was never me. It was Hope and her parents. Your friends mattered more than me. And as for my *daughter—*" she practically spat the word "—she is my curse and an abomination."

Grace glanced at Viv, who shrugged. "Mother dearest believes that she was cursed with me because she had premarital sex or because you died or because she's delusional. I can't keep track of the ways she detests me at any given time."

Gwen pointed a long, pointy finger at Viv. "You consort with demons, you left me for Hope the same way my baby sister did, and you commit unnatural, unbiblical acts."

Viv translated for Grace. "I'm friends with Luc because when I was growing up, Evie was my best friend and her mother, Hope, gave me a home to go to whenever I wasn't welcome here. As for the abominable, unnatural, unbiblical stuff… I'm not straight—not heterosexual—and made the mistake of coming out to my mother first and then not having the good sense to admit it was a phase or a childish joke or something. And worse? I mostly date women and lack the decency to hide my 'proclivities' from everyone else." Viv meant her explanation to be light, bordering on self-deprecating humor, but the bitterness crept through anyway.

Grace looked at her sister, then stood up. "I am so disappointed," she said. "Maybe it is my fault. You were already turning into a bitter woman when Quinn showed up and chose me over you, no matter how hard you tried to get him to notice you, but I see the intervening years haven't softened you at all. If I'd stayed, maybe I could've helped…"

Viv bit back a sigh of relief. They were finally going to leave. She was about three minutes from bolting out, regardless of her responsibility to her newly resurrected aunt, but now it looked like she wouldn't have to abandon Grace.

"You need to get out," Gwen said. "This isn't your home, and you have no right to be here. Both of you can go scrounge for scraps from the Addams like you always have."

Grace smoothed down the skirt of the dress she'd borrowed from Evie and walked towards the door. "Oh, one more thing," Grace said, looking back over her shoulder. "I'm going to hire a lawyer to help me figure out how to legally raise myself from the dead and find out if the assets that were in my name will revert to me now that I'm back."

"You can't," Gwen sputtered. "You've been dead for fifty years, and there's no way to prove otherwise. You look the same age you did when you died. No one will believe it. No one will give you what's mine."

"I won't kick you out when I get my house back," Grace said. "You're family, and you'll always have a place here." She glided out of the room and out of the house.

"The house is yours?" Viv asked once they'd turned off the front walk to the sidewalk that led to the park. "How? Weren't you twenty?"

Grace slowed her walk but didn't look at Viv. "Mom died when Gwennie was fifteen and I was seven. Cancer. She'd been sick for a while but refused to go to the doctor. When she finally did go, it was too late, and she died a couple months later. Dad was devastated and started working more and more, and when he wasn't working, he still wasn't home much. He tried to be there for us, but it was too hard for him, I think. When she was a teenager, Gwennie looked just like Mom. Looking at her was like looking at a ghost." Grace heaved a sigh. "I should've known better than to thrust myself on her today. I don't know what would've been better, but probably just about anything else."

"Mom never talked about her parents. Or about you—I didn't even know you'd existed until last spring. What happened to your dad?"

"When Gwennie graduated from high school, he offered to pay for her to go to any college she wanted. She'd always wanted to be a teacher. But somewhere in the three years between Mom's death and high school graduation, she'd found Jesus." Graced worried at her lip.

Viv glanced sideways, but when Grace didn't continue, she filled in the silence. "I don't have a problem with religion in general. If people feel that faith makes them better, gives them hope and comfort, it's cool with me. If they're not hurting anyone else, who cares, right?"

"That seems reasonable," Viv said. She wasn't sure where they were going and was having trouble keeping up with the ride her aunt was taking her on.

"But whoever was feeding Gwen their beliefs was not a good person. She changed, became dour and dark and judgmental. I was ten when she graduated and decided to stay rather than go away to school. She wanted to 'do her duty and care for her poor sister.'" Gwen paused at the gate that marked the entrance to the park. "Mind if we find a bench? The park hasn't changed much in forty years, and it's a lot easier to sit here than look at things that bear no resemblance to the town I knew."

"Of course not," Viv said. "Do you want to sit in the park, or somewhere overlooking the lake?" Viv gritted her teeth as she asked. Grace had spent the last forty plus years in the lake. Or under it. Or lake adjacent. Sitting and looking at it, complete with brand-new island, probably wasn't the most soothing suggestion.

"Looking at the lake," Gwen said. "There's a bench I used to gravitate to when I wanted to be alone with my thoughts. I hope it's still there." She walked through the park and down the path on the other side that led to the lake.

Grace slid onto Viv's bench and let out a long breath.

Viv sat next to her and looked at her aunt. Grace's eyes were closed, and her face was pinched.

"You're doing remarkably well for someone who wasn't alive twenty-four hours ago," Viv said. "I wouldn't be handling this nearly as well."

Grace opened her eyes and looked at Viv. "I'm really not. I'm five minutes away from losing my mind and needing the men in little white coats to lock me in a padded room and throw away the key. It helps that so far it feels like I was here yesterday. When I think about the passage of time and where I spent the intervening years, I have trouble breathing, so I'm trying not to think about it." She hunched over and closed her eyes again. "Did Quinn and Lilith ever come back? I tried to find them, but I guess the lake lied to me... They weren't there."

Viv shifted uncomfortably. "I didn't even know you—any of you—existed before last April. Mother—Gwen—never spoke of you, and the town sort of...forgot, I guess. Except for Hope. I know they're alive and in hell—Sam had heard of them when Quinn and Lilith came up, but it didn't sound like they knew each other. When we get back to

Evie's, I'll find Sam and see if she'll look in on them, make sure Lilith is okay. If they ever came back to visit, it was before I turned nine. That's when Gwen and I returned to Eden Valley."

"She left? Willingly?" Grace sounded more shocked by this news than she had about anything else she'd learned since returning from the deep.

"After she got pregnant and before I was born. I don't know the whole story—what she told me and what I've heard from other people are vastly different. She said she left to elope with my dad, and then after a brief but glorious marriage that resulted in my birth, he died. She tried to make it on her own as a single mom for a few years, but eventually moved back to Eden Valley so she could raise me in a small town full of people with good moral character. But what Hope told me—accidentally, she thought I already knew—was that Gwen was enamored with Greg Masters and chased him until she got pregnant. She was convinced that Hope wanted Greg for herself, even though Hope had left town after you...disappeared...and didn't come back for five years, after Mom was already pregnant. When Greg found out, he left town rather than stick around and be a dad. Mom left town before I was born, then returned ten years later, moved back into the house that'd been vacant the entire time, and pretended her story was the right one. She told everyone she was widowed, a single mother to a difficult child, and had to come home where I'd be away from the bad crowd I'd started hanging out with." For the first time in forever, Viv laughed at a memory involving her mother.

"What kind of a bad crowd is a nine-year-old spending time with? Drinking? Drugs? Crime?" The tension had left Grace's body while Viv had been talking, and she looked relaxed.

"Grade school book club," Viv said shaking her head. "There were a few of us bored with what we were reading in school, so we got together to read more advanced books. Some of it was genuinely inappropriate for a bunch of third graders—we should've stayed away from VC Andrews—but a lot of it was just YA fantasy and coming of age stuff. Mom found my stash of library books—dragons and magic and witchcraft—and decided I was being led astray. She tried to get the books out of the school library, and when they declined to ban Lord of the Rings, she packed us up and moved back to Eden Valley."

"That's heavy," Grace said. "I'm sorry. If I'd stayed…"

"It would've been something else," Viv interjected. "But you were telling me about the house and why it's yours."

"Right." Grace planted both feet firmly on the ground, propped her elbows on her knees and her chin in her hands. "After Gwen graduated but didn't leave for college, she started getting very religious and took to lecturing everyone—but especially Dad—about our moral shortcomings. It was exhausting being constantly damned to hell for the most minor infractions. If I was late coming home from school, or Dad stopped for a beer after work… Everything was a sign the devil had taken hold." She lapsed into silence.

Viv stared at the island interrupting the flatness of Eden Lake willing herself to be patient. She knew it was there, she'd seen it appear. But when it wasn't in view it faded to the back of her memory as if it was trying to disappear from notice. She closed her eyes until the island's existence receded and she was fully present with Grace again. Every moment they sat here getting to know each other was time she didn't have to think about what to do about amnesia-inducing islands, Kevin, or Sam.

"We got sick," Gwen said. "Dad more than me. After what'd happened to Mom, we didn't delay. We visited so many doctors, but none of them could figure out what was going on. Dad started getting sicker and sicker. And every day, Gwen would plead with him to repent so he wouldn't have to spend eternity burning in the pits of hell for his sins. She was out of control, and Dad was afraid of what would happen to me if he died and she had control over everything. He wrote a will leaving everything to me and named Edward Addams —Hope's father—trustee until I was twenty. There wasn't much—the house, his pension benefits, and a small nest egg he'd put aside for Gwennie and me to go to college. The only thing Gwen got was the right to live in the house until everything was transferred to me. If I died before the trust passed to me, the estate, such as it was, would go to the secondary beneficiaries—the Imperial Cancer Research Fund."

Tears were streaming down Grace's face, but she made no move to wipe them away. "He died when I was fifteen, the same age Gwen had been when Mom died. I was so worried I was next. I was really sick at this point, but after Dad died, I started getting better. When my daughter was born, I made a will leaving everything to her and Quinn. I don't know why I didn't make provisions for Gwen, but I do know that if I can prove I'm alive or if Lilith was to return, it makes sense that everything would come back to us."

While she'd been listening to Grace talk, a dark suspicion had taken hold in Viv's mind. She needed to voice it, to get it out there, but couldn't find the right words to make it happen. Finally, she just blurted it out. "You and your father got sick at the same time, and when he died, you got better?"

Grace nodded and crossed her arms over her chest. "Yeah. It was a real bad trip."

"Did you get better immediately, or after the will was read and got through probate?" Viv cringed. What she was implying was abominable, and she couldn't believe she was even suggesting it.

Grace froze, reaching the same conclusion where Viv had landed. "After it was confirmed that everything was iron clad. Do you think...?"

"I don't know. I feel gross even suggesting it, but the timing is suspicious." Viv's skin crawled as the full realization of what it would mean if her mother was a murderer hit her. "It can't be true. I'm still here, right? And I'm way more hellhound that either you or your dad."

"I can't do this right now," Grace said. "It was too long ago to do anything about it now, and there are so many other things that require my attention now."

"You're right," Viv said. "We can always talk about it later. If it was poison, you probably still have traces of it in your system, and your dad might too... I'm not actually sure how poison breaks down after death."

"Enough!" Grace shouted and put her hands over her ears. "Take me back to Hope's, please. I need a break."

Regret and fear and confusion swirled through Viv, forming a familiar cyclone of anxiety. She stood up, looked out over the lake, and pushed everything aside but her concern for her aunt and her desire to help Kevin and save the town.

Peace washed over her and—at least for the moment—she was grounded and centered. She held her arm out to her aunt. "I'll take you home."

CHAPTER SEVENTEEN

Once Grace was tucked away in a guest room with an Agatha Christie novel—she'd rejected the idea of watching a movie or reading a book on an iPad—Viv sat down with Evie and Luc.

"Now what?" Viv asked. "Grace is back. My mom might have committed patricide. Kevin reappeared on a brand-new island covered with old growth forest. And we have no idea what's going on or how to save Kevin and Eden Valley. I'm in over my head, but the kids trusted me to figure out a solution, so let's problem-solve."

Evie glanced at the clock over the mantle. "Bev will be here in about an hour. I called Elle, but she didn't answer. Luc went over there to make sure she was okay, and she said she was fine through the door. If we don't hear from her in a couple hours, I'll go over."

"What about Sam?" Viv asked, trying and failing to sound casual.

"She left this morning," Luc said.

"When will she be back?" Viv's heart was in her throat. She hadn't had a chance to apologize, to grovel, to set things right, and tell Sam how she felt.

"She stopped by and dropped off her keys this morning." Luc grabbed his phone and looked at it. "Want me to try Elle again?"

Luc looked unruffled by the audible shattering of Viv's heart, and Evie sent a sharp look his way before turning her attention to Viv.

"Did you not know she was leaving?" Evie asked, reaching out and squeezing Viv's hand.

"She didn't say anything when she dropped me off this morning." Viv was so busy trying to tape up her heart she didn't hear how that sounded until Luc perked up.

"She dropped you off this morning?" he asked. "Say more right now."

Viv looked at Evie who shrugged. "He throws in standup between his 'documentaries' and is particularly fond of John Mulaney. Apparently, humor is a window on the human condition or something like that."

"Making someone cry is easy—finding out what makes them laugh is magic." Luc adopted a beatific expression, and Evie rolled her eyes.

"Pretty sure you're misquoting someone," Viv said. "But distraction noted. I will deal later when I know what's really going on."

"Whoa," Evie said. "So mature. I guess being the oldest of us all has some benefits. I hope someday to reach you level of maturity."

"Bitch," Viv said.

"Jerk," Evie replied. They smiled at each other while Luc looked on in confusion.

"I don't get it," he said.

"Time to move on from your documentaries to some of the good stuff. Plus, I bet watching shows with demons in them would be fun for you!" Viv said.

"You'd think so," Evie agreed. "But since I made him watch the Exorcist, he's flat out refused to watch anything else with demons."

"Did you tell him it was Lily's misinterpretation of a Supernatural demon summoning that pulled him here in the first place?" Viv asked. "He's almost obligated to watch at this point. I need to know if he'd cheer for his namesake or for the gay angel.'

The doorbell rang and all three people in the living room swiveled their heads to the door.

"It's probably Elle," Evie said. "She doesn't just walk in like everyone else. I'll get it."

Viv had never before felt awkward being alone with Luc, but for some reason—probably her obvious distress at his sister's departure—she was now.

Fuck it. "Where'd she go, and when will she be back?" Viv asked, bracing herself for the worst.

"I don't know the answer to either question," Luc said. "I didn't know she was leaving loose ends behind; she said there was no reason not to go."

The weight of that almost crushed Viv, but she held her head high. It was reasonable for Sam to think that. They weren't more than a fling. Maybe there were feelings—at least on Viv's side—that were unrequited, but she hadn't had a chance to share them with Sam. And she'd been actively dismissive every time Sam had brought up their relationship, or wanting to help, or wanting anything. It was unrealistic to expect Sam to hang around forever. How often had she walked away from potential relationships? Was it heartbreaking that the first woman she'd finally admitting to wanting had left? Sure. But did it break any kind of track record she'd put into place? No.

Evie walked back into the room, jolting Viv back into reality. Elle was right behind her, and she looked haggard. There was no other way to describe the tightness at the edge of her eyes accentuated by dark shadows and an unhealthy-looking pallor.

"You look exhausted," Viv said. It wasn't polite, but they'd long passed polite.

"I know," Elle said. "It's my first time feeling like this, and I don't like it."

Viv couldn't decide if she was kidding or not, but another glance at Elle showed that regardless of her sarcasm meter, Elle was exhausted. "Did you sleep last night? Or this morning?"

"I didn't, but that's not weird. I don't often sleep. But something in the last day was different. I'm tired. I'm never tired. I only have the emotions I allow myself to have. I'm an immortal being who doesn't need food or sleep. I exist, and that's enough." Elle crossed her arms and glared.

"It's normal to worry and not sleep when you're worried about your child," Evie said.

"He's not my child. He's a monster I wasn't able to contain," Elle said. "My entire mission was to contain him if possible or eliminate him if it wasn't."

"Can you eliminate him?" Luc asked. "He's a primordial creature, and I imagine not that easy to kill off."

"Of course I can," Elle said, puffing out. "I am a celestial being."

"But can you bring yourself to do it?" Evie asked. "Celestial being and primordial creature aside, you've been living as mother and son for more than eleven years."

"That is irrelevant," Elle said. "I have a job to do, and I always do my duty."

"So last night, when you screamed Kevin's name and sobbed over his unconscious body, that was…?" Viv asked.

"Playing a part," Elle said stiffly.

"Aurielle," Luc said. "There is no shame in having emotions. It's freeing. And there's no need to lie to any of us. We aren't the type of people who'll judge you for feeling something for someone you've taken care of for the last eleven years. It's an adjustment, at least it was for me when I found out I had a child."

"How long did it take you to adjust?" Elle snapped.

Luc wrinkled his nose. "That's not important. But a few hours. After that, the only person who had to adjust was Evie."

"What about Brandon?" Evie asked. "How is he taking everything?"

Elle crossed her arms over her chest. "He's fine. Mostly. Of course, it's been a shock to him, too. But he's holding down the fort. He's the thing that keeps me grounded here."

Viv rewound Elle's words. "The thing?" She'd never heard a person refer to their partner—or any human, for that matter—as a thing.

"Is that not the right word?" Elle asked. "Sometimes, your language still confuses me."

Bev walked through the door. "I left work early. I don't know what's happening. I don't know why. But I know we are going to fix this before anyone else dies. So let's figure this shit out."

Viv's eyes widened. Bev almost never cursed. Something had changed for her since they'd talked the night before.

"What's going on, Bev?" Viv asked. "Are you okay?"

"Peachy," Bev bit out. "I'm just motivated to fix whatever is going on here that's screwing with Eden Valley and my friends. Let's get it done."

Viv opened her mouth to probe further, but Evie's hand on her wrist stopped her. Between Elle's assertion that she had zero parental feelings and Bev's cursing, there were too many signs that something was up.

"Where are the children?" Bev asked. "I'd like to see Shelby."

"They're on the dock," Luc said. "I've been keeping an eye on them. They're fascinated by the island and have spent most of the day developing new and increasingly ridiculous theories about its origins." He fixed his gaze on Elle. "But that's just the girls. Where's Kevin?"

She didn't meet Luc's gaze but didn't look away. "Last time I saw him, he was still unconscious. But that's not the point."

"Then what is it?" Luc asked. "You've spent a lot of time avoiding any and all questions about you, about Kevin, about Brandon, and yet you claim you're invested in Eden Valley and the outcome of the crisis we're facing now. You can't have it both ways. Either you care or you don't. Either this is just a job, or you're ready to step up and do what it takes to protect your son and your town. But no matter where you are, it's time to make a stand. It's easy to walk away and pretend nothing matters. It's much harder to do the right thing. So tell us, Angel, are you going to do what's easy or what's right?"

Elle opened her mouth as if to speak, then closed it again. "That's not a fair question."

"Life isn't fair," Viv said. "You're here now. Do what's right or get out of the way. I'm going to save this town and figure out how to save Kevin, and I can do that with or without you. It'd be easier if you were on board, but either way, I will make it happen."

Elle stared at Viv, then stood up and walked out of the living room.

Disappointment hit Viv like a sneaker wave. She'd been so sure Elle would step up.

The angel opened the front door, stepped through, and paused on the other side long enough for Viv to wonder if she was frozen in place. Elle turned around and came back in, closing the door behind her. "I don't know who I am anymore, and I don't know who the monster of Eden Lake is to me. But my job was to protect the Valley, and I'll be damned before I give up on the task given to me in service of my lord."

Viv nodded at her friends "We have some of the brightest minds available here. A demon, three immensely brilliant humans, and an angel. We can figure this out, save your kid, save the town, figure out if my mom is a murderer, and get some justice for my zombie aunt. Definitely not too much to manage." She took a breath and looked at the people in front of her. The two women who'd been her best friends since she was nine, the angel who was pretending she hadn't caught human maternal feelings for her lake monster son, and the demon who'd swept her bff off her feet, learned to be an amazing father, and was the brother of the woman she'd fallen in... Focus. No more Sam. She's gone, and you're here with today's problems. "So, let's fix this. Any ideas?"

CHAPTER EIGHTEEN

Viv looked around the room, and the beginning of a plan started to form. "We'll need to talk to Kevin to make sure we're doing what he wants, but I think we have everyone we need to end this. I know the who, the where, and kind of the what. I just don't know the how."

"That seems like one of the more important parts of any plan," Bev said. She was tapping her fingers on the arm of the couch.

Viv tried to catch Bev's eyes, but her friend was determinedly staring at the clock hung over the mantle. "Okay. I don't know a lot about magic. I'm not even sure it exists, but the presence of so many people who I wouldn't have believed in two years ago makes me think there's a lot more out there than I know about. And if a ten-year-old can use a magic book and a fictional ritual from the internet to summon a demon, there must be some kind of magic in the world we can harness."

Luc shrugged. "I don't know if she would've been able to summon anyone if she'd been one hundred percent human. But I will grant you that there are rituals that exist that most mortals would call magic."

"Get on with it," Bev ground out.

"What is going on with you?" Viv asked.

"Nothing. I left work early to be here, and I kind of thought you'd have more by now than a plan that has aspirations of being half-baked. You're wasting my time." Bev was looking everywhere but at her friends, and her eyes were moving rapidly, never focusing on anything.

"Okaaaaay," Viv said slowly. "I'm going to keep going, but you're worrying me."

Bev didn't respond. Viv looked across the room at Evie. Evie's eyes were wide, and her mouth was hanging open a bit. She saw Viv looking at her and shook her head slightly. Viv wasn't sure if that meant she had no idea what was going on or if she was encouraging Viv to drop it and finish the barely formed plan she'd started explaining. Probably both.

"Okay. So, ritual, magic, spells, whatever. I've been getting flashes of things I don't understand for the last couple weeks, and I think they're related. What stronger bonds exist than the bonds of a parent with their child or the bond between friends. You reminded me of that, Bev, when we talked about how you anchor me in all the best ways. Kevin has two amazing friends who would do almost anything for him, and a mother who—regardless of whether she'll admit it—is fiercely devoted to her son. In addition, we have a demon and an angel and three women whose friendships mirror that of the kids' ties. There has to be something we can do with that."

Evie nodded. "I don't like that you're suggesting Lily be involved, but what you're saying is making sense to me."

"Any chance we could get an angelic boost?" Viv asked Elle. "Is Brandon an angel? Do you have any friends you could encourage to drop by?"

"I don't have friends, and Brand is not an angel. There is no one you can count on from heaven." She paused and appeared to be thinking. "But depending on your plan, it is possible Brand can help in its special way."

Its? If Brandon was going to be involved, they could address the mystery he presented at that point. "Do you want to give him a call and see if he'll help?"

"We don't need to ask. If there is a role for...him...he will fill it. I can call him then." Elle's arm twitched, and for a moment it looked like she was reaching for something behind her. She stopped though and folded her hands in her lap.

"What about you, Luc? Anyone on your side who'd be willing to help out with knowledge and demonic energy?" Viv's thoughts were racing as she tried to put together the puzzle pieces that had been tossed at her over the last few days.

"Maybe," Luc said. "Mat's usually around unless we need him and he decides to adhere to my directive that he stay out of Eden Valley—I found him slinking around again a couple days ago and tossed him out again. But if he felt like there was enough chaotic energy, he'd probably help. Without knowing what you're thinking, though, I don't want to commit to calling anyone else. My father is... Well, I know he'd love to be involved in anything we're doing here, but his help isn't always what one needs."

"Son! I am hurt you think so little of me." Abaddon materialized in the middle of the living room. He was wearing a fire engine red suit and tie with a matching fedora perched between the ebony horns curling up from the sides of his head. It set off his mahogany skin perfectly. "I would love to help with whatever scheme your humans are planning." His million-watt smile was enough to win over anyone.

"Why are you here?" Evie asked. "It's not your weekend yet, and you're not supposed to show up without an invitation from either Luc or me. You signed a contract."

Abe whipped a scroll out of his pocket and shook it, unrolling several feet of paper. "If you'll read the fine print..."

Evie rolled her eyes. "You're so dramatic." She snapped her fingers and a folder appeared in her hands. She opened it and pulled out a few sheets of paper. "The contract is two and a half pages long. Luc wrote it, we both reviewed the fine print, and there is nothing in it that says you can show up without invitation."

Abe rolled up his scroll. "Look who's being dramatic now. You don't need to snap your fingers to wish things into existence. You're just showing off." He pouted as he stuffed the contract back into his jacket. "Please review the exceptions. Read them out loud."

"We don't have time for this," Bev said. "You two can wrangle about your stupid demon contracts later. Let's just get this over with."

Abe turned his attention to Bev while Evie flipped to the last page of the contract and read with a furrowed brow.

"Beverly, isn't it? The one who feels left out because she believes she didn't get anything to go with her demon brand. Not so sure anymore, are you?" He walked towards her and sat down in front of her on a chair that hadn't existed a moment before. Chair might be too mild a word—this was an oversized chair with deep burnished gold upholstery and intricately carved arms and legs. A throne.

Bev looked him straight in the eyes and a sad smile, telegraphing defeat and exhaustion, curled up the corners of her mouth. "You knew, didn't you. The whole time I thought I was the odd one out, the normal one, but you knew."

"Of course I did. Whose marks do you think adorn the shoulders of you and the psychic over there? Did you think they were my son's? My granddaughter's?" He laughed, and the windows vibrated with the noise. "My innocent child, the door that you fell into was mine. Liliana's will helped form it, and Lucifer's compulsion to walk through it and into this town to claim what was mine forced it open, but nothing happens in my kingdom without my knowledge and, in this case, without the groundwork I laid. Those marks are mine— mine and my siblings'."

Lily ran into room, Shelby trailing behind her. "Papa Abe!" she squealed.

Abe stood and held out his arms. Lily threw her arms around his neck and kissed his cheek. "What are you doing here? Are you going to help us with Kevin?"

"I would do anything to help you and your dear friend," Abe said, laying a hand over his heart. His throne moved from in front of Bev to the periphery of the room. "Your father was just speculating on what help from hell might be forthcoming, and so I am here. I am excited to hear your Aunt Viv's plans. Please do continue, Genevieve. I am all ears."

"Dammit," Evie said from the couch where she'd been reviewing the contract. She handed the page over to Luc who read what she pointed out and then closed his eyes.

"That's a very loose interpretation of the exception," Luc said. "No one here is in mortal danger."

"Are you sure?" Abe asked. "What she's—" he pointed at Viv "—planning is daring and dangerous. There are no guarantees everyone will survive the ritual. And since my granddaughter was named as a major participant in the ritual, I am here to lend my aid to protect her."

"Fine," Evie said. "Please, Viv, continue."

Viv gathered her thoughts and tried to remember where she'd been before Abe's dramatic entrance. "We have an angel and a demon. We have Kevin's mother—and possibly his father. We have his two best friends. There's support from hell. Nothing from heaven. That should be enough people to anchor Kevin to this world and help cut his tie to the lake and make him mortal. If that's what he wants."

"Or else it's enough people to sever his tie to the lake and let him rest forever," Abe said.

"Yes," Viv said. "Whichever he prefers."

"It doesn't matter what he wants. He's staying here." Shelby looked around the room and glared at each of the adults. "That's what I was told, anyway. And if it's true for me, it's true for him."

Bev got up. "Someone find me when you know what you're doing." She stalked out of the room, the sound of the screen door slamming signaling that she'd left the house.

Evie stood, but before she could follow Bev, a wailing sound permeated the house. Evie looked up the stairs, then checked her watch. "I have to go get Alex. Someone else needs to go after Bev."

"I can go fetch my second favorite granddaughter," Abe said.

"Not unless you've suddenly started lactating," Evie said. "And before you say that it's within the realm of possibility, stop, just don't."

"I'll go get Bev," Viv said after Evie disappeared up the stairs.

"She'll be okay," Shelby said. "It's just noisier now, and it's difficult for her. There are so many voices, and she doesn't know how to filter them out. Imagine if there was constant conversation, yelling, screaming, pleading, but you couldn't quite make out what anyone was saying or what they wanted... That's what it's sounded like since the island showed up. If she doesn't come back soon, I'll go get her." Shelby dropped into the spot Bev had vacated, and Lily took Evie's place. "What's next?"

Viv spread her arms wide. "I've gotten through my entire plan. Now we need to figure out the how."

"Where's my book?" Abe asked. "I know just the thing, but it'll take someone with mortal blood and ties to two worlds to read it."

"Your book? You mean the book Kevin gave Lily to do the 'demon summoning?' I thought Evie had given it back." Viv narrowed her eyes at Abe. "You gave it to Kevin to pass on, didn't you?"

"Of course." Abe permitted himself a small smile and steepled his fingers in front of his face. "He might be an ancient being, but he certainly doesn't have access to books like this. Liliana, my princess, is it in your room?"

"Um. Maybeeee?" Lily looked at her father who'd started slowly shaking his head.

"We'll talk about this later. If you have the book, you might as well get it," Luc said.

"Don't tell Mama," she said as she headed to the stairs.

"There is no way I'm keeping that from your mother," Luc said. "Get the book. Repercussions can wait until after we save your friend."

Viv watched Bev from the porch. Her friend was at the end of the dock staring at the island. Elle, Abe, and Luc were looking through the book for the ritual Abe was positive would work. Viv wasn't so sure... He was a demon who loved attention and enjoyed drawing things out way past the point of appropriateness. He knew where the ritual was, she was positive, but she also knew there was probably no way to rush him.

So she came outside for some air and to keep an eye on her friend. She'd really messed up everything and had been so convinced she had the worst of it she hadn't even considered anyone else's experiences. For a group of mature women in their forties, they were all really bad at asking for and accepting help.

Viv walked down the path, searching for the words to say to her friend that would help. She hadn't come up with anything better than, "Sorry about the voices in your head. How can I help?" by the time she'd reached the dock.

"Hey, Bev," Viv said. "I'm sorry about the voices. How can I help?"

Bev turned around. "I'm sorry, too. I'm exhausted—I barely slept last night, and when I did, I had zombie horror movie nightmares all night. That's not a great excuse for how rude I've been, but it's the best I've got."

"Is it easier here away from the voices of alive people?" Viv asked. She moved up to stand next to Bev.

"Yeah. When I don't have to concentrate on distinguishing between the voices in my head and those of the actual people in front of me." Bev slipped her hand into Viv's and leaned her head on Viv's shoulder. "It isn't often that I wish I had a partner, but I do now. I don't want to put too much on Shelby—she's just a kid and has been through a lot—but she's going through the same thing, but with infinitely more grace. And you and Evie and now Elle are my best friends, but at the end of the day, it's just me alone with my thoughts. Well, not alone. Never alone."

"I'll stay as long as you need me to," Viv said. "As long as you want to put up with me, that is."

"I know how badly you must want to get back to Seattle, and that makes your offer even more meaningful, but it's not quite what I meant." Bev huffed and made a dissatisfied hum in the back of her throat. "I don't know how to describe it. I don't want a boyfriend and all that implies. But I do want a someone. It's all jumbled up in my head. Too much information about what an adult relationship is and isn't to reconcile with what I want and need. Sorry. I'll figure it out, and maybe once I do, I can find what I need."

"Whatever you need. Always. Can I bring you a chair and a glass of wine? I'll let the others know you're fine."

"I'd rather have my hat and shades," Bev said. "But I wouldn't say no to a chair and some rosé." She heaved a sigh and lifted her head from Viv's shoulder. "But I'll come back now. I feel better enough that I can participate without snapping at anyone."

"If it helps, my plan is at least in the oven now," Viv said. "We're getting closer and closer to half-baked."

Bev squeezed Viv's hand and laughed. "Hmmm… You have many talents, but I'm not sure baking is top of the list. Maybe I should come back and help."

"We'd be lucky to have you."

They turned around and walked back towards the house. A loud pop like a mini sonic boom followed by voices that Viv couldn't quite understand but knew were curses made them switch direction and skirt the house towards the front.

Three people stood in the drive brushing dust off their bodies. Two of the people were facing Viv and Bev. They were almost impossibly beautiful. The masculine looking one was wearing an impeccably tailored dark navy suit and a white shirt unbuttoned at the neck. He had lightly tanned skin and light brown hair a little longer on top than the close-cut sides. A hint of a beard darkened his chiseled jaw, and although she couldn't see them from here, Viv just knew he'd have the piercing blue eyes of every rakish romance novel hero.

The woman next to him was almost as tall, and just as beautiful. Her honey brown hair flowed down her back in gentle waves. Her skin was lighter than the man's—almost porcelain—and her lithe, willowy frame was set off with a peach and blue spaghetti-strapped sundress that gathered at the bodice and flowed down loosely to the hem that fell halfway down her thighs. She had on jute espadrilles and her toenails and fingernails were the same scarlet as her lipstick.

"Wow," Viv breathed.

The third person, who'd been blocked by the gorgeous pair who'd captured Viv's attention, turned around and leaned in close to the man and whispered something in his ear. He smiled, his full, sensuous lips curving up and pulling Viv's libido up with it. Then he moved his head to answer and Viv saw the person who had an arm around the gorgeous man's waist. Her height was the only average thing about her. Her black skin glowed against her tank top framed by a leather jacket and body-hugging leggings.

"Is that Sam?" Bev asked. "I thought she'd taken off."

"So did I," Viv said. "Guess the only thing she left was me." She turned and walked around to the back of the house, followed by Bev. Viv was hoping the few extra minutes before she was forced to greet Sam and the man she'd brought to the ritual planning meeting would be enough to remind herself she was being mature and dealing with her feelings later, after they'd saved Kevin. A literal child's life and the entire town's future mattered more than her relationship woes.

"I can do this," she said. "No problem. I have a ton of experience pushing my feelings down and pretending they don't exist. This won't be any different."

"Is it helping?" Bev asked.

"Not even a tiny bit," Viv said. "But what else am I going to do?"

"I got you, babe," Bev said.

"Same back at you," Viv replied.

CHAPTER NINETEEN

Viv parked herself in the dining room—close enough to hear Luc and Elle catch Sam and her new friends up on the plans to save Kevin, if he was willing, but far enough away that she wasn't visible to anyone except Lily and Bev. She'd have to go in soon, it was her plan after all, but she was going to soak up every second she could to solidify her composure.

She missed introductions—too busy drowning her sorrows in an ice cream sandwich she'd found in the freezer—but she hadn't wanted to hear them anyway. She'd already seen enough. The newcomers were obviously demons, and that made a lot more sense for Sam than Viv did. Demons who were in it for the long haul with humans were pretty few and far between. Luc was the only exception she could think of. Not that she knew that many demons. Her case study included Luc—who'd left for ten years rather than settle down with Evie. Grace and Quinn—and that demon had kidnapped their child and taken off to the underworld, leaving Grace behind, devastated and broken. And... That was it. She and Sam hadn't been enough of a thing to determine either way.

"...Viv?"

Dammit. She'd missed the question and whoever had asked it. Time to put on her big girl pants and brave the room.

"Sorry." Viv pasted on her biggest, fakest smile. "I was scarfing down some ice cream and missed a few beats."

"Daddy just wanted to give you credit for your idea and see if you had anything else," Lily volunteered. "And if you ate my last ice cream sandwich, I will give you pimples on your butt forever."

"I'll buy you some more," Viv promised. "Please leave my butt alone."

Lily considered a moment. "The really expensive ones?"

"As many as you want. Cross my heart." Viv drew an X over her chest with her index finger.

"Fine. Your butt is safe." Lily drew her legs up in front of her on the couch and crossed them underneath her.

"Did you find the ritual?" Viv asked. She slid Lily over and sat down next to her.

"We think so," Elle said. "But there's something missing. Someone. We need another person to complete it. We have his friends who can anchor two of the eight points. We have me, his mother, for lack of a better word, who will take a third point. Points five and six will be Evie and Bev—the mothers of Lily and Shelby and powerful beings in their own right. You should take point seven. The visions on how to solve this came through you. The eighth point will need to be a demon to read the ritual. Luc has volunteered, but I am not sure that's wise since Evie and Lily will also be taking part. He should stay in the background to mind the baby."

"That'll be me, then," Sam said. "Unless you want my twin."

"No," Evie and Luc said at the same time.

Viv counted on her fingers. "There are friends to form a triad, and you need a second triad that's you, Kevin, and someone else who fits. This is where Brandon should be, don't you think?"

Elle squirmed. "I don't think that'll work. Brand isn't exactly... father material. There is no familial bond."

"The other four are creating links with the first four, correct? Are they also triads?" Viv asked. She kept her eyes focused on Elle and didn't even notice when Sam took off her leather jacket and hung it on one of the hooks near the door. Nor did she see that Sam was wearing a tight, black tank top that dipped in a vee between her breasts. She was paying attention to Elle and the book. So much focus. She shook her head. Elle was answering her questions, and Viv had missed the beginning.

"...balance. There's an angel, so there has to be a demon. There are children, so there has to be their mothers."

"And who am I balancing? Who's the missing person?" Viv racked her brain, trying to figure out the solution. Who would balance her that would also be someone who was close enough to Kevin to form that relationship?

"I don't know," Elle confessed. "Maybe Kevin will have an idea, though."

"We probably shouldn't do too much more until we talk to him, though," Bev said. "After all, this is his future and his fate on the line."

"So mature and boring," Abe said. "Glad I could help. I'll be back for the fireworks. You might not need me in a point position—which is decidedly unfair, I'm a demon who is very much attached to Liliana, but if you want my daughter, far be in from me to get in the way—but you'll need some hellfire as backup in case things go wrong." He disappeared in a puff of yellow, sulphurous smoke that left everyone coughing and plugging their noses.

"He does it because he thinks it's funny," Lily said. "I told him no one liked giant stinky farts, but he doesn't care."

"Now what?" Viv asked, desperate to change the subject away from the king of hell and his fart jokes. "Do we go get Kevin?"

"I'll go see if he has awoken yet," Elle said. "And if he has, I'll bring him here. There is one thing we haven't discussed—the where. Viv, you said you knew?"

Viv glanced towards the lake. Even though she couldn't see it through the walls of the house, she knew everyone would follow her line of thought.

"I don't know where that island came from, but it's here, and it's perfect, don't you think?" she asked.

Elle bowed her head in acknowledgment. "There is nowhere else that would work. I don't know how or why it appeared, but it's connected to Kevin and the lake that created and sheltered him for centuries."

Footsteps on the stairs announced Evie's return. "Hi! I hope you solved it all without me. Grace will be down in a second. She's done with her nap and ready to brave the twenty-first century again."

Grace walked in the room as Evie finished speaking. She looked rested and radiant again, but then her jaw dropped.

"Quinn?" she whispered. "Is that you? Is it really you?" Her skin lost all color and she fainted, falling in a heap on the floor before anyone could catch her.

GRACE WAS in the dining room having a glass of water and steadfastly refusing to see anyone but Evie. Elle had gone to find Kevin. Lily and Shelby had retreated to Lily's room with Sprinkles. Luc and Alex were on a walk. Bev was down at the lake again.

That left Viv with Sam, Quinn, and the yet unnamed demon that accompanied them.

"Hey," Viv said. "I don't think I caught your name?" She held out her hand to the gorgeous woman in a blue sundress sitting between the demon who was apparently Quinn, her aunt's ex-boyfriend and Sam, Viv's ex-girlfriend.

The woman looked at Viv's hand until Viv withdrew it. "Lilith, Queen of Hell." Quinn gave her a look over Sam's head and Lilith heaved a sigh. "Lilith, future Queen of Hell."

"Oh wow," Viv said. Every last drop of anger at Sam and jealousy of the beautiful demons Sam had brought from hell disappeared. "You're Grace's daughter. My cousin."

Quinn narrowed his eyes at Viv. "You're Guenevere's child?" His mouth twisted in distaste.

"I am," Viv confirmed. Quinn clearly knew her mother, and Viv searched for a way to tell him she was nothing like her mother without sounding defensive.

"She is nothing like her mother," Sam said. "Viv is the one I told you about. She has repudiated her mother."

"The one you told them about?" Viv asked. "What did you tell them? That you changed your phone number so I couldn't call you? That you left town, dropped your house keys with your brother, and again didn't tell me? You keep talking about how you want more, how you have my back, and you keep disappearing when I need you." Viv's voice was rising, but she didn't care. She glared at Sam.

Sam crossed her arms. "I told them about the human woman who'd captured my interest, much in the way Evie caught Luc." Red light sparked in Sam's eyes. "And I didn't change my phone number. I forgot to pay the bill. For several months. Money is so tedious, and the phone people turned it off. So I got a new one."

"But you left without telling me where you were going. After you dropped me off and I thought something was happening between us. I thought..." Viv's voice trailed off before she exposed every facet of her broken heart.

"Luc asked me to take a trip to hell to see if I could find Quinn and Lilith. I wasn't going to be gone for more than a few hours. I didn't think it was something I needed to run by you." A tendril of smoke rose from the sofa.

"He said he didn't know where you were or when you'd be back. And you left the keys to your cabin with him," Viv practically shouted. "He never lies."

"Luc is my brother, and I love him dearly, but he is the worst at providing all the correct information sometimes. I dropped off my keys because I didn't know how long it would take to find Quinn and Lilith and get back, and I needed someone to...check on a couple things." Sam's hard stare met Viv's eyes. "And last night aside, when have you ever given me reason to think there was anything between us? You pushed me away at every turn, rejected every offer of help, and showed little desire to explore what was between us other than brief physical encounters before you once more turned away from me."

Quinn and Lilith watched the argument with the polite expressions of spectators at a particularly genteel tennis match.

"It's been a really rough year and a half. So sorry that I couldn't figure out what you wanted and match those expectations perfectly. I guess us humans aren't intuitive enough to figure out what a demon wants and when and adjust themselves to fit in with someone else's plans." Viv knew she was babbling and had stopped making sense, but she plowed ahead anyway. "You wanted me to change who I was, to give up everything I'd built for myself outside of Eden Valley, to move back to the town where my mother lived and refused to consider a compromise."

"I'm the one who wouldn't compromise?" Sam scoffed. "You were so dead-set on leaving Eden Valley, on going back to your sterile life in the city where you had no friends, no connections, and nothing to keep you grounded and connected to the powers that were growing in you. Did you never stop to wonder why your visions were so devastatingly awful away from here?"

The weight of what Sam had told her hit Viv in the chest like a ton of crystal balls. "Staying in Seattle is what made the vision hangovers worse? And you didn't tell me?"

"Are you a psychic or not?" Sam asked. "Seems like that information is something that should've come to you." She crossed her arms.

"All my visions of Eden Valley were of destruction or my mother. Why would I want to come back here? I've never met anyone who admitted to being a real psychic and no one here bothered to tell me the distance from Eden Valley was why things were so difficult." Viv blinked away the tears of anger forming in the corners of her eyes.

"I tried! I told you it would be better if you stayed here. That it would be easier. That I couldn't help you if you were in Seattle, but you were so hell-bent on leaving town and maintaining your aura of independence that you didn't listen." The hellfire in Sam's eyes dimmed to a faint glow. "I wanted to help you, but you wouldn't let me. You never let me."

The fight drained out of Viv. "I thought you wanted me to stay for you, to give up my whole life for you."

"I would never ask that... I wanted you to stay for *you*. Having you here was a bonus for me. I wanted to explore what we had, spend more time in your bed and in your arms. I wanted to guide you through what you were experiencing, help you hone the visions and learn how to harness and direct them." She sighed and looked human for a second. Human and sad.

Viv heard "wanted." Past tense. She'd messed up everything. Again. "I'm sorry, Sam. You're right. I was so intent on what I thought you were trying to take from me, I didn't hear what you were trying to give me. I know I don't deserve another chance with you, but since I walked away, I've been lonely. I know I'll never be able to find anyone else willing to put up with me the way you do. What we have—had—is one-of-a-kind."

"Is this how it was with Mother before her sister banished us?" Lilith asked Quinn.

"Our passion was different, if just as fiery," Quinn replied. "We channeled it into love and sex, not anger and miscommunication. Perhaps if we'd been able to stay, Grace and I would've learned to fight like this, if only to find forgiveness and peace in each other's bodies. It is hard to say."

The speech Viv was preparing, complete with groveling and yanking out her heart to sew on her sleeve, vanished. "Did you say my mother *banished* you? Both of you? How?"

"And how were you able to return?" Sam asked. "I didn't realize you'd been banished when I asked you to come back. I believed what the mortals believed—that you'd absconded with Lilith and returned to hell with the half-demon child you'd gotten on Grace."

"I felt the force that kept us in hell and out of Eden Valley weaken a year ago as the mortals reckon time," Quinn said. "It snapped completely yesterday. I don't know the cause of either, but I also didn't know a human had the power to banish a demon, and to create such a strong barrier that no matter how many times I tried, I could not return."

"What happened a year ago?" Viv asked.

"I did," Luc replied as he walked into the room. "Or, more accurately, Lily happened. A gate to hell was opened in Eden Valley. It must have weakened the binding enough to let Grace's resurrection yesterday finish the job."

"Weren't there gates before? You came and went pretty freely that summer you lived here," Viv pointed out.

"I didn't use a gate, though. Those are almost never necessary. I came the usual way—through the door." Luc looked like he was going to elaborate, but he paused, eyes focused on something across the room.

Grace stood in the doorway. Her color hadn't yet returned, but she was looking less terrified and more angry now.

"You didn't leave me?" she asked. "I thought you'd left me."

Quinn stood and crossed the room, taking Grace into his arms. "I would never leave you. You were my everything, you and Lilith. If I'd returned to my father's court, I would have done so with you or not at all."

"Gwennie," Grace said. "Gwennie did all this… She took everything from me. Father. You. Lilith."

"Grace, why did you go into the lake?" Viv asked. "We know Evie tried something similar when Abaddon spirited Lily away last year, and she said a voice compelled her, called to her, promised to reunite her with her daughter. Is that what happened to you as well? I'd assumed it was Kevin who'd done that, but now I have questions."

Grace pulled back from Quinn enough to turn and look at Viv without leaving the circle of Quinn's arms, wrapped protectively around her. "It was much the same. I remember a voice in my head telling me that the water held everything I wanted, that it would give me peace. That I would be…saved."

Evie stood behind Grace and Quinn. "The lake told me that I could save myself and save Lily if only I came to it. That we would be saved."

"Oh no," Viv said. "We need to talk to Kevin, but I only know one person connected to both of you who is obsessed with saving others from the temptations of hell."

CHAPTER TWENTY

V iv stared out the kitchen window at where Quinn, Grace, and Lilith were huddled close together, catching up on fifty years of missed opportunities. Viv wanted to join them— she was family, too, after all—but she was also Gwen's daughter and didn't want to force herself into their intimate moment, not with the cloud of her mother's actions hanging over her.

They were waiting for Elle and Kevin to return, even though Quinn had suggested—strongly—that he leave to have a "conversation" with Gwen while they waited.

He finally conceded that Gwen would wait—the damage was already done, and no one was likely to invite her for a potluck any time soon. The less she knew about who was in town and why, the better. No one knew how she'd banished Quinn and lured Grace and Evie into the lake, and the timeline was too fraught now to risk it.

Viv shivered with the imminence of the disaster. Something had shifted in the last forty-eight hours. It'd been ten days since Viv had returned home, and the tension in the air had grown so palpable that even the tourists felt something was up. No one commented on the new island that had appeared—perhaps more of that Eden Valley magic that made everything seem normal—but the stream of tourists, usually torrential this time of year, had slowed to a trickle, and even some long-time residents decided to pack up and go on vacation at the typical height of the tourist season.

"Are you ready?" Sam asked, walking forward to stand next to Viv.

Viv turned her head to look at the gorgeous demon at her side. "Ready for what?"

"For the end. Everything's going to change, and it's because of you." Sam paused, then looked into Viv's eyes. "I wasn't patient enough. You are so confident, so poised, and so powerful. I should've explained better or figured out a way we could be together without you giving up your whole life. If I'd tried harder, you could've had the training you needed, the time to get used to the visions, and the skills to steer into what you need to know. I let my own pride get in the way, and after accusing you of the same sin, I find myself feeling more than a little hypocritical."

Viv turned her attention back to the window. It was hours until dark yet, but the sun was starting to flirt with the horizon and the shadows were growing longer. "It won't be tonight. Tomorrow, I think. Tomorrow, if Kevin agrees and we find the missing piece."

"Do you know what the missing piece is?" Sam asked.

Viv heard her voice, but it sounded like it was far away, across space that was constantly folding in on itself. "All I see is a woman cradling a child. The woman's face is hidden in the folds of a scarf. I see tears fall from her eyes and splash on the baby's face. They're burning through the child's skin, marking him as hers."

Viv tried to get closer, to catch a glimpse of the woman's face, but every time she got near, the figures would rotate, and Viv would find herself back where she started. "I can't see her face." Frustration laced through Viv's body, and she ran towards the woman, but no matter how fast or how hard she ran, the woman stayed the same distance away.

"It's okay, Viv," Sam said. She was closer now, and Viv felt pressure on her arm. When she looked down, nothing was there, but the pressure didn't lessen.

"I need to see her face," Viv said. "I can't walk away yet."

"It's okay to come back," Sam said. She was even closer now, and when Viv looked, the outline of a hand that matched the pressure she felt appeared on her arm. "You've figured it out. It's enough."

Viv opened her mouth and gasped. She was drowning. Water was flooding her lungs and she didn't know which way to swim.

"I'm here," Sam said. "I have you. You are safe. Follow my voice."

Viv grabbed onto the sound of Sam's voice and swam towards it. Soon, her head broke through the water and sunlight hit her face. She took a long, shuddering breath, then opened her eyes. She was standing by the window looking out over the backyard, Sam by her side. When she shook her head experimentally, no water flew off the ends of her hair. She was completely dry and could breathe without choking.

"What was that?" Viv asked. "Chair."

Sam pushed a chair behind Viv and helped her sit. "That was you having a directed vision," Sam said. "You had a question, you knew what you needed, and your mind took you there."

"I don't have a headache," Viv said. "But I'm thirsty AF."

"I'll grab you a glass of mineral water," Sam said. "Then we can talk about what you saw."

Viv turned in her chair to watch Sam cross the kitchen and pull a water out of the fridge. "I didn't see anything. At least not anything useful. I thought I was going to, but every time I tried to get closer, it felt like I was moving farther away."

"Don't discount what you saw until you think it over," Sam said. "Visions aren't always literal, you know. Once Elle and Kevin get back and he agrees to the ritual, you can share what you've learned with the group. Surely, with that many great minds in one place, we'll be able to figure out what it meant." She handed over the water and grabbed herself a beer. After cracking it open on the bottle opener fastened to the wall next to the fridge, she took a long drink and sighed. "Beer is one of the things mortals do exceptionally well. It's so good, it seems like a demon must have had a hand in it." She glanced at the label and laughed. "Maybe a demon did have a hand in this one."

She turned the label around to show Viv. It was an "Infernal IPA" from "Pour House, home of devilishly good brews."

"Ha!" Viv laughed. "You figured it out. The monks who perfected brewing were actually Satanists, and their secrets have been passed down from demon to demon."

"Weirder things have happened." Sam took another drink of the beer. "This is devilishly good. No false marketing here. I wonder if the owner has any need of legal assistance." She looked at the label again. "They're in Washington, and a short trip to check them out might be a good idea. Maybe I could tempt them into joining our portfolio."

Viv took a drink of water and watched the gears in Sam's head turn. "You're gorgeous when you're plotting evil," Viv said.

Sam flashed a grin at Viv and leaned in to drop a kiss on her forehead. "When this is all over, we need to have a very long, very naked discussion about our futures."

Viv tipped her head up in time to brush her lips against Sam's. "Too bad we're stuck in Eden Valley," Viv said. "Anywhere else would be a much better place for the kind of privacy discussions like this need."

"I'll erase everyone's memories of our whereabouts, and it'll all be fine." Sam held out her hand and hauled Viv off the chair. "I think I hear Elle and Kevin approaching. Time to see if the subject of all our work is amendable to the solution."

"Can you do that?" Viv asked. A flutter of fear vibrated in her chest.

"Can I...ask Kevin what he wants to do?" Sam turned back to Viv. "Yes, but I think it'd be better coming from you or Elle—someone he knows better than me."

"No, I mean can you erase everyone's memories? Can you erase mine?" Viv cringed as she realized her voice was laden with fear.

Sam paused. "No. I can't erase people's memories. I can influence them to forget, give them something to hold on to they'd prefer to remember, but I can't make anyone forget something they don't want to. And even if I could, I would never do that to you, not even if you asked me to. You don't have to be afraid of me, Viv. I would never hurt you. I will never abuse you."

"I'm sorry," Viv said. "I'm not afraid, not really." She pulled her hand back from Sam's and tried to hide her hands in her non-existent pockets. "Stupid clothes without pockets. Whose stupid idea was this anyway? The patriarchy needs to be taken down."

Sam recaptured Viv's hand. "It's okay to be afraid. Even if I was mortal, I'd still be able to hurt you, it's just that my powers are different than the typical human's abilities. If you think of the person who's hurt you the most, I think you'll find that they're very, very mortal. All I ask is that you talk to me about your fears before knee-jerking and pulling away. Give me a chance."

Viv squeezed Sam's hand back. "I can do that. I'll try, anyway. Let's go talk to our resident monster, shall we?"

KEVIN SAT at the head of the dining room table. Dark circles under his eyes highlighted his sickly pallor, and his hands trembled on the table. "I thought it was over," he said, looking at Viv. "I found the woman your mother blames you for. She wasn't mine, but she was there. There are a few like her, dead but not, suspended in time. Because they weren't mine, and because whoever they belonged to didn't encroach on my territory, I left them alone."

"How many are there?" Viv asked. "How long have they been there?"

"Not many, maybe a half dozen or so. Your woman, your aunt, she was there the longest. It took almost everything I had left to break the ties that bound her in my lake. I thought it would finally be over." He leaned back in his chair and closed his eyes. "I can retrieve someone else. Maybe. I don't know what will happen to them if I expend all I have left before they're freed, though."

"No," Shelby said. She stood up and ran around the table to Kevin and slipped an arm around him. "You do not give up. We think we have something that will help. It will break your tie to the lake and end your hunger."

A wry grin, too old for an eleven-year-old, flashed on Kevin's face. "And did they tell you what would happen when the tie is broken? Did they tell you that without the tie, I will cease to be me? I will cease to be. If I am not the Eden Lake monster, I am nothing."

"I don't think that's true," Viv said. "The ritual, which requires eight people, four to tie you to this world and four to hold back the dark, will hold you here. There is a catch, though, and that's what you need to consider before we go forward."

"Of course there's a catch," Kevin replied. "You consort with demons who love to find catches and loopholes and write the fine print that drives you mortals mad. Might as well tell me and get it over with. I am weary and need to return to my home to sleep and feed."

"The catch is that you'll be mortal," Lily said. "You'll be a real boy, like Pinocchio, but less creepy."

"That's impossible," Kevin said. His eyes glinted emerald for a second, then dulled again. "There is no such ritual."

"Guess you should've read the book Abe gave you to pass on to Lily," Luc said. "Of course, you also shouldn't have been passing demon tomes on to impressionable children, but since it gave me back my daughter, I'll overlook it this once."

"Let me see the ritual," Kevin demanded.

Luc passed the book over, and Kevin read through the page several time, brow wrinkled.

"This might actually work," he said. "But only if everything is exactly right. Who will you have stand with me?"

"Lily and I will be two of your anchors," Shelby said.

"No. Out of the question," Kevin said. "I will not risk you."

"That is not your choice," Lily said. "Shelby and I believe in you, and we believe in the adults who say this will work."

"The other anchors will be Elle and the one person we haven't yet figured out," Viv said. "But we will. I had a vision."

"Bev and I will stand against the darkness," Evie said.

Kevin scoffed. "What good will two mortals be against the primordial dark?"

Evie smiled at him, and it was terrifying. "Look me in the eye and tell me there is anything that could get through me to hurt my child. I don't do this for you. I am doing this for her. She believes in you, and I believe in her. Don't screw this up."

Kevin looked suitably taken aback. "Good choice," he murmured. His eyes drooped. "Sorry. So tired. I am losing my grip on my mortal self. I hate it when I talk like a weirdo and not like Kevin. Who else?"

"Me," Viv said.

"Good," Kevin said. "Your visions are what brought us together and found a way through this. But you need someone to balance you."

"Me," Sam said. "A demon is exactly what you need to see the darkness and push it back."

"So everyone is in place but one," he mused. "We will need to find the final piece. I don't have much time left."

"Tomorrow at noon, when the darkness is at its weakest," Sam said. "On the island that was born for you."

"Tomorrow at noon," Kevin said. "And now, I need a nap."

"We'll take you upstairs," Lily said. "You'll be safe with us."

The girls led Kevin out of the room, and all eyes turned to Viv.

"We have less than seventeen hours to put the final touches into place and find our missing person." She ground her teeth. "It's so close I can almost see it. If Brandon isn't the anchor we need, it has to be something similar. Who else... Oh. Oh no." Viv shook her head.

"If you don't spit it out right this instant, I will hop over this table and shake you until you tell us what you realized," Evie threatened.

"It's Brandy," Viv said. "A mother's tears... I should've seen it. There is no part of this that will not be fantastic." She hung her head into her hands and closed her eyes. "Guess I should go talk to her?"

"I'll come with," Sam said. "She doesn't hate me as much as she hates the rest of you."

"Thanks, Sam." Viv stood and headed to the door. "Might as well get it over with before I chicken out and risk all our lives for nothing."

As she reached for the handle, the doorbell rang, causing Viv to jump back several steps and tread on Sam's foot.

"Sorry," she muttered, then pulled open the door.

Gwen and Brandy stood on the porch, identical expressions of suspicion and simmering anger on their faces.

"I brought brownies," Gwen said, handing over a large container that smelled like chocolate and comfort. "I want to apologize to my sister and see if I can make things right."

"I'm just her ride," Brandy said.

"Please, come in, both of you," Viv said, opening the door wide. "I'll go put these brownies in the kitchen and remind the kids that they've already brushed their teeth, so they'll have to wait until tomorrow for their sweets."

CHAPTER TWENTY-ONE

V iv was busy sliding the container of brownies into a box, trying to touch everything as little as possible when Sam came in.

"Your mother is vibrating with some kind of power I don't recognize," Sam muttered. "I've never noticed it before, but we need to be very, very careful. Don't antagonize her until we figure out what's going on."

"Antagonize her? I never antagonize her. She is a toxic person who it full of bitterness and hate. What could I possibly say that would antagonize her?" Viv shouted under her breath as she glared at Sam. Viv finished taping up the box, wrote "GWEN'S BROWNIES: EVIDENCE, DO NOT EAT," on the box, and slid it on top of the fridge.

"I'm sorry. I said it wrong. I should've said, 'Don't take her bait, no matter how awful she is.' I don't know what'll happen if she decides her black magic brownies aren't fast enough. Black magic. Of course. How could we all have missed it? Whatever you do, don't let her leave before I get back." Sam turned and sprinted out of the house, wings streaming out behind her before the door even closed.

Viv shook her head and stared at the door. Sam was often impulsive, but usually she managed to at least offer an understandable explanation before disappearing. She shrugged; maybe she'd start working on the virtue of patience. Viv grabbed a stack of glasses and the pitcher of lemonade and walked through the swinging door to the dining room. "Lemonade?"

After dropping off the drinks, Viv headed to the back to talk to Grace, Quinn, and Lilith.

"My mother is here," Viv announced with zero fanfare. "She says she wants to apologize and make things right, but she brought a tray of brownies. Sam said Gwen's vibrating with strange power and requested that no one fight with her."

"Is that why she flew out of here like a bat out of hell?" Lilith asked.

"Children," Quinn said. "Always with the bad jokes. We will come in and not pick fights. Does she know I'm here or should Lilith and I wait behind so as not to 'freak her out' as the kids say?"

"I need you there," Grace said, shrinking into the circle of his arm.

"I will not be far behind. I will never endanger you—we lost too much time already." Quinn pulled her closer. "We will be just out of sight, but close enough to intervene if necessary. If it even looks like she's planning an encore of her act fifty years ago, Lilith and I will grab you and take you home. If that's okay with you."

Grace took a deep breath. "Yes. I'd like to stay longer, tie up loose ends, get to know my niece and maybe visit Hope, but I'd rather go now than risk being separated from you again."

Grace and Quinn rose as one and walked into the house. Viv and Lilith followed.

"Say the word," Lilith said under her breath, "and I will blast her out of this world for what she's done to my family."

"Like Grace, I'd rather it not come to that, but I will not allow anyone here to be in any more danger than we already are." Viv held the door for Lilith and walked into the kitchen.

Quinn kissed Grace, and there was so much longing and passion in that kiss that Viv had to look away.

"I'll be right here," Quinn said, moving to the side of the doorway. "You will be safe."

Grace walked through the door and faced her sister. "I know what you did to father, what you tried to do to me."

"Dammit!" Viv said and rushed after Grace. So much for not antagonizing her.

"I don't know what you're talking about," Gwen said. "Fifty years is a long time, and all I remember is my grief when father died compounded when you committed suicide. I don't know where you've been for the last fifty years, but I imagine it messed with your memories."

Viv grabbed Grace's hand and squeezed hard. "It's been a trying twenty-four hours," Viv said. "Evie? Do you want to get us all some of those brownies? They smelled magical."

Gwen smiled, and if Viv hadn't been watching for it, she would've missed the dark spark of satisfaction that shone and winked out.

Evie returned with a plate of brownies, much too quickly to have opened, cut, and served Gwen's, but hopefully she wouldn't have noticed. She grabbed one for herself and passed the tray around.

When it got to Gwen, she eyed it regretfully. "I'm afraid I licked the bowl and ruined my appetite for chocolate today." She passed the tray to Brandy, who hadn't said anything since she'd walked in.

Brandy took a brownie, but before she could take a bite, Gwen put a hand on her arm.

"Do you really want to eat that?" Gwen asked. "The other ladies here are slim, well except for Bev, but you..." Gwen stared at Brandy until the woman dropped her brownie.

"I feel silly not knowing this, but have you two hung out a lot in the last thirty years?" Viv asked.

"Oh yes," Gwen said. "She's like the daughter I never had. So willing to repent of her sins to make things right. A proper church goer who is alight with the love of Jesus."

Viv, Bev, and Evie exchanged a glance. This explained a lot.

Brandy nodded, and the expression Viv was used to seeing on her face—smug superiority—replaced the hurt Gwen's words had installed. "You might have noticed if you'd been a better daughter and paid a little attention to her instead of running off to spend time with your stupid little friends."

Bev laughed, and it startled everyone at the table. She grabbed a brownie and took a big bite.

Viv watched Gwen watch Bev, and at that moment, she knew it was all true.

"Guenevere, you should leave," Viv said. "You've dropped off your brownies, and I'm sure someone here will send you a thank you note tomorrow. But right now, we have more important things to do than sit around and let you gloat at us. Whatever you game is, you need to play it later."

Gwen stood. "You don't have to be so cruel. I just wanted to see my baby sister, found after all these years, and bring her one of my famous brownies. She used to love them as a kid. She'd gobble them up...couldn't get enough. The Lord works in mysterious ways, and He never gives us challenges we can't bear. This town, and especially you, Genevieve, are my crosses, and I will not rest until you're all saved. Brandy, if you'd be so kind as to drive me home."

Brandy started to rise, but Luc, who was sitting next to her, put a hand on her shoulder. "We'd like you to stay. There's something we need to discuss with you."

"I have nothing to say to any of you, and Miss Gwen needs a ride home." Brandy pushed past Luc's hand and shoved her chair back to stand next to Gwen.

"It's about your son," Bev said. "He needs your help. We all need your help."

"What help could she give you that you can't talk about in front of me?" Gwen scoffed. "She's not strong nor particularly bright. Or is that why you need her? Someone too stupid to ask questions?"

"Wow," Viv said. "That sounds so much worse when it's directed at someone else, even when that person is Brandy. You can walk home and think about everything you've done."

Gwen sat back down. "I'm not leaving."

"Good," Sam said, striding into the room. She dropped a large, slate mirror framed in tarnished silver and a soft-ball sized unpolished jet-black rock with sharp edges and the barest hint of striation —almost like a hunk of coal but emanating an energy that felt like air before lightning strikes. "Look what I found in Gwen's room. Wonder what would happen if we put the rock on the mirror and requested an audience?"

"What are you doing?" Gwen shrieked. "Those are mine! Give them back."

"Black magic? Really?" Luc asked. "That's something not even a demon would stoop to. Aren't there verses in the Bible specifically forbidding witchcraft?"

"It's not witchcraft," Gwen said, making a grab for the stone. "There's no such thing. But how dare you break into my house and steal my private belongings."

Sam dropped a book on the table next to the mirror and stone. "If you want to check the bookmarked pages, I think you'll find a spell of compulsion and stasis. That's the one she used on Grace and tried to use on Evie…and who knows how many others are down there. Kevin said a half dozen. There's also a spell to bind and banish demons, which I'm assuming is what happened to Quinn and Lilith. I'm a little surprised she hasn't used that on anyone else here, but I guess Gwen does work in mysterious ways."

"Why would I waste this on the demon familiars of the family who stole mine away?" Gwen scoffed. "You were beyond saving, and I like watching your descent into hell."

Sam dropped one more thing on the table. It was a tin, like the kind you'd package Christmas cookies in, and the beatific face of a very white Jesus smiled up at them.

"I was following everything up until now," Viv admitted. "What's the Jesus tin have to do with anything?"

"No one take a deep breath. And Luc, why don't you keep hold of Gwen for us." Sam popped the lid and revealed several small bottles, each filled with a light grey powder. "Look at that. Someone wears her Jesus on her sleeve but keeps arsenic in the cupboard. I'm not an expert, but that doesn't seem like the answer to 'what would Jesus do?' does it…"

"You have no idea what you're talking about. You are a creature of hell and you and everyone here are damned to burn for eternity."

"You're one to talk," Bev said. "If anyone here has committed unforgivable sins and damned themselves, it's you, Gwen. I don't know how you're doing it and what you're doing, but the dead are crying out for your soul."

"Hell doesn't want her," Sam said. She put the lid back on the Jesus tin and dropped it on the sideboard behind her.

"Heaven has already closed the gates to you," Elle said. "You are not acting on behalf of the God you claim you serve."

"What happens if you have nowhere to go?" Bev asked.

"You are claimed by the spirits of those you destroyed in life, and they feed on your soul until you're nothing but pain and memories." Sam grinned at Gwen and the older woman shrank back and paled.

A moment later, she regained her composure. "I have done everything with the aid of an angel who came to me when my mother died and showed me the way to save everyone I loved. I am worthy of heaven. Now I'm leaving. Come on, Brandy."

Brandy was staring at Gwen with dawning horror. "You're a murderer," she whispered, then glanced around the table. "The brownies! Oh no, you all ate them!"

"It's okay, Brandy," Evie reassured her. "They're not the ones Gwen brought. But why don't you stay here. It'll be safer. Kind of."

"We should call the police," Brandy said. Her voice was barely audible, and for the third time in less than two weeks, Viv found herself feeling sorry for her.

"Hi Gwen, remember me?" Quinn walked into the room with Lilith behind him. "Since everyone else has gotten to have their say, I wanted to make sure we got a chance to reunite before human justice catches up with you."

Gwen jumped to her feet and pulled the crystal and mirror from the center of the table to the space in front of her. She pulled a feather out of her pocket—it was black and iridescent, and it didn't look quite right, not like any bird feather Viv had ever seen.

"So that's how you did it; you stole one of my feathers," Quinn said. He started backing away from the table but froze after two steps. "Get out of here, Lilith. And could someone stop her?"

"I'm trying, but whatever power she's tapped into, whatever dark magic she found, it's holding us all." Lilith's voice was steady and even —the exact opposite of how Viv was positive she'd sound if she spoke.

Gwen cackled loudly, and madness flashed in her eyes. She moved the crystal to the center of the mirror, dropped the feather next to it, pulled a pocketknife out of the pocketbook she'd set on the table, and pricked her finger. With her eyes fixed on Quinn, she let fall a single drop of blood onto the feather. Dark smoke burst forth from the feather and pushed outward, first in an expanding bubble, but soon, it found its target and became a rapidly solidifying net locked on Quinn.

"No! You won't take any more people," Kevin yelled, running into the room and placing himself between the demon and the net. The net wrapped itself around the boy, obscuring him from view.

Viv watched in horror, still unable to move, as Kevin started to fade from view. This was not how it was supposed to happen.

Water dripped from the darkness that had been Kevin. It was black and oily and foul smelling.

Viv reached up to cover her nose and only after she'd moved did she realize she could.

Kevin wavered in and out of view, and the water flowed faster.

"It's dissolving from the bottom," Bev said. "Like it's melting."

She was right, and Viv's attention was captivated by the scene unfolding in front of her. Soon, Kevin's feet were visible, and after what seemed an interminable amount of time, he was free to the waist. The more the net dissolved, the clearer the water became, washing away the foulness that had gathered on Evie's floor.

As Kevin was freed, everyone else in the room found they were able to move more freely. First hands and arms, then shoulders, torso, waist.

Gwen watched in horrified shock. "This isn't possible. How can that evil child block the demon binding?"

The net was almost to Kevin's chest now, but the rate at which it was disappearing slowed to a crawl, then reversed itself, knitting back down Kevin's body. A stream of thin, twisting fog reached out and wrapped itself around Gwen, holding her in place.

Gwen sagged against the table, and the net unraveled, quickly now. When Kevin's arms were completely free, the water from his body was running clear and the mist holding Gwen coalesced into a watery rope.

Kevin freed himself, but the face that broke free from the net no longer resembled the little boy Viv had known for the last six years.

He was grey, and his head had elongated into an almost squid-like shape. Brilliant green eyes stared at Gwen, and his arms lengthened and split into tentacles.

Gwen slumped against the table and started to slide out of her seat before Viv figured out what was happening.

The monster of the lake had woken, and in order to save Quinn, had burned through the remainder of its energy and was replenishing itself.

"Kevin, no!" Shelby screamed.

"Stop! You can't do this!" Lily ran into the room, skidded across the wet floor, and threw her arms around Kevin.

Shelby followed and grabbed him from the other side.

Bev and Evie were on their feet in a flash.

"Lily, let go! You have to let go." Evie sounded panicked. She grabbed Lily and tried to pull her off, but Kevin's new tentacles had wrapped around the waists of each of the girls who were so desperate to save him.

Bev didn't say anything, just put her arms around Shelby and held on.

Slowly, the rope of water released from Gwen and traveled back into Kevin. Once he'd completely reabsorbed it, his tentacles shortened and joined, turning back into arms as his head regained its human shape. He collapsed on the ground, Lily and Shelby guiding him down.

Elle rushed forward, gathered him in her arms, and sobbed.

The scraping of a chair was all that alerted Viv that her mother had revived.

Gwen stood up on shaky legs, grabbed the mirror, feather, and crystal in front of her, and ran.

"I'll keep an eye on her," Lilith said. "It's about time I spent some quality time with my aunt."

"See if you can figure out who—or what—is feeding her this power," Quinn said. "It's beyond the realm of human abilities."

"And don't hurt her," Grace said. "At least not too much."

Lilith flashed a quick, predatory smile at her parents. "I'll be good, Mom and Dad. Promise."

CHAPTER TWENTY-TWO

Viv stood in the small crowd who'd gathered at Evie's dock. There were—she counted—ten people ready to row to the island and five on the shore who were staying behind.

Evie and Lily had their arms around Luc who was holding baby Alex while Grace, Quinn, and Lilith stood back, not interacting, merely observing.

Viv wanted to reassure those being left behind that this was a formality, it'd be easy and safe, and they'd all come back, but she couldn't.

"If we thought this was a suicide mission, we wouldn't be doing it," Bev said, coming to stand next to Viv. "I love that little lake monster, almost as if he was my own, and I might risk my life to save him, but I'd never risk Shelby's. And you know Evie well enough that she wouldn't be doing this if she believed Lily was in mortal danger. So, take a breath and let go of whatever fears are riding you." Bev leaned in close and whispered, "We both know that's not what you want riding you…"

Viv gasped and tried to stifle her inappropriate laughter. "Beverly Hill, you are a degenerate. My mother was right about you." At the mention of her mother, Viv stopped laughing. "Yeah. Too soon, I guess. Maybe I can make jokes about it when I'm confident my mother can't hurt anyone and I figure out why I'm still walking and talking instead of six feet under—either the lake or the ground."

"We're safe from her, at least for the moment. I know we just met your demon princess cousin, but when she says Gwen's not going to escape, I feel inclined to trust her." Bev bumped Viv's shoulder lightly with her own. "I'm going to subject my kid to some hugs and see if Elle needs anything."

"You're going to subject your kid to some hugs and try to figure out what Brandon's deal is," Viv countered. "He hasn't said a word since he showed up with Elle."

"He's so weird, right? Really hot, but weird. He hasn't said a word today and doesn't even seem remotely interested in what's going on. I can't figure him out, but we have a few moments, so I'm going to try." Bev bumped Viv again, then walked the few feet to the other side of the dock, slipped an arm around Shelby, who was standing next to Kevin, and said something Viv couldn't hear.

Brandy was standing alone and looking more than a little forlorn at the end of the dock, and Viv was trying to make up her mind whether or not to go talk to her. Brandy'd had a rough couple days to cap off a rough couple weeks...and probably a rough few decades if Gwen had been standing in as a surrogate mother who refused to be seen with her in public.

"The canoes are ready," Sam said. "But remember, if you don't want to boat, I can take you across the speedy way." Her wings popped out and she spread them, letting them waft in the breeze.

"Tempting," Viv said, lips pursed.

"I hope so. I am a demon, after all. Tempting is in the job description." Sam leaned forward and brushed a kiss across Viv's lips.

Viv moved forward, pressing into Sam and deepening the kiss until they were skirting the bounds of propriety. They broke apart, breathing heavily. Goose bumps erupted across Viv's skin, and she shivered. "We're definitely getting through this, because I refuse to live in a world where I never get to kiss you again."

Sam trailed a finger along Viv's jawline. "We're going to live. It will be enough—we will be enough. In a couple hours, we'll be back on shore. Brandy will call her bff the sheriff and present the evidence of Gwen's wrongdoing. She'll be arrested and eventually convicted of attempted murder and, if they can exhume your father's body, probably murder as well. Once she's been hauled off in the paddy wagon, you and I are going to take a very extended vacation."

"A vacation? Where?" Viv was hypnotized by the heat in Sam's glowing amber eyes.

Sam pulled a key out of the pocket of her black leggings. "I paid Bev through the end of the year for her cabin. I don't know what we'll end up doing or where we're going, but at least for the next six months, that can be our refuge." She captured Viv's hand, turned it over, and dropped the key into her palm, pressing her fingers tight around it. "Now, go talk to Brandy while I round everyone up and hand out life jackets. I'll be your cruise director for the day."

Viv reluctantly pulled away from Sam, tucked the key into the zipper pocket in her leggings, and went to round up Brandy.

THE THIRD AND final canoe drifted onto the shore of the mysterious island.

"I hope this island doesn't disappear when we break Kevin's tie to the lake." Viv winced when two sets of eyes turned towards her and glared.

"It'll be fine either way," Sam said. "There are enough wings in the area to get everyone to safety if you start to get a sinking feeling. Between Elle and me, we can probably drop everyone into a canoe before you even get your socks wet. Faster if Lily's wings have sprouted." She looked at Lily who shook her head, an expression of profound despair on her face.

"Not yet, Aunt Sam. Papa Abe says because I'm half human, I might never get wings." Lily sounded so dejected Viv was torn between snickering and dropping to her knees to comfort her honorary niece.

"It's fine, kiddo," Sam said. "You're a couple years from puberty yet, and I'll bet they'll show up then."

"It'll be a nice balance to menstruation," Shelby said, affecting an academic air and pushing up imaginary glasses.

"Two sets of wings will be enough to get us to the canoes," Sam said. "And if we need more, Luc, Quinn, and Lilith—a half demon with gorgeous wings—aren't too far away. We will be fine."

Viv took a deep breath, conscious of everyone's eyes on her waiting for instruction. She should've had Sam bring her over early so she could scout the lay of the land and find the best place for dark rituals. She turned her back on the shore and scanned the tree line starting less than five feet away. Branches shifted in the breeze, and a path appeared between two large conifers that were the absolute opposite of anything Bob Ross had ever painted.

"This way," Viv said, trying to project more confidence than she felt. Viv walked towards the trees and onto the path. The branches of the firs brushed against her shoulders, and for a moment she thought they were going to hold her back and refuse to let her pass, but then they yielded, and she plunged into almost perfect darkness.

No one had told the interior of the island it was nearly noon, and Viv was forced to pull her phone out of the pocket of her leggings and turn on the light to see where she was going. The path was perfectly smooth without a rock or root to trip them up and straight enough that the light was almost unnecessary.

They walked for about twenty minutes and Viv was uncomfortably reminded of the trip she'd made into hell with Evie and Bev the year before, although that'd been too bright, while this was too dark.

"I don't suppose anyone brought snacks this time," Evie commented. "We definitely prepared more for our last spooky hike."

The island seemed to be bigger on the inside—Viv could've sworn they'd walked long enough to come out on the other side already. Finally, it spit them out into a perfectly round clearing. The trees ended abruptly, and blue sky framed by the crowns of the old growth trees appeared above. The grass was soft and spring green, and a stream burbled forth from a spring in the center of the circle.

"Guess this is the place," Viv said. She glanced at her watch. "It's almost noon. Does anyone have any questions before we get started?"

Everyone shook their heads except Brandy, Kevin, and Brandon. Kevin walked to the center and sat in the spring, crossing his legs and closing his eyes.

"Okay. Kevin is in position. Lily and Shelby, if you want to get into position, then Brandy and Elle, we can start the ritual."

Lily and Shelby sat down on either side of Kevin, facing each other with him in the middle. Lily took Kevin's right hand with her left, reached behind Kevin with her right hand to clasp Shelby's left, and Shelby held Kevin's free hand with her right. They leaned in and rested their foreheads on either side of Kevin's head.

"It's all gonna be okay, Kevin. We're gonna be bffs forever," Lily whispered, her voice carrying across the clearing that was devoid of any sounds other than those made by the current occupants.

"Bffs forever is redundant," Kevin said.

"Smartass," Shelby retorted.

"Better that than a dumbass. Let's get this show on the road. My butt is getting super wet." Kevin shifted a bit, and the water started flowing over him and reaching out to ripple lightly against the other children.

"Brandy and Elle?" Viv said. "And whatever you're doing with Brandon, I guess."

Elle walked forward and stood behind Kevin. Brandon walked with her and knelt between her and Kevin. He was silent and slack faced. Less himbo territory and more soulless automaton.

"Elle, is Brandon okay?" Viv asked. "If he's not, he can wait at the edge."

"He's fine. We'll do what's needed."

Brandy didn't move. "I don't think this is a good idea."

"That would've been a good thing to say last night. Or before we hopped in the canoe. But now? We're kind of all in. Without you, this won't work." Viv smiled encouragingly at Brandy, hoping the pseudo-flattery would motivate her.

Brandy crossed her arms. "This is stupid, like some magic trick kids do at slumber parties. Light as a feather stuff, or bloody Mary. It makes zero sense. I don't know what happened yesterday, and I don't know why I'm here today, but this is all bullshit, and you're all crazy."

"We went over this last night," Bev said with infinitely more patience than Viv felt as she watched the minutes tick by on her watch. "You know Kevin's conception wasn't typical. Jer's not his father, so where did you think he came from?"

"It had to have been Jer," Brandy said, thrusting her chin forward stubbornly. "Nothing else makes sense."

"You saw what happened last night. You're trying to stave away your fear with defiance and petty meanness, but you know he's not human. However, he's still your son, and now he needs your help to stay here, to *become* human. If you help him now, you'll not only save his life, but the lives of so many people who come to Eden Lake and can't resist the water. Please, Brandy." Bev's soft voice pleaded so gently and convincingly that Viv was ready to agree to anything Bev wanted.

"I can make you," Evie said. "But I'd rather you do this because it's the right thing to do."

"I'll play your stupid games on one condition. Kevin comes to live with me and Jer. If I 'save his life,' it's because everyone here recognizes me as his mother. I should get him back." Brandy stared defiantly at Viv as she carved the air quotes out of the space between them, then turned her attention to Elle. "You tricked me into giving him up. I would've kept him if it wasn't for you."

"Brandess Miller, I chose you to bear me and Aurielle to raise me. You are both my mothers, and you do not get to fight over me. When we get through this, I'd be happy to spend more time with you, but there are reasons Aurielle was chosen for this role, and you were not." Kevin opened his eyes and glanced towards Brandy. "If you want me to live, however, then take your place. The reason we cannot do this without you is because you are my mother as much as she is."

Brandy hesitated and shifted from foot to foot, looking suddenly less certain now that her needs were in danger of being met.

"Please." Kevin closed his eyes again and once more settled into the meditative pose flanked by his two best friends.

Brandy snorted in disgust and stomped over to take her place at Kevin's head. She sank to her knees in front of him and reached out and touched his face. "I'm sorry I wasn't enough for you," she said, almost too quietly to be heard by anyone else.

"It's okay. You were enough then and you'll be enough now." Kevin smiled at her until her face softened, then closed his eyes looking more exhausted and run down than any child should ever look.

Viv and Sam took their places, facing each other. They were a quarter of a turn around the circle and slightly further out. Viv was between Elle and Shelby and Sam stood between Brandy and Lily. Bev and Evie completed the circle, each closest to her own child.

Thunder clapped when Evie and Bev settled into place, and dark clouds rolled in to block out the sun.

"This is it," Kevin said, voice vibrating with tension. "I hope it's enough."

CHAPTER TWENTY-THREE

Tension pulled Viv's body taut like a bowstring ready to release an arrow into the oncoming horde. Sam had the lion's share of the work now. She was responsible for saying the words that would bind the ritual; a demon ritual needed a demon to make it work.

The wind whipped up, and although Viv could see Sam's mouth moving, she couldn't hear the words. The effects of the ritual were made known almost immediately. The darkness of the storm clouds swirled down, and the spring in the center of the island bubbled up to meet it. A waterspout and a tornado joined forces in a localized vortex with Lily, Shelby, and Kevin at the core.

It was hard to stay still, to not rush forward and pull the children out, but Viv forced herself to stay put. She concentrated her gaze on Evie. If Evie was staying still, so could Viv.

The vortex began to thin and become translucent, and the children were visible again. They looked serene and unbothered.

Obviously more fearless and resilient than me, Viv thought. Brandy did not look serene. Her eyes were wide, and terror vibrated her body. She wrapped herself in her arms and rocked back and forth from her position on her knees.

Viv tried to will her to stay in place. They wouldn't get a second chance at this.

Brandy kept rocking but didn't get up.

It was Elle, though, who captured most of her attention. She stood behind the still-kneeling Brandon, and she was glowing. Where her light touched, the darkness began to recede. Silver wings with gold barring erupted from her back, and her face was almost too bright to look at. The vortexes began to separate and return to earth and sky from whence they came.

The earth shook, and Elle lost her balance. The darkness shot back into place, and the children once more disappeared from view.

It pressed outward, palpably. It didn't feel evil, but it was oily. Old. From a time before good and evil had separated. It was primordial and hungry, and it was testing each of them to feed that aching hunger.

Images flickered around Viv, and she didn't know where to turn her attention. Should she look at the one where she held Sam's lifeless body? The one watching Evie and Bev mourn their children? The one where Kevin morphed into the monster they'd gotten a glimpse of the night before and devoured everyone on the island, then in Eden Valley, before spreading across the state to consume everything in his path.

She shook her head. These didn't feel like the flashes of the future she'd gotten before. It felt like something was forcing them on her from outside.

Still, the darkness spread, pushing against the four women whose strength contained the tenebrosity that had created Kevin and wanted him back.

Tendrils explored the unseen barrier, looking for weakness. Viv's knees wobbled. She was getting shakier. She could no longer see anyone else nor hear Sam and had to hold onto the hope that everyone was holding on. Viv couldn't tell how long it'd been, minutes or hours—either seemed likely.

When she was about to give in and admit defeat, a sound finally permeated the smothering blanket that was wrapped around her. She stood a little taller and concentrated on the sound.

Again, she heard it, but it was too far away to identify.

Once more, and this time she recognized it. It was the deep, booming three-part barking harmony of an overprotective and fiercely loyal hellhound. Sprinkles had followed Lily and found them.

As Sprinkles ran into the circle, the darkness was disrupted, and Viv could see everything Sprinkles left in her wake.

Elle was standing behind Kevin, light once more streaming from her body and wings spread out behind her, piercing the darkness. She reached down and placed her hands around Brand's neck.

For a moment, Viv thought Elle was going to strangle the man she'd been living with for eleven years, but before that thought could come all the way to completion, Elle raised her arms and the man-shape that was Brand transformed into a burning sword.

Elle held the sword over her head, and the flames shot skyward. Then she swung and severed the rope of darkness binding Kevin.

The darkness fell away and leached into the soil of the clearing. The clouds rose into the sky, which still roiled and flashed with lightning, but no longer lay like a shroud over the clearing. The grass in the clearing had died in a perfect circle that extended six inches beyond the circle Viv, Sam, Evie, and Bev had created with their bodies.

Sprinkles sank to her haunches in front of the children and laid one head in each of their laps.

Viv heaved a sigh of relief. This was what was supposed to happen. More or less. She'd seen Elle cut the ribbons that tied Kevin to the lake but had assumed that was either metaphorical or would involve a good pair of scissors, maybe a pocketknife.

A flaming sword had not entered her imagination, and she was having a hard time reconciling what'd happened and what she was seeing now with what was possible.

Viv looked across the circle to Sam. "Is it over? Can we move?"

Sam's chin dipped down in the beginning of a nod when Bev screamed.

"The dead are coming," Shelby said. "The barrier holding them back is gone."

Bev fainted.

THE GROUND BOILED and erupted around where Viv sat, cradling Bev in her lap, arms wrapped protectively around her. It was like the worst zombie horror movie Viv had ever seen. Hands appeared first, then arms, pulling themselves out.

Evie and Elle had rushed forward to shield the children, and Brandy was keening shrilly from where she still knelt. Sam had gone to Brandy's side and was trying to convince her to get up and join Viv and Bev but was having zero luck getting her to move. Sam's wings burst forth from her back, and she wrapped one arm around Brandy and launched into the sky.

Or tried to. Her feet didn't leave the ground. There was a hand locked around her ankle holding her back. The harder she strained, the further the arm came out of the ground.

The bodies kept coming. Many were free to their waists now, and Viv was getting an up close and personal glimpse of their faces. They were dripping and coated with green, slimy algae. Seaweed hung from their hair and limbs. They were naked, mostly, their clothes rotted away from years and decades and centuries under the water, and every single body was missing its eyes.

Sticks started pushing through the ground, like rapidly growing leafless trees. Soon, they branched out, then a head appeared beneath them. An elk broke through the ground, then the beginnings of a bear appeared.

Everything that had ever died in this lake was rising, and they had no way to leave. Never in her wildest imagination or most alarming visions had "zombie apocalypse" been a possibility. If she made it through this, Viv was asking for a refund on her psychic powers.

Panic fluttered in her chest as the first human completely emerged from the ground, turned around, and started towards her and the still-unconscious Bev.

"STOP!" Shelby burst to her feet and spun a slow circle, taking in the dripping corpses of people and animals that were filling the clearing.

Everything froze, living beings included. Everyone but Shelby. A slow smile crept onto Shelby's face, and an icy tendril of fear, colder even than the bodies of the dead surrounding her, ran across Viv's skin.

The dead rotated to face Shelby, moving in a perfect unison that turned the creep factor up to eleven. When she had everyone's attention, Shelby reached out her arms. Her smile now exuded warmth and calm. She held out her hands. Aurielle took one, stepping forward with her flaming sword to join Shelby in the center of the clearing. Sam walked forward and took the other.

"You can rest now, if you want," Shelby offered. "If you want to cross over, we will make a doorway for you. You'll no longer simply exist with nothing but anger and pain. You can move on." Shelby lifted her arms into the sky, lifting Sam's and Elle's with her, and their bodies made two doorways, both churning with golden light.

At first, nothing happened. Viv held her breath, afraid to even move lest she disrupt whatever Shelby was doing.

The elk to Viv's right scrambled the rest of the way to its feet and shambled forward. When it reached Shelby, it dropped its great head in a facsimile of a bow and walked towards the opening between Shelby and Aurielle. Its antlers dissolved in light, and the great beast disappeared.

A bear was next, following the elk through the same doorway, then the first person stepped forward. He, too, paused when he reached the three figures—nearly all the same height now. After a moment, he ducked between Shelby and Sam. The golden glow sparked red and orange, then returned to the golden swirl. A second person followed the first, then a child approached and, without a pause, walked between Elle and Shelby. This time, the doorway sparked silver and blue.

The dead were pulling themselves out of the ground, faster and faster, but it seemed there was no end to it. Animals of all sizes, predators and prey, pushed through the doorway between Shelby and Elle that Viv was starting to think of as heaven. The humans were split evenly between the two doors, and all the child-sized bodies except one walked through the heavenly door.

Finally, the rush slowed to a crawl. Shelby's arms were trembling with effort and sweat dripped down her face. The last body in the clearing was the first one who'd emerged. He was a little shorter than Shelby and hesitated in front of her. He glanced right, then left, but seemed unable to decide.

"I didn't know," he said, his voice carrying across the clearing. "I wanted to live forever." He turned around in a complete circle. Mud was molded to him, and he was draped in rotting algae, but his face was familiar.

It was Kevin.

Viv jumped to her feet. There was no way she was going to let this end like this. They'd been through too much to allow Kevin to walk away.

Before Viv got to him, though, the figure still cross-legged on the ground next to Lily got to his feet.

The zombie Kevin—Viv didn't know how else to describe him—reached out to human Kevin. They clasped hands for a moment before the Kevin who'd risen through the earth moments before spoke, his words enveloping everyone in the clearing. "I'm sorry. Goodbye."

He walked towards the doorway made by Sam's and Shelby's arms, then stopped, arms raised as if standing on the edge of a pool, before diving into the ground in front of the swirling gate. As he disappeared, tentacles streamed out behind him, waving in the air until the earth swallowed him completely. Shelby dropped her arms and sat hard on the ground.

Two pairs of arms snaked around her waist and held her close.

Kevin rested his face against Shelby's shoulder. "For a moment, I thought I wouldn't be able to stay, that the lake would take me after all. Thank you."

"You're scary," Lily said against Shelby's other side. "That's pretty cool."

Shelby grinned, but her eyelids were drooping in exhaustion. "I want to go home."

Sam stumbled a bit, then picked Shelby up. "I got you tiny necromancer. Hold on tight."

"I am not tiny. I'm almost as tall as you." Shelby put her arms around Sam's neck while Sam scooped the girl into her arms.

Viv returned to Bev who was finally starting to come to.

"What'd I miss? Is it over?" Bev rubbed her eyes as she looked around. "Where's Shelby and why does the ground look like a cross between the aftermath of a rodeo and a music festival?"

"Sam's taking Shelby back to the house," Evie said, helping Lily stand up. "She's fine—saved all of our lives."

"Ugh," Bev groaned. "I hate getting shown up—again—by my preteen. I might need to do some work on myself so I can handle the...whatever that was."

"Zombie apocalypse. You missed the whole thing." Kevin was flushed, and for the first time in days looked healthy and energetic. "It was awesome."

Sprinkles ran around the perimeter of the clearing barking and chasing the army of dragonflies that had filled the space above them.

"Brandy? You okay, girl?" Viv asked.

"No, I am not okay. You all are crazy, and I am getting out of here as soon as I can. I don't care if Jer wants to come with me or not. He can stay here with his stupid horses and his stupid trucks and his stupid farm and his stupid bleeding ulcers. I am done with this town and with all of you." Brandy climbed to her feet and marched across the clearing and into the trees.

"She's gonna take one of the canoes, isn't she?" Evie asked.

"Definitely," Viv replied. "I guess we should follow her. "Elle, how are you? How's your husband's sword?"

Evie snorted.

"What's so funny, Mama?" Lily asked.

Viv tilted her head at Evie. "Yeah, what's so... Oh my god. You are a monster."

Bev dissolved into giggles, and even Elle cracked a smile. Nothing like a dick joke to bring a bunch of middle-aged women together.

"I wouldn't know. I've had this sword for millennia, and still nothing... Not even in human shape. Huge disappointment." Elle smirked, eyes dancing in amusement under her curly dark hair.

Sam landed hard in the center of the clearing, sinking several inches into the muddy ground. "We need to get out of here fast. I left Shelby on the shore so I could come back and warn you all. The island is starting to sink."

"Finally, something we anticipated!" Viv took a step forward and squelched in the mud. It sucked at her feet, threatening to unshoe her.

"Elle, why don't you grab Kevin and wing him back to the house. Tell Luc, Lilith, and Quinn it's their time to shine." Evie was in her element now. There was a plan, and she was confident. "Sam, go grab Shelby and take her back home. Those of us who can walk will hightail it to shore and take the canoes."

Elle shot up in the air with Kevin, and Sam took off behind her.

"We have to get going." Bev pointed at the rapidly rising water—or was that the rapidly sinking land?

"Right," Evie said. "Lead the way, demon child. We are right behind you."

When they left the trees behind and hit the shore, the water was ankle deep and still rising. None of the three canoes they'd arrived in were on the shore. Two were floating in the expanse of the lake between the island and the public beach and the third was rapidly paddling towards the same beach.

"Did Brandy shove the rest of the canoes away or did they float away with the rising tide?" Bev asked.

Luc swooped down onto the beach and grabbed Lily. He smiled at Evie, then took off towards their house.

Viv, Evie, and Bev stood on the edge of the shore and watched as three figures flew towards them.

"Well, ladies, this was another great Eden Valley vacation," Viv said. "Maybe next time we can try hanging out somewhere else. My friend Charlie left Cairdeas to start making her own wines. She managed to score a parcel of land with built-in caves for aging and storage. That's got to be better than anything else Eden Valley can offer."

"I think a girls' wine weekend sounds fantastic." Bev slipped her arm around Viv's waist.

"If we can convince Sam and Elle to come along, and get Charlie to hang out instead of working, it'll be a whole party," Evie said. She leaned into Viv's other side.

Viv watched the three figures winging their way closer. "Do they seem awfully slow to you? And not very demonic? I was expecting Sam, Lilith, and Quinn, but none of those fliers look familiar to me."

Bev shielded her eyes against the glare of the mid-afternoon sun. "You're right. One has silvery wings, but the other two have wings that look like Elle's."

"Oh no," Evie said. "Do we have more angels? This cannot be good."

The three figures landed in front of Viv and her friends, splashing gently in the water.

"Hi. My name is Barachiel, this is Uriel, and the other guy is Andras. We're angels of the Lord. Kind of. Well, I am. And they were. Andras is a fallen angel slash risen demon, or whatever. Uriel is usually out and about seeking redemption or offering it... I'm actually not quite sure what he's doing most of the time. And I'm reviewing my options and getting sent on boring errands. Anyway, we're here for Aurielle and her fiery sword." The angel's wings moved in time with his arms and their expansive gestures as he rambled.

"Elle isn't on the island anymore. But since you're here, maybe you could fly us back to shore and we can look for her together?" Viv suggested.

"Your wings are gorgeous. May I touch one?" Bev asked Barachiel, reaching out a hand.

"Are you the necromancer?" Barachiel asked, stepping back out of arm's reach. "Russell says hi!"

Viv sighed. "I'm so glad y'all made it, but if you want to talk to Elle, you have to take us to shore. Please. The island is disappearing and none of us particularly want to swim for it."

"We could, though," Evie said. "Now that the monster is gone, it should be safe, right?"

"We'll take you," the one Barachiel had called Andras said. He picked Evie up and took off towards her house.

Barachiel gave Bev a wide berth and grabbed Viv. "You smell like a demon. Are you one?"

"No, but my girlfriend is, so you'd better be nice." Viv glared at the ethereally perfect face above her.

"You're safe with me! I am not interested. In anything." He scooped her up and took off.

Moments later, she was deposited unceremoniously on the dock and into Sam's waiting arms.

"Why did we end up with a bunch of angels—or flying creatures questioning their role in life?" Viv asked, watching Bev hit the deck as she jumped out of her angel-taxi's arms.

Sam shrugged. "They were on their way already, and Quinn said they were trustworthy. Apparently, he knows the handsome one."

"We're all handsome. We're angels." Barachiel crossed his arms and glared at Sam.

Sam stuck her tongue out at Barachiel, and he grimaced at her.

"Where's Aurielle?" Uriel asked.

"Here." Elle walked out of the house and down the path to the lakeside. "The kids are taking turns in the shower and plan to hang out quietly for the rest of the day. I am free to accept whatever punishment you are here to mete." She bowed her head and spread her wings out.

"No one is getting punished," Andras said. "Barachiel and Uriel felt your power escaping from its leash this morning and dragged me along to make sure you were okay. I don't even know why they needed me, but Ceri—Ceridwen, my…person—insisted I come along, so here I am. And unless you need me for something more—brewing advice or a direct line to the underworld, which it appears you already have—I'm going home."

Sam snapped her fingers. "Brewing? Are you the maker of the devilishly good brews? I love your Infernal IPA!"

Andras smiled, and it lit up his face. "You know my beer? You should come to the brewery sometime. There's a lot on tap there that doesn't make it into bottles. Distribution is pretty new. My brewery manager is trying to make us a 'thing.'"

"I am going to take you up on that once we get things straightened out here." Sam winked at him.

Andras laughed and launched himself into the air.

"We do need to talk." Barachiel pointed at Elle's sword, the hilt of which was visible behind her. "I have some very pointed questions for you."

Bev snorted. "Love a good sword pun," she said when Barachiel looked at her.

Barachiel furrowed his brow. Viv watched his lips move as he repeated what he'd said two or three times. Finally, comprehension dawned on his face, and he laughed out loud, sounding delighted in his inadvertent joke. "Sword pun! That *was* funny. I am still getting the hang of Earth humor, but I like puns."

The stench of sulphur rolled over them, nearly bowling Viv over. She glanced at Sam who shrugged.

"Not me, and Luc's up at the house." She looked around. "It'd better not be Mat... He can't avoid the situation in case he's asked to help, then show up at the end."

A burst of yellow smoke made Viv step back several steps.

Abaddon appeared, this time in an electric blue suit. He looked around, widened his eyes when he spotted the angels, but didn't say anything to them. "Did I miss it all? He pushed his lower lip out in a grotesque parody of a pout. "Oops." His gaze returned to the angels. "Do not think you can have what is mine. This town, these people, they belong to me, and you and your Lady cannot take them."

Uriel spoke for the first time since he'd shown up. "Your people are safe from us, but do not think you can claim this town. This place is ours; it's always been ours."

Abe laughed, and the sound waves curdled Viv's stomach and caused a frisson of terror to spread over her body. "If it was yours, I wouldn't be here and none of us would've ever been able to breach the gates. Look to your defenses and ask why we're allowed to walk freely."

Uriel turned to Elle who shrugged. "It's been millennia since the gates were first breached, and I refused—on Her orders—to tell you how then. I'm not going to give up my secrets now, even if I was able. But Abaddon is right. Eden Valley isn't ours any more than it's his. It's neutral ground, and if you take me away from here, we'll cede this territory. We have so few such places left… Do you really want to give up this one?"

Uriel glared at Abaddon who returned the hard stare.

"Watch yourself. I'm going to check on my *granddaughter*." The demon king turned towards the house and the suit melted off him as large wings sprang from his back, and his tail snaked out and up.

"We will be back. There is no reason to worry about what will happen if your town falls to the power of the demons." Barachiel smiled brightly, and his light forced back the stench Abe had left behind.

"That's not as comforting as you might have intended it to be." Bev hadn't taken her eyes off Barachiel since they'd returned to shore.

"Lolz." Barachiel grinned. "I am hip with your tweeting lingo."

"I have so many questions," Evie said, eyes darting between the angels and her future father-in-law. "And at least two of them are why you are the way you are, angel."

"You're not the only one," Viv muttered.

"There are no answers a mortal would understand," Uriel said. "Come, Aurielle. No more delays."

The angels walked to the edge of the water and flew off.

Viv watched them as they disappeared into the distance. When she looked down again, the island had almost disappeared. As the tips of the last redwoods sank below the water, green eyes flashed once before the entire island disappeared with not even a ripple to remind them it had been there only moments before.

"What now?" Viv asked. "We saved the kid and prevented the lake zombie apocalypse, I'm too old for Disneyland, and too tired to hit the bars and do some celebratory dancing."

Sam slipped her hand into Viv's. "You're filthy. Why don't you come back to my place and get cleaned up?"

"I don't have anything clean to change into there." Viv squeezed Sam's hand.

"Exactly." Sam picked Viv up and they flew off.

Evie yelled after them, "Don't do anything I wouldn't do!"

Viv leaned back into Sam's arms and closed her eyes. "Thank you."

"For what?"

"Carrying me when I need it." Viv slipped into sleep, the exhaustion of the last few days dragging her under.

But before she fully succumbed, she heard Sam whisper, "Always for you."

EPILOGUE
THREE MONTHS LATER (MORE OR LESS)

The snap of a rubber glove hitting skin had Viv whirling around. Bev and Evie stood in the doorway, gloves on, hair up, and their grimiest work clothes on.

"Are you read to tackle this?" Evie asked. She looked around the house, nose wrinkled in disgust. The air was permeated with must and dirt that all the open windows and box fans did nothing to chase away.

"I guess so. I'm clearing out my condo and moving all my stuff here in a couple weeks. I don't want it to go into storage, and we can't live in Bev's rental much longer, either. This is my place now, legally and everything, according to this document Grace gave me before she jetted off with Quinn and Lilith. It's time to change things up and make it my own." Viv docked her phone in the speakers and cranked the volume. "We have gloves and mops and gallons of bleach, and now the best playlist in the land. Might as well see if we can make this place livable."

"You're sure there's no more arsenic anywhere?" Bev asked as she reached up and ripped the loose wallpaper, peeling it down the wall in a thin, brittle strip.

"The cops and forensics people were pretty thorough. They took bags and bags of evidence, cleared out everything in the kitchen that could've ever been in contact with arsenic, and destroyed a lot of things that probably didn't need to be destroyed, like light fixtures and the antique sideboard that belonged to my great-grandmother." Viv looked around at the dreary wallpaper weighing down the room. "Didn't check the wallpaper, though. Old wallpaper can be full of arsenic according to at least three true crime documentaries I've seen."

"Cops." Bev shrugged. "I mean, I guess it's good they got your mom off the streets, but..."

Viv walked to the corner of the room and pried up the carpet tack strip. She followed it to its end, then went around the room to get the rest.

"Is Sam joining us?" Evie asked. "Seems like she should be helping if she wants to live here, too."

Viv laughed. "She had 'pressing business' somewhere else today. People need tempting, contracts need signing. You know, day in the life." She pulled up the corner of the shag carpet and started rolling it up. "There's hardwood under here! I was hoping there would be."

"That's better than what's under this brown and gold 70s wallpaper." Bev pulled another strip down. "In case you care, it's more wallpaper. This one is blue and silver and almost as ugly."

"What if it's wallpaper all the way down?" Evie asked. "You could be destroying the structural integrity of the house!"

Bev took the rag she had hanging out of her back pocket and tossed it at Evie. "Whatever, slacker. Get to work."

"Can I help?" Elle asked from the doorway.

"You're back! We were beginning to think you wouldn't return." Evie ran forward and hugged Elle.

"Time passes differently where we took counsel. To me, it seemed like only a few days, and not months. I stopped at home to see Kevin, but he wasn't there. Did Brandy take him?" Elle's teeth worried at her lower lip.

"He's an actual child now and can't be on his own. He's staying with us for now. Brandy disappeared, leaving Jer behind, and no one's heard from her since. The DA is pretty mad because she wanted Brandy to testify against Gwen, but here we are." Evie shrugged. "Guess that 'I want to be a mother' talk was just talk after all."

Elle sighed in relief. "I hope he'll want to come live with me again. I kind of miss being his mom."

"You can ask him yourself," Evie said. "We're doing dinner and wine tonight at my place to celebrate day one of fixing up Viv's new place."

"That sounds wonderful. How can I help?" Elle pushed up the sleeves of the gold shirt she was wearing and looked around.

"As long as you don't expect me to pitch in," Barachiel grumbled from the porch.

Elle rolled her eyes. "No one expects anything from you. Why don't you head to the cafe and bore the locals with your theories about the island no one else seems to remember. And then you'll need to find a place to live. You are not staying with me for more than a week. I don't know if it's possible for an angel to murder another angel, but we would definitely find out."

"Later alligators! Or is it crocodiles?" Barachiel walked away, running through an exhaustive list of water-loving reptiles.

"Glad you're back," Viv said. "You can head into the sitting room and…clean the fireplace? I don't know. This whole place is disgusting, and I hate asking anyone to get dirty for me."

"No problem." Elle walked into the sitting room. There was a flash of light, and she returned. "I think I'm done, but you might want to check it out. Also, I found this." Elle held out a small book to Viv.

Viv took the book and walked into the room Elle claimed she cleaned in seconds. It was spotless. The carpet was gone, the wallpaper had been replaced by clean, white walls—a blank canvas—and the fireplace was almost sparkling.

Viv took a deep breath and exhaled forcefully. Her shoulders straightened, and she stood tall instead of hunching. She tipped her head from side to side loosening the muscles in her neck. Something was different, something more than what she could see. The oppressive aura that had blanketed the house for as long as Viv could remember was gone.

"You'd make a fortune as a housecleaner," Viv said. She turned her attention to the book Elle had found. "The greatest of these is love" was emblazoned in gold on the pink cover. "Where was this?"

"Inside the fireplace; it fell out when I was cleaning," Elle replied.

"Huh. She refused to ever use the fireplace, so I guess that's a great place to hide stuff." Viv opened the book. "Oh my god. It's my mother's diary. Are there any more?"

Elle reached inside the fireplace and moved her arm around. She pulled out five more journals, each with an inspirational Bible verse on the cover.

Viv leafed through them quickly. "Every detail of everything she did is in here. I'll have to hand them over to the police, but first..." She looked through them, scanning for her name. "I'm not mentioned in here at all. Not once. There's a lot about Brandy, random rage about sin, and a lot of pages devoted to how much she hates Hope. But nothing about me at all." Viv deflated and sat down on the floor.

Bev sank down beside her. "If I can't get up again, you'll owe me big time. But in the meantime, why don't you talk it through."

"I was hoping this might finally be the answer, that maybe this is where I'd find out that the reason she didn't poison me or send me into the lake, despite my continuous and obvious sin, was because deep, deep down she loved me too much to hurt me. But I'm not in here at all. It's like I don't exist to her. I'm not even a minor character in her narrative. I know it doesn't matter in the long run. She's an awful person, a murderer, and I should be happy that I flew beneath her radar, but..." Viv's voice trailed off and she sniffed back the tears. "This is stupid. Why am I crying? I am almost forty-five, and it's been a long, long time since I held my breath waiting for her to love me, and to be sad she didn't prove her love with arsenic? Ugh."

"It's not weird to want your mom to love you," Bev said. "But you know that even without that, you are very much loved, right?'

Viv dried her eyes, smearing dust across her face. "Yeah. You guys are the best, and you've made my life so amazing."

"Oh, I think I'm having a vision!" Evie said, holding out her hands to Bev and Viv and hauling them to their feet.

"Hey, that's my gig." Viv stuck her tongue out at Evie.

"Wait!" Evie held up one finger. "I am seeing...what could that be? Oh yes, it is you, Viv, in the very near future. And who's that with you? Could it be... Yes! It is a not-so-tall, dark, stranger. When you meet this woman, you must hold onto her and never let her go, only that way lies true happiness."

"You're a dork, Evie. But you're my favorite dork. Let's get to work so we can get to that sauvignon blanc I know you have chilling in the fridge." Viv looked around at the sitting room. "I don't suppose you want to go tackle another room, Elle?"

"Anything I can do to help." Evie and Bev followed Elle into the room where Gwen had slept. Viv stayed behind in the sitting room and pulled the dank, dark brown curtains, the only thing of her mother's that was left after Elle's magic cleaning spree. The windows behind them were clear, no trace of grim left behind. The sun streamed in, lighting up the room in a way it hadn't been lit in too long. A sunbeam caught a corner of the leaded glass window and rainbows danced around the room. She turned back to the window to see if it would open, and what she saw outside stopped her in her tracks.

Sam was at the end of the sidewalk holding a bottle of wine and a full canvas bag with the end of a baguette and several roses visible. She was wearing a tight red dress that wrapped around her figure, leading Viv's imagination down a very sexy road.

Sam walked up the path and Viv heard the sounds of her friends' laughter over the playlist blasting through the house. Viv pulled the door open and yanked Sam into the house.

Everything here was practically perfect. Her friends. Her Sam. Her house where she could sit in the parlor whenever she wanted.

Viv kissed Sam, and an angel sang. Poorly—Elle was off-key and didn't sound one bit like Britney—but it felt like a good omen.

Viv slipped her hand into Sam's and pulled her further into the house. "Welcome home."

FALL FROM GRACE
COMING YOUR WAY SOON!

One last, perfect summer—that's what Grace Kane and her best friend Hope have promised each other. They're young, beautiful, and have their whole lives ahead of them.

Grace has just graduated from high school and wants nothing more than to get as far away from Eden Valley and her overbearing older sister as possible. When James, Hope's on-again/off-again boyfriend returns and monopolizes Hopes attention, and Grace receives a rejection notice from the university she'd planned to attend, she's left watching life from the sidelines as her perfect summer slips away, and along with it, the belief she'll ever be free.

Enter Quinn, the hot as hell newcomer to Eden Valley who only has eyes for Grace. When a summer romance turns into something more, will the choices Grace makes lead her to happiness? Or will she end up trapped in Eden Valley forever?

Fall From Grace is an origin story novella in Eden Valley, a magical new paranormal women's fiction series from USA Today Bestselling Author Amy Cissell, author of the Eleanor Morgan novels and the Oracle Bay series.

Fall From Grace has romantic elements, but it is not a romance.

Eden Valley
Book Three

Valley of Angels

USA TODAY BESTSELLING AUTHOR

AMY CISSELL

CHAPTER ONE

"Hello, this is Beverly Hill. How can I help you?" Bev winced as she did every time she said her whole name. She'd had it for forty-four years and still wasn't used to it.

"Miss Hill? This is Principal Ives. I'm afraid I'm going to need you to come pick up your niece. She's been suspended for the rest of the week but will be welcome to return on the twenty-sixth. Since this is her first offense of the year—and the first as a middle-schooler—her suspension is only three days long. As you know, she gets two more before expulsion."

Bev massaged her left temple with her free hand, trying to get rid of the sudden-onset tension headache. "It's Ms. Hill. I'll be there in a half hour. Can you tell me what happened this time?"

"She was fighting in the lunchroom and sent another student to the nurse's office. She'll be in the office when you get here. I look forward to meeting you. I understand you knew the elementary school principal well."

The principal's cheery tone made Bev want to reach through the phone and punch him in the face. Maybe calling parents with suspension notices was a daily part of his job, but he didn't have to sound so happy about it.

"See you soon," Bev said through gritted teeth. She hung up and went back to the email she'd been composing when the phone had rung. She finished, hit send, grabbed her purse, and stepped out of her glass cubicle. As soon as she stepped foot into her boss's office, he sighed audibly.

"Shelby?" he asked.

"I'll be back after I pick her up. I'm just taking my lunch early today." Bev hated the way she sounded, but she couldn't cover up the placating tone she adopted every time she talked to Neil Tallant. Her new boss was beige—white, medium height, lightly tanned, sandy hair, light brown eyes, forgettable face, and a body that was neither hard nor soft. He'd started a couple months ago after Bev had been passed over for the promotion into that position. Again. The fact that they'd worked together for less than eight weeks and he already assumed, correctly, but still, that she was leaving to get Shelby meant his predecessor had warned him and that made losing the job to him even worse.

"If you're gone more than thirty minutes, you'll have to use PTO." His smile was borderline smug and for the second time in ten minutes, Bev felt like punching someone in the face.

"I'll keep that in mind." She pasted a smile on her face.

"Beverly!" he called when she was ten steps out of his office.

She turned around, but before she could walk back into his office, he raised his voice and said loud enough for everyone in the branch to hear, "You'll need to work on your absenteeism if you ever want to advance your career. You've been the assistant manager for how long?" He shuffled through some papers on his desk as if he was looking for the date while heat suffused Bev's cheeks and a wave of humiliation failed to provide a complementary hole in the floor to sink into. "Fifteen years?" He whistled low in surprise. "That's longer than I've been old enough to drive. Maybe you're a middle management lifer…"

Bev walked out of the bank before she fulfilled the fantasy that had been building for weeks. Every time he was awful to her, she added another layer to her elaborate revenge scheme. Currently she was contemplating paying Lily, her niece's best friend and genuine demon child, to magic permanent boils in between his butt cheeks.

When the fresh air hit her, Bev stopped and took a deep breath. "In with positive, out with the horror that is a mediocre white man."

"Do all humans talk to themselves, or is that an affectation only necromancers have? Ooooh, maybe you're not talking to yourself! Is there a ghost around?" The man turned around, eyes alight as he looked for the non-existent ghost Bev might have been talking to.

"What are you doing here, Barachiel?" Bev asked. She side-stepped him and headed to the parking lot without waiting for an answer.

"Elle says I need to have a bank account so I can buy things and get a place to live that is anywhere but her house, so here I am!" He grinned and fell into step beside her. "And you're supposed to call me Barry."

"I am not calling you Barry." Bev unlocked her car and slid into the driver's seat. Barachiel got in on the other side and fiddled with the seatbelt, trying to buckle himself in. "What are you doing?" Bev wasn't even trying to keep the exasperation out of her voice anymore.

"I'm putting on my seatbelt. Evie says it's the law." The latched clicked home. "First try. I'm getting the hang of your weird travel vehicles!"

Bev started the car. She was at the end of the thirty-minute window she'd given Shelby's principal and didn't have time to argue with an angel. "Fine. We're going to the school to pick up Shelby. You are not coming in with me. In fact, as soon as we get there, you're getting out of the car and heading back to the bank to deposit your money and open an account." She turned on the blinker, looked right, left, right before making a cautious left turn out onto Main Street, which was currently almost devoid of traffic.

"What money?" Barachiel asked absently, rolling the window up and down.

"The money for your bank account." Bev stopped at a four-way stop sign, waiting to ensure no one was coming too fast to stop, then pulled into the intersection. The two-mile drive was punctuated with several stop signs, two blind curves, and underbrush too close to the roads that could be concealing foolhardy animals ready to jump in front of the next vehicle that sped by. Driving safely—two miles under the speed limit, complete stop at each stop sign, and high alert through the curves and forested section of the road—took fifteen minutes. She was going to be late.

"I thought the bank account was supposed to pay for everything I needed?" Barachiel rolled up the window and pulled the lever next to his seat and leaned all the way back.

"You have to put the money in. The bank holds your money for you, keeps it safe, and, depending on the account and how much money you have in it, pays interest. But the original deposit comes from you." Bev slowed down as she approached the next intersection. She had the right of way, but you never knew. Better safe than dead.

"Where do I get money?" Barachiel pulled the lever again and shot upright.

"A lot of people have jobs." She turned on her blinker and turned right.

"What kind of jobs? How do I get one? My friend Andras owns a brewery. You work at a bank taking people's money. What else is there?" Barachiel pressed the lock button and tried to open the door.

"What are you doing?" Bev yelled. "That's dangerous. You sit there and leave the door alone until we're parked."

"Sorry. But you don't have to yell. Nothing bad will happen. I'm an angel of the Lord and immortal." He flashed another one of his million-watt grins at her and, for a moment, every bit of tension Bev was holding disappeared.

"Please don't do that again, no matter how immortal you feel." She took a deep breath as he dimmed his light and the stress of the last eighteen months—strike that, twelve years—returned. "Evie owns the Silver Dollar, Viv is a graphic designer, Sam and Luc work for their dad. Kind of." She thought about it for a minute and grimaced. "Actually, you don't have a lot of good examples of people with jobs. But you know my cousin Russell, right? He manages a bar, doesn't he?"

"A lot of my associates work in alcohol management. Have you thought about quitting your job? Taking people's money doesn't seem like the best use of your talents." Barachiel rolled the window down again. "You could be a detective and solve crimes by interviewing dead people. Detectives are very cool."

Bev signaled, then turned into the school parking lot. After creeping forward and into a space as far away from any other cars as possible, she put her Prius in park and turned it off. "Like there are so many crimes to solve in Eden Valley. Besides, I don't want to be a cop."

"Oh no, not a police detective. I meant a detective like Miss Marple or Jessica Fletcher! They're old ladies in small towns who are always surrounded by murders they get to solve, showing up the police! You could be just like them." Barachiel opened the door to get out, but his seatbelt yanked him back. He struggled with the seatbelt, getting more and more tangled, until Bev reached over and unlatched it. Barachiel stumbled out of the car. His wings popped out as he tried to get his balance.

"Wings!" Bev hissed.

Barachiel huffed, and they disappeared back to wherever they went when they weren't visible.

"Please leave now," Bev said. "I need to go pick up my kid and sit with the knowledge that you compared me to two elderly women who were probably serial killers inserting themselves into the investigations. There's no other explanation for the sheer number of murders around them." She walked to the front door of the school, purse clutched closely to her body.

Barachiel caught up with her. "School isn't over yet, is it? There are no other children around."

"It's not. School doesn't let out until three, but today I am picking Shelby up early. Now go." Bev hit the buzzer to notify the office staff she'd arrived.

"Yes?" a voice crackled through the intercom.

"It's Bev Hill here to get Shelby." She turned her back to the brick wall and scanned the area in front of her, alert to any potential dangers that might exist.

"Your name is Beverly Hill," Barachiel said while they waited for the buzz signifying they were being allowed in.

"It is." She hated her name and had ever since she was a student at this school and a couple classmates decided it was hilarious and deserving of mocking. She'd sworn then that the minute she was eighteen, she'd change it.

But then she'd used it to enroll in college and after that assumed she'd get married and could change it later. She got busy with work, then being a doting aunt, first to her sister's child, then to her best friend Evie's daughter. When her sister and mother died in a horrible car accident when Shelby was [age], her name seemed like the least of her problems. She'd taken Shelby in and raised her and hadn't had time to reflect on the twisted senses of humor her parents—Richard Wood and Chloe Hill—had called on to name their children. She'd gotten her mother's last name, and her sister Holly had been given her father's.

The door buzzed and Bev yanked it open and fixed Barachiel with her steeliest gaze. "Weren't you leaving? I am going in here, and you cannot."

The angel looked completely unfazed and peered over her shoulder into the school.

"He can come in with you, Bev!" the school secretary called from her office across from the door. "As long as you have ID to pick up Shelby and he doesn't wander off."

"Thank you, Miss…" Barachiel trailed off as he strode across the hallway and walked into the office.

"You can call me Dawn." Dawn Ives, who had been the middle school secretary since Bev had been a student there thirty years ago, giggled at Barachiel.

Bev walked into the office just in time to see his friendly grin replaced by an expression of mild horror. His eyes widened and darted around the room, clearly looking for an escape other than the doors he'd just walked through.

"I'll wait for you outside," he said and fled outside.

"Who's your friend?" Dawn winked.

Bev sighed. Eden Valley was small enough that Dawn already knew the answer—or at least the answer that had been spread around when he'd returned with Elle two weeks ago. "Cousin of Elle's," Bev said. "He's in town to help her through this difficult time."

Dawn's face drooped down and a look of deep compassion overtook her. "I heard. Poor lady. And how Kevin must feel, losing his father so suddenly." She looked at Bev expectantly, waiting for her to fill in the blanks left by Brandon Jones's "death" at the end of July and Elle's three-month departure to mourn, leaving Kevin behind to stay with Evie Addams, her two children, one of whom, Lily, was Kevin's best friend, and her fiancé Luc. Short for Lucifer. Last name Morningstar. Descendent of the original.

"It was very sad," Bev murmured and wondered what Dawn would say if Bev told her that Brandon Jones hadn't been a real person but was instead a flaming sword in a human body, the same sword that had once protected the gates of Eden and had been used to cut the ties Eden Lake had on Kevin, former Eden Lake monster and current sixth-grade student. She bit her tongue to keep from blurting it all out. "Shelby?"

"Of course, you want to collect your niece." Dawn clucked her tongue and handed Bev a form to sign.

Bev scanned it. "It says she's being suspended for fighting in the lunchroom. Do you know what instigated the fight?"

"They don't tell me that kind of information. I just know what's on the form. Shelby punched another student, sending him to the nurse's office with a black eye." She shook her head mournfully.

"He knocked my lunch tray out of my hands and called me a very bad name," Shelby volunteered as she walked into the room. "He's also an eighth grader, about a foot taller than me, and at least fifty pounds heavier. The only reason he got a black eye is because he hadn't finished straightening up from running a hand down my back looking for a bra strap."

"Nice job, sweetie," Bev said, holding out an arm and pulling Shelby in for a side hug. "Let's go see the principal now. I'm excited to hear how he's going to address the bigotry and sexual assault perpetrated on a younger, smaller student. I'm assuming that if you suspended Shelby for three days, you expelled the other student?"

Dawn didn't reply, just picked up the phone and said, "Miss Hill here to see you."

Bev channeled every bit of rage she had simmering as she marched towards the principal's office.

"I'm sorry," Shelby whispered. "I know I'm not supposed to lose my temper and hit back, it's just…"

"You are not in trouble," Bev said loud enough for anyone in the vicinity to hear. "If I wasn't an adult, I'd find that kid and…" She bit her tongue. Threatening to assault middle schoolers probably wouldn't look good on her permanent record. "You are not in trouble. If you want, I'll push for them to reverse your suspension, but if you'd rather spend the rest of the week home, I'll just force them to remove it from your record—this is not a first strike."

"Thank you." Shelby squeezed Bev's hand, and together, they breached the principal's office.

Valley of Angels is available for preorder! Grab yours today!

NOT IN THE CARDS
ORACLE BAY BOOK 1

Not in the Cards is the first book in the Oracle Bay series—a paranormal romance series set on the Washington (state) coast. It's a separate series but in-world with the folks of Eden Valley (and you might even find the connecting character!).

Welcome to Oracle Bay, the town where the local psychics were already expecting you!

Oracle Bay has always attracted the preternaturally clairvoyant. When anyone with seers' blood in their veins steps foot in this quaint coastal town, their powers awaken. They receive a visit from the Psychics Union, and shenanigans ensue.

Sandy Franklin is on the run from her old life and her almost-ex-husband. Lured to Oracle Bay by a too-cheap-to-be-believable apartment with attached tarot reader shop, she has found new friends and a job she didn't know was possible. Hiding from her past while building a new future.

When Vincent, the handsome stranger who owns most of Main Street, announces he's selling Oracle Bay to stave off personal problems, Sandy and the other resident psychics devise a plan to save the town using their divination skills and a little old-fashioned sleuthing.

The one thing Sandy couldn't predict was how hard she'd fall for the one man who could crush Oracle Bay and her hopes for a new life without blinking an eye... Will Sandy get a second chance at true love with the man whose past might be even more dangerous than her own?

TAKE A TRIP TO ORACLE BAY. Come for the scenic Pacific Northwest, stay for the paranormal romance in these (mostly) standalone novels.

Once Sandy has you hooked, check out the rest of the psychics in Oracle Bay.

ABOUT THE AUTHOR

 Amy Cissell is a USA Today Bestselling Author of urban fantasy and paranormal romance novels. She lives in Portland, OR with her husband, her haunted house-obsessed daughter, their three cats, and the murder of crows she's conspiring to turn into her vengeful army.

When she's not working or writing, she's sleeping because that's all she has time to do! There are few things Amy loves more than a well-timed pun, a good book, a glass of wine, and time at the Oregon Coast.

Although she reads anything and everything, her first love is fantasy. Eleven-year-old Amy discovered fantasy when she 'borrowed' her father's copy of The Hobbit and an enduring love affair (mostly with dragons) was born.

facebook.com/acissellwrites
twitter.com/acissellwrites
instagram.com/acissellwrites
bookbub.com/authors/amy-cissell
goodreads.com/acissellwrites

ALSO BY AMY CISSELL

Paranormal Women's Fiction

Eden Valley

Raising a Demon (June 2021)

Devil and the Deep, Blue Lake (September 2021)

Valley of Angels (November 2021)

Guardian of Eden (February 2022)

Eden Valley World Novellas

Match Made in Hell (June 2021)

Fall From Grace (September 2021)

Hell's Bells (December 2021)

Heaven Sent (February 2022)

Paranormal Romance

Oracle Bay

Not in the Cards (October 2018)

First Hand Knowledge (November 2018)

Belle of the Ball (December 2019)

Hell and High Water (2022)

Tempest in a Teapot (2022)

Bad to the Bones (2022)

Oracle Bay World Novellas

Wing and a Prayer (January 2019)

Contemporary/Urban Fantasy

The Eleanor Morgan Novels

(complete series)

The Cardinal Gate (February 2017)

The Waning Moon (June 2017)

The Ruby Blade (October 2017)

The Broken World (March 2018)

The Lost Child (June 2019)

The Iron River (May 2020)

The Dark Throne (February 2021)

The Eleanor Morgan World Novellas

The Throneless King (March 2020)